MUSE

DU

Mixed
Blessings

J.M. Muse

MUSE

J.M. Muse for Mocha Girls Productions, LLC
In cooperation with
Muse Communications, Inc.
2001 Wilshire Blvd. Suite 600
Santa Monica, CA 90403

Manufactured in the United States of America
Library of Congress Control Number: 2018915145

Print ISBN: 978-1-54395-370-1
eBook ISBN: 978-1-54395-371-8

Body & Soul Lyrics permitted by Alfred Music, Van Nuys, CA. 91410

This book is dedicated to Carol and Bill for having the courage to read my first draft before knowing how truly awful it was, then having the grace to encourage me to start over.

SOMETIME
AROUND NOW

1

The Sanchez Reunion

The temperature was a delicious seventy-two and the glint of the Southern California sun made seeing shapes and shadows difficult without sunglasses. The display of manicured lawns and green beltways took their shapes under the supervision of the leaf-blowers and Mexican gardeners that dotted the landscape like animated lawn jockeys with cannons strapped to their backs. The well-cut plots betrayed the uneven and impulsive lives that the people of Los Angeles lead.

Kimberly Solberg unzipped her brown Samsonite luggage with its neon yellow nametag and flipped it open on the double bed in her room in her mother's apartment. She carefully folded her go-to oversized beige sweatshirt with the words *Valley High* embossed on the front. Into the bag it went. Next came the dressy jeans she could wear on any occasion. On the cherry walnut secondhand dresser was a round-trip economy-class ticket from Los Angeles International Airport to Ciudad Juarez de Mexico. Kimberly tussled her long auburn hair and thought of if her jeans were right—maybe she needed her fat jeans? Struggling with her slightly pear-shaped body had led Kim to diets without cause. She was just a little thick around the middle like most teenage girls.

Her elegant hands were beginning to smell of flop sweat. Mexico was a long way from the San Fernando Valley, but not far enough to sustain a sense that she was getting away from her childhood and adolescent identity of growing up Jewish.

"Mom, now is a good time to go to Juarez? Right?"

"You're going to be safe. Magdalena guarantees it," said Rachel Solberg, a no-nonsense Jewish girl with salt and pepper hair cut short to show her pride in maturity and the ability to tell the truth without doing harm. Her long walks in The Palisades and advance Pilates classes helped keep her trim enough to wear leggings but with a long tailed shirt to cover her ample assets. Today she would be careful with the truth she knew about Mexico.

"Easy for her to say. It is the freaking murder capital of the world. Where's my Uzi?" Kimberly mockingly looked around her bedroom.

"Kim, you're tripping. It just isn't like that. When I was there, lots of stuff jumped off, but the locals knew how to stay safe and keep us students safe, all the while keeping it real."

"Keep it real." Kimberly made a face. "You've been reading *Urban Dictionary* again? Safe I get. Real? That's another story." She reached for her English/Spanish dictionary. "Somebody better speak English, or I'll be a slave to this thing."

"Can you say *cómo está*?"

Kimberly humored her mother. "*Muy bien, y tú*?"

"That's a start. During your week there, be a sponge. I'm sure your brother and sister will help you get by."

"Yeah, but that Magdalena scares the bejesus out of me."

"Remember, she's the boss of the family. Stay on her good side."

"Yes. The bastard kid's gonna be her new best friend. Give me a break."

"I think I know what you mean. Just be charming."

"Come on, Ma, you know she hates me. And Dad's a wuss around her."

. . . .

The next morning they reached LAX with plenty of time for customs. Rachel guided the red Honda Civic with the care and attention usually reserved for chauffeurs driving VIPs or FedEx men hauling precious cargo. Her hands were poised at ten and two on the steering wheel, and her left foot gently caressed the brake as she looked for any reason to delay her careful approach.

She wanted the trip around the airport loop to last at least until the tension in her stomach ceased and she felt better about sending her only child to godforsaken Mexico. Rachel pulled the Honda to the curb, and Kimberly looked at her mom with the eyes of an adventurer ready to launch into the unknown. Rachel's eyes moistened as a lump rose up somewhere in the space between her throat and Adam's apple. She gulped.

"They will like me. It's not every day you meet your American half-sister. I think my brother and sister will be easier to love than Lady Magdalena," Kim said.

Rachel got out of the car and reached into the back for Kim's suitcase.

"It's her family that offered you safe passage," she told her daughter. "Just be careful."

"I know. I'm sure the freaking armed guards will have more to do with that than me."

"Just remember that your father is a good guy," Rachel reminded her. "You just have a mother who didn't want to share you. I hope you find everything you are looking for, and then you come back to me."

"I will see you next week."

Kim gathered her bags and turned toward the terminal.

"Promise?"

Kim turned back, dropped the bags, and gave her mother a bigger hug.

"Promise."

Kim went into the terminal and Rachel headed for the exit, both thinking of Juarez and Los Angeles, and what it would mean to understand who she really was as both the daughter of a Jew and a Mexican National.

• • • •

As the Boeing 937-900 commercial jet descended into the smog and airborne pollution that draped Mexico's second-largest city, Kim was surprised at how it looked compared to El Paso on the other side of the border. Ciudad Juarez was sprawling with a hodgepodge of architecture that had more of a third-world look than anything befitting a modern metropolis. The ciudad of two million people also was kissed by slums and poorly maintained commercial buildings. Such a clear sign that there were two classes of people in Juarez: those who had money and influence and those who didn't.

Once on the ground and into the terminal, Kim saw her father at baggage claim. Hector Sanchez was practically vibrating with excitement. He was a skinny little man, dressed in designer khakis and a white polo shirt to represent his status as not only a reporter, but an in-law of the powerful Rodriguez family. Kim was sure Magdalena had chosen the entire outfit for him, right down to the slip-on loafers without socks and the scented hair cream that she could smell when she came closer. The only sign of freedom he wore was his clunky black eyeglasses, which he needed to remain the best investigative reporter in Juarez.

"Kimberly, welcome to Mexico. How was the flight?"

Just behind Hector was a two-man security team that had the bulges on their backs to prove they were carrying concealed AR-15 semiautomatic rifles. The guards watched the perimeter of the arrival area with particular attention to anything that might indicate the presence of kidnappers.

Kim gave him a hug and allowed her hand to casually rest inside of his. As she kissed him warmly on the cheek, she noticed the glare in the eyes of the security team. Hector noticed her noticing them.

"No worries, young lady, they're here to keep us safe."

"Okay, Dad. I just need to breathe. They got guns."

"I'll get your bag, just point it out. Can't wait for you to meet Juanita and Hermando."

"Can't wait either. It's that brown one," she said and caught it herself.

• • • •

The trip to the ranch where the Sanchez family lived took an hour from the airport. The brown stucco hacienda was replete with the round ornate facade and red tiled rooftops, reminiscent of a time gone by when wealthy *caballeros* employed *vaqueros* to work the land and tend to the livestock.

The Sanchez family stood ceremonially at the steps of the main building as the lead black SUV made its way down the horseshoe driveway. The second car stopped precisely by the marble stairway that led to the foyer and courtyard. As Hector opened the rear passenger door, Magdalena approached the car, looked in, and smiled pleasantly.

"Kimberly, welcome."

Juanita and Hermando were dressed in sophisticated daywear straight out of Nordstrom's Rack. Both teenagers stood precisely in place at the opening of the foyer and were about the same age as Kim, but more trained and restrained. Juanita was sixteen, and her figure seemed to suffer the good life. Her black embroidered skirt was a tag sight around the waist but revealed her thick legs and ample thighs and calves covered in white stockings. Her black hair nestled nicely on top of her delicate shoulders draped by a fine white silk blouse with a large bow in the middle.

Hermando wore the beige pants and green polo shirt and looked like he was forced to dress conservative. He smiled politely and followed the lead of his mother. His athletic build and strong handsome face made it tough for Kim to see him as a brother.

Magdalena was impeccably dressed in a white cotton sundress with comfortable shoes and a flowing wide-brim straw bonnet with a champagne-colored silk hatband.

Magdalena was slim, trim, and of average good looks and maintained the appearance and charisma of a member of the Mexican ruling class. Kim knew for a fact that she also practiced the art of concealment and pretense. Hosting the bastard child of her husband was a sign of her virtue and not that of her disloyal husband. Her children would have to suffer through it.

"It is so great to finally meet you. Don't worry about your bags and have a cold drink in the courtyard with your brother and sister."

Kimberly could feel her flop sweat returning, but she took a deep breath and stepped forward to greet them.

The beautiful foyer was adorned with classic paintings and sculptures from the great masters—Diego Rivera, Ernest Silva, and Ruben Ortiz-Torres. The carved-wood floors were polished to a high gloss. The small cadre of servers and workers completed a remarkable scene of Mexican hospitality. A white-coated waiter offered summer punch to Juanita and sangria to her parents, along with Hermando and Kim.

"No, thanks. I will have one of those pretty drinks," Kim said, smiling at her siblings.

"Como está?" said Juanita as she offered Kim an agua Fresca scented with grapes and mangoes.

Kimberly stumbled over her ninth-grade foreign-language competency before reaching for her pocket dictionary. Juanita continued in English.

"The punch is made here. Do you like it?"

"It's awesome."

Hermando talked to his parents on the other side of the courtyard, giving the girls a chance to bond.

Kimberly felt the warmth of the Mexican sun on her face and had a sense of home. She counted a half-dozen members of the wait staff just milling around the grounds, making sure everything on the beautiful dining table was perfect. She smelled the roasting of meat on a brick barbeque pit across the courtyard. Kim knew her other family was well off, but this was right out of a novella. She enjoyed the sweet, cool citrus taste of the purple concoction.

"I understand you live in Hollywood. Do you know any movie stars like Brad Pitt? He's so cute," Juanita said, giggling to break Kim's trance.

"No. Southern California is just so big. I did see Britney Spears on Mulholland Drive one day. At least, the woman looked a lot like her."

"I hope that one day I will get a chance to visit you in America. Spending time with my new big sister would be fabulous."

Juanita moved close to Kim, who reached out for her hand.

"I think that will be great." She pulled Juanita into a hug.

"No need to be stuck with my sister," Hermando cut in. "I think you and I enjoy the same music, but her taste is so whack."

Magdalena interrupted the sibling rivalry with smooth courtesy.

"We are putting you in a beautiful guest house," she told Kim, "where it's cool during the evenings yet warm in the morning sun. You'll love it."

As Magdalena led the progression into the hacienda, Juanita held Kim's hand gently. The children followed with their father close at hand. Kim whispered into Juanita's ear.

"We're going to be best friends."

As dinner approached, Magdalena instructed a young service boy to take Kim to her casita, while the rest of the family went to their rooms in the hacienda to change for dinner.

In her well-appointed guesthouse, Kim was impressed not just by the obvious wealth of the family, but by the way the room was decorated. It was stocked with pieces of Hollywood memorabilia, including what appeared to be Michael Jackson's silver-speckled glove. A dress that looked remarkably like the gown worn by Mariah Carey in her debut performance at Caesar's Palace was draped on a life-size wax mannequin of Ms. Carey.

Musical instruments were littered among the celebrity costumes of Lady Gaga, Justin Bieber, Ciara, Shakira, Justin Timberlake, Christina Aguilera, and 50 Cent. In the center of the spacious room was a stuffed lion—not a carnival plush toy, but a real skin mounted and posed as if it were on the prowl. Stuffed toy animals were also placed around the room, interspersed with beautifully dressed dolls. The cabinets and other furniture were authentic antiques from seventeenth-century France. There was an English Tudor bed with a pink silk canopy in the center of the large one-room *casita*. The room's colors were bright combinations of red, pink, and white. It was a girl's room, but one that looked like it hadn't a resident in months. Kim was breathless.

"Whose room is this?" Kim asked the white-jacketed teenager who was carrying her luggage.

"It was Señorita Juanita's favorite room until she moved to the main building. You like it?"

"I think it's interesting and colorful."

As she was left to unpack and dress for dinner, Kim thought that it might not have been a good idea to come to Mexico. For one thing, it was going to be hard to go back to California and not think that somehow she had gotten the short end of the family deal. Her father was rich, but none of the resources she saw on display here were available to her in the States. She wondered if her mom knew how the Sanchez Rodriguez family lived.

The garden patio where the reception dinner was being staged was just a short walk away. The arid ranch was rejuvenated by a massive sprinkler system that transformed the dusty land into earth that could produce beautiful avocados, grapefruit, olives, and a host of vegetables. The grounds also contained beautiful lawns that made brief walks in the late afternoon enjoyable.

Juanita met her on the pathway.

"What do you think?"

"About what?"

"You know. My room. A little too much, huh?"

"It's so much fun. Was that really Michael Jackson's glove?"

"Of course, silly. Everything there is real, including Socrates."

"Socrates?"

"Yes, my lion. Dad shot it on a safari last winter and had him shipped and stuffed. Isn't he cute?"

"Amazing. I've never seen anything like it."

"Then you should see what my other girlfriends have. Some have leopards and panthers, and Cecilia has a wildebeest. Such an ugly thing."

Hector approached the girls as the family guests mingled about the courtyard.

"Kim should meet a few of her new relatives," he said, leading her to a small group near her.

"Say hello to your new uncles, Manny and Roberto. And your new aunts, Wilhelmina, Clarisse, and Esmeralda."

As Hector informally introduced each one, they politely held out a hand to shake Kim's. Except for Roberto.

"Oh, come on. Give your uncle Roberto a big hug. That's what these big arms are for."

"Uncle Roberto. You're already becoming my favorite." She leaned into his embrace.

Aunt Clarisse was Magdalena's older sister, a slender, elegant woman in her early sixties. She had skin like alabaster. Her strikingly blond hair did not come out of a bottle. Kim had never seen a Mexican woman like her.

"I hope your trip here was safe."

"It was very smooth. No muss, no fuss."

Uncle Manny, a short, stout man in his thirties drinking a glass of top-shelf rum, interrupted.

"I think your Aunt Clarisse was referring to once you arrived in Juarez. You know we are known as the murder capital. With the drug warlords fighting for dominance, killing is a commonplace occurrence here. Even reporters like your father live in peril."

"Now, let's not scare Kim," Aunt Wilhelmina said. "We all have to thank God for the lives we lead and the fact Jesus keeps us safe."

Aunt Willie was clearly the baby of the family and was still in her late thirties, voluptuous but Kim noted, without a wedding ring on her finger. Next to her was a well-groomed short woman with striking plain facial features wearing a pair of large unattractive yellow-wired glasses. It was Aunt Esmeralda and her claim to fame in the Rodriguez family was her tenure as a Fulbright scholar. She was completing her doctorate in education at Duke University.

"LA is not all that much safer with the gangs and drugs. USC is in a war zone." Esmeralda said.

Magdalena approached, and the conversation went silent.

"Dinner is served."

With the children, the dinner table on the veranda was set for twenty. Place cards revealed the seating arrangements. As the room settled, Hector stood and offered a toast. All glasses were raised. Hector started slowly and with great affect.

"It's not every day that a wife gives a man a chance to be forgiven for putting a stain on the family's reputation and honor. Today is a blessed day for me today because I have permission to introduce my daughter, Kim, from America."

Hector continued to speak and as he stood at the head of the table, he shifted his weight from one foot to the other repeatedly.

"I thank our family for having the grace and courage to accept Kim as a member of our family. Salud."

Magdalena brought her glass of champagne to her lips and smiled politely. The rest of the clan followed her lead. Hector sat down without saying a word more.

The polite talk ensued far beyond the dinner toast, and it was clear that Kim's presence there was going to be a short one. As dinner arrived, Kim noticed the gelatinous head of a pig being prepared for roasted Carnitas tacos. Soon the waiter was carrying the steaming head toward her. The eyes were black holes and the teeth of the pig formed an insidious grin. Kim knew what this was. She was about to be presented with the cabeza de cerdo, a sign of respect and good-will. She steeled herself, willing her face not to show her anxiety.

"Kim," Juanita said abruptly, "do you like my bracelet?"

Reflexively, she looked over and smiled politely. "It's lovely." Then she looked forward again.

The pig's head was twelve inches from her face.

She screamed in horror. Before she knew it, she was out of her chair and had spilled sangria all over her dress. Hector tried to calm her.

"Kim, it's a pig's head. You have to eat some of it, please. Just a little piece."

"But my dress is ruined! I have to go and try to fix it. Please, Dad."

Hector stood there motionless as the family tried to ignore the commotion.

Juanita rescued them both.

"Some seltzer water will do the trick. Follow me."

Together the two sisters dashed off to the nearby bathroom. When they returned, dinner had given way to dessert.

"This is homemade ice cream," Juanita told her by way of a peace offering. "The best in Mexico."

Kimberly put the creamy concoction to her lips and swallowed deeply. The cool, frozen confection settled her stomach and made her forget about the invasion of the horrid pig's head.

· · · ·

After dinner, the young adults, Kimberly, Juanita, and Hermando, stayed in the courtyard to talk. They hatched a plan to take Kim to see the notorious nightlife of Ciudad Juarez.

"I have a plan," said Hermando drinking his fourth beer.

"For me?" Kimberly asked curiously.

"All of us are going to the city to have some fun," he added as he signaled to the security team to get ready for the trip to Juarez.

"Can I go, please?" Juanita begged.

"You got a fake ID?"

"No…."

"Then you're going to miss it."

"I'll see you when I get back."

Juanita turned on her heels, waved goodbye, and headed back inside the main house.

• • • •

Inside the SUV, Kim took a deep toke from a joint being passed around and took in more smoke than she could handle. Without warning, she was overcome by a frenzied coughing fit. Her brother came to the rescue.

"Drink more tequila."

Kim took a shot, and a minute later, she was stoned out of her mind.

"Good shit, huh? Only the best for my sis," he boasted.

Inside Juarez the Rodriguez Family Trust babies were driven to *El Mulato*, a house music discotheque with amazing lights and video displays. Hermando took on the role of tour guide for Kim.

"That's DJ Karma, from Brussels. Have fun, but stay away from the stoned-out cowboys from El Paso. There's Rico from school. He thinks he's a player, so stay away from him. I'm gonna chill with my boys."

"So, why I can't talk with your friend Rico? I think I'd like that."

"Not Rico, he's a hound," Hermando emphasized.

"Let me be the judge of his 'hound-ness,'" Kimberly said while weaving and swaying from the tequila and weed. Her brother frowned at her tipsiness and pointed to the bunch of girls laughing and joking.

"That's where you should be. Stop being a spoilt brat and just go back and hang with the ladies."

Kim felt the tiny hairs on her neck stand up and her pulse race.

"That's a hell of a way to try to get rid of me. I can find my own party."

Kimberly sensed the tequila in her stomach start a trip up her throat. The sour taste of vomit began to pass through her teeth. Her flop sweat was returning.

"Where's the bathroom? I got to go," Kim pleaded as she stretched her neck like a giraffe looking for acacia leaves. She saw the flashing neon sign and headed there before Hermando could answer.

The ladies' room reminded her of the restrooms in the States with one exception: the boys lingering around the bathroom door.

"Hey, Americana. Enjoying our nightlife?"

Kim smiled and just kept walking. The bile in her mouth was at capacity. She cupped her mouth with her hand to catch the overflow.

Inside she rushed past the girls at the mirror and pushed open a stall door in time to stoop to her knees and pray to the goddess of Earl.

"Let's go to San Felipe's. This place is just not happening anymore," said a girl primping at the mirror.

"The boys are also cuter there. Let's get out of here and ditch those boys at the bar," said another.

"Do you have some blush?"

For a moment, Kim heard the English being spoken outside and forgot she was in Juarez, but the tequila had other plans.

Kim used her left foot to keep the door closed as she expelled the fermented cactus juice. She grunted and groaned silently as the señoritas left the room, paying no attention to the American girl heaving out her insides in a Mexican toilet. Gagging led to pockets of air and spitting in the basin. Her gut was empty, and she was closer to being sober. She rinsed her mouth at the sink and headed back outside.

Kim felt like dancing. Her energy was back, and the DJ's frantic house style was making her booty shake and her feet twitch like they were wearing tap shoes. She headed for the crowded dance floor, where the hypnotic rhythms made her legs and arms sway like slaves to the pulsating beat.

"Young lady. Allow me to introduce myself. I'm Jorge."

His sandy-brown hair cupped against the back of neck and shirt collar made his appearance more rakish than polite. But against the backdrop of the pulsating beat in a south of the border meat market his clean button down shirt and woolen charcoal plaid sport coat looked acceptable. His fit body and unkempt hair five-day stubble made him look interesting.

"You speak English," Kim blurted. "Jorge means George in Spanish. Right?"

"And vice versa, Senorita. I'm ambidextrous."

"I like that. Where are you from?"

"I was born in Juarez. As you say, I'm a native son. I assume you are American?"

"Yes, of course, and yes before you say it, I'm from California. My brother says I have an accent."

"And you're a movie star. So beautiful."

"Sure. Haven't you seen my films?" She laughed. "So what do you do?"

"I'm a photographer, and I have a studio in El Paso. Here's my card."

Jorge blew on the card as he handed it to Kim. Almost immediately, she felt her heart race and got dizzy. She tried to catch her balance, but stumbled. Jorge caught her.

"What's happening? I'm sorry. I feel weird."

"No worries. I'll help you outside to get some fresh air."

"No. My family is here."

Kim found the words she spoke to have little meaning. She knew something was very wrong but couldn't resist Jorge or scream for help. He was moving her toward the exit. Her body did not react the way she wanted it to. Within nanoseconds, she knew she was being taken, but she couldn't resist. The feeling was like being in a coma while her mind raced. She felt like a ghost; her body was in another time and space.

Kim was led outside, down a long dark alley heavy with the rancid smell of garbage. She dragged her feet aimlessly as her flop sweat caked around her neck and between her legs. Her underarms were soaked.

"Kimberly, we're going to stop here for a second. First, I want you to say, 'Jorge, is there something I can do for you?'"

The command was irresistible.

"Jorge, is there something I can do for you?" she whispered.

"Yes. I'd like you to unzip my pants and put your hand in."

It was like she was under his control.. He had barely stopped before she was deep in his crotch.

"Now stroke my dick and make it hard."

"Okay."

Kim screamed inside her skull.

"Oh my! That's it. Harder."

She obeyed.

So she did. Her face was dead, her mouth was ajar, and a little line of drool trickled down her chin.

Hermando walked out the club's back door and saw them.

"Stop. Let her go!"

Jorge zipped his pants and held Kim up like he was helping her. Two of Hermando's security team emerged at the end of the alley.

"Hey, Hermando, do you know this lady? Seems like she needed some air, so I was taking her for a walk."

"You're still up to your tricks. This time you picked the wrong girl."

Jorge let her go and ran toward the other end of the alley. Hermando grabbed Kim as the men caught Jorge like two football players chasing a running back. They pistol-whipped him while he pleaded.

"Mercy, brother. I didn't know. I'm just fucking around looking for a little fun. I'm so sorry. You let me go, and I'll never use this stuff again."

In moments, guns were pointed at his bleeding, crumpled body.

"Rid the world of him. Quietly," Hermando ordered.

A guard swiftly pulled a knife from his belt and slit Jorge's throat. Kim watched, numb. Jorge bled like a slaughtered pig as they threw the body in a nearby dumpster. Hermando assisted Kim toward the car. He spoke to his team leader.

"My sister just needs a good night's sleep. We'll tell everyone she had too much tequila and needed to sleep it off in the car. Tomorrow she won't remember a thing. Devil's Breath is rough shit."

Hermando and Kimberly strolled through the streets of Juarez like any young couple dazed in the moonlight.

"Next time," Hermando murmured in her ear, "I'll tell you not to take any cards from strangers."

2

The Day after Tomorrow

5:00 a.m.
The Mayflower Hotel
Washington, DC

Michael Kublai Khan from The House of Jeremiah Temples woke to the barks of spotted hyenas and the grunts of black wildebeests emanating from an electronic dreamscape machine that was programmed with the sounds of ocean waves, rainstorms, and animal noises. For the minister, this jungle symphony was a stirring way to command consciousness in a strange hotel room. In the seconds after waking—before he had the experience of knowing where he was in space and time—the screeching howls transported him to the Serengeti. After that brief second, the honorable minister was forced to remember what city he was in and which hotel he'd checked into the night before. But in that moment when the unreal trumps real life, Michael Kublai Khan felt at home in the Motherland.

After his morning prayers and meditation, Kublai Khan showered, shaved, and prepared himself for a day of long meetings in the nation's capital. The man of God admired his image inside the ornate hotel bathroom mirror and then tuned the twelve-inch Seura LCD TV to CNN. The news reports gave him a sense of what was *not* happening in Washington. The politicians fought like single women attacking one another's digital dating habits, with both adoration and disdain for a process where winning was losing. The bipartisan dance was more for effect than effectiveness, and the minister felt he could bring about more change for his people by being of the community and not in Congress.

He lathered his cheeks, chin, neck, and medial cleft with an aloe-vera-infused shaving cream and then carefully sharpened the straight razor on the rawhide strap he traveled with. Once the soothing cream conditioned his face against razor bumps, Khan pressed the sharpened tool against the tender skin of his neck. After a few precise upward strokes, he washed the straight razor in the sink under scalding water before continuing. His graceful cadence allowed the razor to dance between his skin and the flow of steaming hot water like his hand, body, and blade were one. After the shave, the pastor cradled his face in a frigid towel he had immersed in a bucket of ice water before the after-shave ritual began. Then he tenderly treated his skin with specialized creams and lotions until he was satisfied that his chiseled features were properly protected against the freezing temperature that accompanied a mid-January day in the capital. The image in the mirror showed the taut face of a man who defied age, and proclaimed the true meaning of the adage *Black don't crack*.

Kublai Khan's grooming routine would not be complete without ensuring that his hair was properly coiffed. He wore a modified natural, trimmed short enough to be combed with a two-inch

Afro comb and softened with a strong bristled brush. Fifty strokes later, Khan used an olive-oil-infused pomade that he rubbed into his scalp, smoothing out the coarse texture of his hair before using the comb to finish off any stray kinks the brush had missed. To finish the job, the minister patted down the edges with his hands until he was pleased with the shape and look of his do.

Today there was no time for his usual military-style pushups and sit-ups. Skipping a day made him feel like he was slacking off, but it also gave him confidence that tomorrow would be a good day to suffer the punishment of rededication to his physical fitness. He took the freshly pressed white-on-white Indian cotton shirt from the plastic skin and felt the warmth of the press as he brought the shoulders of the shirt around his muscular guns and across his ample chest. It fit perfectly as he carefully applied each button to the specially tailored buttonholes. His red silk tie flowed into a perfect full Windsor knot on the first attempt. The final touch was the blue and gold presidential cufflinks he had received at the White House last January.

The minister reached for his suit jacket and brought it over his shoulders as he stretched his arms toward the ceiling. The blue polished silk jacket lining held snugly to his right arm.

RIP!

The jacket tore along the exterior sleeve of the perfectly tailored coat.

Disgusted, he reached for his cell phone. Wyman Jeffries would still be at home in Bethesda, having breakfast with his wife, Yolanda.

"Brother Jeffries. *As-Asalamu Alaykum.*"

"Good morning, Minister Kublai Khan. What can I do for you this blessed morning?" Wyman would know the answer to the question was only a breath away.

"I trust you can have that new worsted wool pinstripe suit you're cutting me ready in about ninety minutes?"

"We were planning to have that one ready next week."

"Need it this morning."

"Then I will call my seamstresses in early to finish it, and will have it ready with a matching tie and shirt when you arrive. About noon?"

"Make it nine thirty sharp. Got to be at the Mayflower by ten."

"Consider it done."

. . . .

Kublai Khan arrived at the DuPont Circle tailor shop on time and found Wyman hovering by the front door. The tailor didn't keep his minister waiting as he hurriedly unlocked and opened the pane glass door with *Wyman Jeffries Custom Tailor LLC* painted on it.

"Good morning, pastor. How are you doing this day Yahweh has given us?"

"Blessed. Where's my suit?"

Jeffries pointed to the naked mannequin centered in front of a four-way mirror near countless bolts of Arabian silks, Moroccan cashmere, and English worsted wool. Wyman deftly moved to the pedestal, where he motioned the minister to stand.

First they fitted the jacket. It fit fastidiously, except for the single vent in the back of the coat. As Wyman took the yellow measuring tape from around his neck to make sure the dimensions were correct, he said, "Minister Khan, the single vent back just doesn't dramatize your athletic build. The double vent would look a thousand percent better."

The minister scowled as if Wyman had pressed a double-edged switchblade against his tender flesh. Then he studied the tailor for a moment, and dipped his head.

"Whatever you think is right," he said. "I count on you to help manage my image in the world. I don't want people to see the pimp in me." He laughed wryly.

Jeffries took two of the pins from his wrist cushion and placed them against the chalk markings he had made where the two vents should be. "Now the pants" was all he said.

Khan admired him grudgingly. Paris-trained, Wyman had been in the same location since the suits were Nehru style and his clients were mostly White. The minister stepped into a changing room as the tailor gave the jacket to the seamstress waiting just on the other side of the looming mirrors. When the minister came out again, Wyman was already sizing up the adjustments he had made to the pants, including a half-inch along the inseam, and finished off the one-inch cuffs. He looked pleased with himself.

"If you wait twenty minutes, I will have the suit finished and you will be on your way. Try on the candy-striped shirt with the white French cuffs, and before you select a couple of silk ties and cufflinks, your suit will be ready."

Wyman slipped the minister into a beige changing robe while he waited for the Vietnamese seamstresses to finish his pants. Khan picked a pair of antique silver circle links trimmed in gold to go with the red silk tie that he'd worn into the tailoring shop, leaving the necktie choices of his tailor on the changing rack. When the suit was completed, Jeffries beamed with pride at the evidence of his grace under pressure.

Kublai Khan merely nodded. For him, the two-hour miracle was just another test—one that endeared the tailor to the pastor while leaving the minister uninspired by the two-hour miracle. It was a routine morning in an ordinary day in Kublai Khan's demanding life. He left his dutiful subject behind as he strode out of the shop in a beautiful custom-tailored suit and exquisite cufflinks.

"*As-Asalamu Alaykum*, my brother." "*Wa Barakatuh*."

. . . .

Close by on Connecticut Avenue, four nonlethal response vehicles, equipped with high-density LED deterrent lighting, seven hundred rounds of tear gas, and beanbag pellets, headed to the site of a civil disturbance. On board the armor-plated three-wheeled transports were police officers from the Public Disturbance Division. They listened to the police radio for the status of the situation.

"A 10-15 reported at the Mayflower Renaissance Hotel on Connecticut at De Sales Street Northwest. Two hundred protesters are blocking the side entrance to the Hotel. Request ETA."

"We're three minutes out," an officer reported into his shoulder microphone. "Will approach off Connecticut and Seventeenth Street. Two by two. Request patrol car for backup."

"Copy that. Proceed with caution."

Minutes later the vehicles arrived at the protest.

Standing at the side entrance of the prestigious hotel was a small, portly man with a big megaphone. It was the good Reverend Tucker Dalton of Chino California who bought an assortment of bible toting and countrified White men and women that wanted to feel as if their words mattered. The underemployed and misunderstood had just dined on a breakfast of rancid baloney, molded cheese, and stale crackers from brown paper lunch bags before being taken to the luxury hotel of the politically oriented.

"Brothers and sisters, we are here against the power mongers. God blessed the White race with its dominion over this world. Can government say who is White and who isn't?"

The crowd shouted back their rehearsed response, thrusting signs skyward: *White Rules, God Made Us! White Makes Right.*

"No!"

"Should a mixed-race mongrel be able to declare themselves black, brown, or yellow?"

"No!"

"Stand with me here at the doors of Babylon. Together we will not be moved."

"We will not be moved. We will not be moved."

The crowd stepped toward the revolving doors of the hotel, and the riot vehicles edged closer. The command officer shouted a warning to the protectors.

"You are in violation of the District's Ordinance 22-1107 against incommoding, which carries a maximum penalty of a $250 fine and 90 days in jail. Please turn back and gather across the street to peaceably continue your gathering or you will be arrested."

The police placed tear gas pellets into high-pressure air tanks for use against the thickening crowd. Pastor Dalton saw the arrival of a news crew and knew he had gained the advantage.

"Do as the officers have asked. I will stand here as a solitary soldier in Christ till Hell freezes over," he said.

A man in a rush so preoccupied by his thoughts he ignored the commotion and cast his looming shadow on the hotel entrance. Dalton stepped contemptuously into his path.

"Pardon me, sir. I'm trying to make a meeting," Kublai Khan said.

"I bet you are Mister Khan. And it's got to do with how mixed-race bastards can call themselves any damn thing they'd like to," Dalton said.

Now the portly white man was up in the grill of the strong black man towering over him. The cameras were clicking with excitement. The minister smiled politely, clearly recognizing the countrified play for attention, and stepped out of the doorway. He leaned into the bodacious preacher's face and whispered.

"If you don't get out of my way, fat man, I will kick your ass."

Dalton went still.

In four gigantic strides, Kublai Khan headed to the VIP entrance of the hotel like he should have in the first place. Dalton remained where he was. The crowd retreated, and the pastor hurried across the street to his followers. A group of men emerged from the crowd and surrounded him.

"Pastor, what happened?" one of them demanded. "And who was that big black man?"

"Turn on the evening news tonight," Dalton said in a conspiratorial whisper, "and you all will see the good news."

3

Keeping It a Hundred

Inside the hotel ballroom were 521 academics, government bureaucrats, civil-rights leaders, school administrators, and corporate executives to review population models and seek a solution for the biggest social challenge to the American way of life.

A government wonk in a cheap blue suit with an obligatory cotton twill button-down shirt and bargain basement red tie and sensible shoes approached the microphone and introduced the first speaker.

"Ladies and Gentlemen, please welcome the Director of Operations of the United States Office of Management and Budget, Jennifer Marcus."

Ms. Marcus, an African American woman in her fifties replete in her St. John dark-blue wool knit suit, offered a rushed good-morning greeting and then spoke about the subject of the conference.

"The Federal Interagency Committee on Education has set categories to allow all government agencies an opportunity to adopt common statistical standards for reporting and presenting data on race and ethnic groups," she said without prompts or cue cards.

"We will discuss today the possible repeal of Directive 15, which allows for the self-classification of racial categories. The designation is allegedly disruptive, costly, and potentially divisive. Our work today is to hear views for and against using self-identification in the next Census."

What followed was an assortment of academics, policy wonks, and civil-rights leaders who spoke on both sides of the country's first self-qualifying statistical category that had been added to the Census. The arguments were about money and power.

Kublai Khan served on a panel with Dr. Federico Garza, Chairman of the Federal Working Group on Population Growth. His work on the expanding Hispanic populations elevated him to the status of lead authority on the subject in the country. Before he spoke, the professor looked over his brown horn-rimmed glasses.

"Race isn't about science, biology, or anthropology. It's about control. The government is controlled by White Europeans, and they use race classifications to control other non-White people."

The panel also included the charismatic presence of televangelist Samuel Foresight from Albany, GA. He was known as one of the most popular televangelists on cable television. His followers were multicultural, and he saw an opportunity.

"The freedom for people to define themselves by their own classification is a right, not a privilege. Don't go back to the old ways. This is the new America."

The last member of the panel was the urban demographer Les Solomon, a veteran demographer from the Institute of Numbers a California-based think tank. He knew Kublai Khan from their days in Michigan, fighting the social wars of the inner city. Together they had developed strategies to counteract the power structures in government that helped make Black people poor and the cycle of poverty endless. Les was a wily man with a habitual thirst for statistics, which grew as fast as his receding hairline. A boor of a man— Les went on about his professional interests.

"Our work is the critical factor in how appropriations, redistricting, and federal grants are dispersed in this country. Anything that impedes one minority over another will foster rebellion. Blacks against Whites."

Khan agreed.

"In America, race is the key factor in politics, education, and the quality of life. For Black people our minority status limits opportunity. We got to increase the flow so Blacks get mo."

Kublai Khan's attempt at humor was a joyful noise in the cathedral of banality. The session ended after a few more questions about race and population. As the panelists dismounted the one-foot platform, a cohort of admirers and seminar groupies surrounded the minister. The most adamant was a case worker from Billings, MT, who had a comment and not a question.

"It doesn't make good sense to try to make things change from the way they are. Black people are minorities. Begging for more is just not going make it happen. Y'all got to make the best of a bad situation."

Khan turned away from the crowd, tugged the lapels of his sport coat, straightened his tie, and spoke directly to the lady.

"Madam, you can kiss my grits."

With that, Kublai Khan left the room.

4

Rigging the Race

Les Solomon and Kublai Khan had coffee in a local restaurant in the shadow of the Vietnam Memorial. The morning workshops had concluded with little closure to the question of mixed-race America.

"So, what do you think, Les?"

The demographer and statistician unfolded some poorly sorted spreadsheets on the coffee table. Khan knew the drill.

"They got it wrong. Bureaucrats have no balls. All population projections are about putting your ass on the line."

Les used his drugstore pen to point to a line of numbers that looked to the minister like complicated algebra.

"Their algorithms are bullshit. When I add the higher fertility rates of mixed-race women with the male promiscuity factors of men of color, it's going to send birthrates through the roof."

Kublai Khan asked questions while Les scribbled unintelligible figures on crumpled napkins he pulled from his well-worn tweed jacket.

"Twenty-five percent?"

"Yes, it's a beautiful thing."

"You mean if we can put the two factors together, it will make the difference."

"America will become a majority minority nation."

"Beautiful. The House of Jeremiah can secure its place in human history as the lost tribe of Israel. Hallelujah!"

Khan jumped to his feet with both arms stretched to the sky, and his fists thrust above his head. No one in the café reacted. Stranger things happen in Washington all the time.

. . . .

In a booth at the rear of the café, Pastor Dalton sat quietly with other men from the church. They nursed cups of cheap coffee as they listened intently to the conversation happening just a few yards away. Dalton smiled.

"He calls himself a Christian. Let's learn more about him."

The little round table that the men sat around was barely large enough for four small women, yet there were six burly men huddled together, trying to hide in plain sight. Only Khan's rapture hid them. Next to Dalton sat Brother Jimmy Blair.

"Jimmy, what do you see? Can you share with us how a soldier sets his sights on a target?"

Brother Blair peered at the minister and studied his mannerisms. Dalton could see the wheels turning behind Blair's eyes and tried to follow his observations as he muttered under his breath.

"Look at those clothes...six feet five, two hundred and twenty pounds...three hundred yards; it'd take a fifty millimeter to drop him...." Blair murmured to himself and then shook his head and looked directly at Dalton with a small smirk. "He's formidable, but no match for the right weapon."

The other proselytes nodded in unison. The lunch-hour crowd at the restaurant buzzed as the customers moved around like drones in a hive, while the waitresses conducted their business like queens.

. . . .

When the Honorable Minister Kublai Khan of The House of Jeremiah was inspired, his voice deepened and he shouted like a country preacher. There was a brazen glare in his eyes. Everyone ignored him except for his well-trained bodyguards, positioned near exits and checkpoints.

In seconds, the outburst was over and Kublai Khan calmly returned to his seat.

"What do you call this strategy?" he asked Les.

"I call it the 'Mocha Effect.'"

Les and Kublai Khan talked about hours how the real impact of their plot would bring a new social order to America. As the numbers man, Les always knew the change he wanted.

"The opportunity is to change the very way people see themselves. That'll change what they do." He slurped his coffee. "Europeans saw Indians as savages, without intelligence or virtue. Africans were brought here as property. It all started with a deep disregard for other groups of people and the need to dominate them."

"It stops here," Khan rumbled. "We'll take the multicultural population in America and turn it into a social revolution based on the one real truth. People who say they're the same—*are* the same."

Les frowned.

"Rigging the statistics is a lot harder than it sounds. This kind of engineering will take exceptional methods, and will require help from the people. Are you ready for that?"

"My men will be the fathers of this new nation. The work to transform America starts today." Khan leaned back in his seat. "There are thirty million Black men in this country, and I've got the two million who can lead it. I call that a good start."

5

Sebastian Knows Best

Pastor Dalton enjoyed tinkering in the utility barn beside his home on his four-acre farm in Chino, California. In the barn, he kept dozens of rats and mice of varying sizes and colors in twenty-gallon glass aquariums. He also had a few large snakes for waste disposal.

In his makeshift lab, Dalton picked the sires and dams he liked best and put them in a glass shelters supplied with water, grain, and exercise wheels. Pastor Dalton put the black, brown, and mixed rats in bins by themselves.

Watching the procedure with indifference was Dalton's pet white mouse, Sebastian. He enjoyed the wrinkles and folds of the inside of the hood on Dalton's heavy jacket he needed for the damp, cold confines of the barn. Sebastian was a good listener.

"This one's so handsome. Isn't he?" Dalton said while gently holding a male by the tail with his head resting against the pastor's upper lip and his tiny feet resting against his lower one.

Sebastian sat on the preacher's left ear and gazed at the specimen squirming in his master's hand.

With a two-milliliter hypodermic syringe, Dalton injected adrenaline into the rodent so he could observe its behavior in a makeshift labyrinth he made out of plywood and chicken wire. Inside the maze was a large black rat.

"Now we will see of the two which one is smarter, faster, and better," Dalton said as he put the two rats side by side and finished final touches on the course.

"I saw the oddest man of God when I was in DC," Dalton told his pet. "He was arrogant, rude, and blasphemous. But more important, he was Black, and in charge of a plan to kill off the White species. I gotta do something about him and his scheme. I must look to the Lord for his guidance and direction. Don't ya think so?"

Sebastian crawled around Dalton's neck and gently nibbled on his ear. Then he nestled inside the peak of the hood at Dalton's nape. Dalton nodded his agreement.

He pulled the barrier separating the maze from the holding station and watched the rats explore the pathways that had to be negotiated to reach the prize of a dab of peanut butter at the end of the race.

6

Of Soap and Shoes

As Kublai Khan left his suite at the Shutters Hotel, he heard the wood crackling in the stone hearth of the resort just a few yards from the hustle of the Santa Monica beach scene. He ignored the scantily clad ladies and beach brutes that occupied the sand and surf just outside the circular driveway that men like the minister used to stack and store their impatient drivers. The tedious crosstown trip would prove almost civilized with his favorite driver, Ahmed Reynolds, there to serve him.

Reynolds had queued up in the crowded driveway for fifteen minutes before he caught sight of the minister. He sprang into action, commandeered the rear passenger door, and greeted Kublai Khan with a no-nonsense smile.

"Good morning, sir. Ready for LA traffic?"

"We'll get there in time enough. How's Nana Rey?"

"Everything's a struggle with her, but Mama's in decent health."

Ahmed still lived with his Nana Rey, who saw him as a failure both on the streets and in life. Nothing he did had pleased her until he got out of the thug life and into The House of Jeremiah.

Behind the wheel again, Ahmed wiggled his butt into the wooden-beaded car seat cushion that he'd bought at the Compton-Slauson Swap Meet a few weeks back, and placed his long and surprisingly elegant young fingers firmly on the wood-grained steering wheel. The cabin held a mild scent of jasmine from the three drops of oil that he'd sprinkled into the ashtray to cover the stench that had lingered since he stopped smoking two years ago. Ahmed looked back to see Kublai Khan secure in his seat belt. The driver's eyes shifted back to the windshield, where he caught a glimpse of the dream catcher that he'd hung from the rearview mirror.

The black town car turned right onto Pico Boulevard and headed east. The brilliant sun washed the cabin in morning light, while Ahmed turned the radio from the hip-hop station that he liked to the morning news program Khan preferred. The minister gazed out of the window and admired a vintage cherry-red Chevy Camaro with a "Seniors Rock" bumper sticker, driven by a white-haired lady. It fit like a salty ocean breeze kissing the shores of Catalina. Ahmed turned down the radio and posed a reckless question.

"Why are you visiting an advertising agency? I don't understand what selling soap and gym shoes has to do with religion."

"Be the driver. No questions."

"Thought I could always ask intelligent questions?"

"Now's not this time. I'm trying to focus."

"Sorry."

Kublai Khan caught Ahmed's eye in the rearview mirror and pursed his lips. He had been too abrupt. Ahmed saw his attitude shift.

"What's your favorite ad?" Khan asked.

"I don't know," Ahmed admitted, "since I'm reading more and watching TV less."

"What about billboards or bus shelters? Anything comes to mind?"

Ahmed thought about it. "I like the antismoking ads," he said slowly. "Like the one with the blindfolded gangbanger smoking a cigarette in front of a firing squad. It said, 'Save the bullets.'"

"Did it make you stop smoking?"

"I don't know. But I do remember it."

"That's the power of advertising. It can help the church."

"I see. Thanks." Ahmed nodded.

"Perfect. You're on the right track, my little brother." Khan leaned back against the seat. "How are we doing on time?"

"No problem. Gibbons and Italia in five minutes."

Gibbons and Italia was located in the Penthouse Suites of the Traper office complex on Museum Row by the La Brea tar pits. Entering the penthouse from the elevator bays revealed floor-to-ceiling windows and a spiral staircase that led to the clouds.

Kublai Khan was ushered into a conference room that featured an exquisite marble table with Aeron executive chairs caressing its perimeter. The widescreen televisions were already cued, and they displayed the gold and black Copperplate Gothic bold initials of its founders, Frank Gibbons and Andrea Italia, both long dead and their firm expanded beyond their wildest imaginings. There were breakfast bagels and croissants, homemade jam, and freshly squeezed orange juice placed on the table. It was a generous act of hospitality, and too much food for Kublai Khan to consume alone. Three women and a man walked into the conference room and came to shake hands.

Khan made a point of shaking hands with Chaka Khoury Jackson first.

Chaka was a chocolate-skinned woman with a flowing natural up-do hairstyle that denoted her sense of individuality and fashion. On her tailored charcoal-gray pantsuits lapel stood a gold alloy-jeweled cherub broach about five-millimeters long. Underneath she wore an ivory lacy tie neck silk blouse and just for this meeting, she had backup.

"Good morning," said a trim well-groomed man who made a fashion statement with clothing straight out of a men's magazine. His fade haircut was flawless, "I'm Malcolm Gilmore, chief strategist, and all of us at G&I are honored to meet you." He smiled and then added, "Once I have shared our strategic insights, our creative director, Susan Morgan, will present our preliminary creative work."

Gilmore nodded to Chaka without saying her name, and then everyone turned eyes toward the woman who had to be Morgan. She was fair skinned, with Irish-eyes and stood six feet tall, with bright-red hair that seemed to be ablaze. It was hard for Khan to take his eyes off her but he did so, wondering whether Chaka would finally address him directly.

She didn't. Instead, she walked calmly away from the conversation and picked up a small black cylinder from a table near the door—a stick microphone. Her fingers brushed a panel on the wall as Morgan began telling him excitedly about some aspect of the ad campaign. He didn't hear a word. He was watching Chaka.

Then a blast of rap music from well-hidden speakers made every head in the room—except Chaka's—snap around.

Chaka stalked to the front of the conference room, hips swaying to the thumping beat, gripping the microphone like the hilt of a sword. She brought the black foam tip to her lips and spat words like machine-gun bullets.

"Only God can judge me, that's right. Only God can judge me now. Only God, baby, nobody else…nobody else. All you other motherfuckers get out of my business, really."

The music slammed to a halt. Chaka dropped the mike on the table as the speaker reverberated. Khan stared.

"Today," Chaka said, locking eyes with him, "we will provide you, Minister Khan, with a brief glimpse at a big idea we call Emancipation Day. It is based on the inspiration we get from the words of Tupac Shakur's song *Only God Can Judge Me*. Mr. Gilmore will take you through what we know about our target and what they are looking for from God."

Malcolm took charge.

"The House's new believers are people who see themselves as self-sufficient and yet seek some greater sense of satisfaction. They are looking for something more," Malcolm said as he straightened his Armani tie on his micro-checkered blue and white tailored shirt. He spoke with a polite yet rushed Northeastern flourish.

"African American men are also a part of the growing younger population that don't identify with color or racial identity. They are not their parents."

"They *are* their parents, even if they don't think so," Kublai Khan interrupted with a deep booming tone that sucked air out of the room.

The silence left the room breathless.

"They see themselves as independent and *not* like their parents," Gilmore said politely.

"I reject that premise," Khan rumbled. "None of us can beat the gene pool. They're Black and will be Black until they're dust."

"Even so," Malcolm said, but didn't contradict him again.

The images on the video screen changed to show young Black men watching movies outdoors in a park, going to poetry slams, updating social-media sites, taking selfies, rock climbing, and feeding the needy.

"Your target feels differently than their parents," Malcolm said. "They have seen the old lines of ethnicity and race blur, and want to be known for who they say they are. If a pet hamster can have a Twitter handle, why can't people be who they want to be? The House of Jeremiah is the answer to the provocative social question—where do I fit in?"

Malcolm was sweating out his designer shirt, leaving moist circles underneath each arm and around the back of his neck. His pulse was twitching at his throat, like he was a neophyte gambler with a royal flush for the first time, although his face showed more anxiety than excitement. The minister rose to his feet, standing face to face with Malcolm, and held out his hand.

"Son, where did you grow up?"

"Baltimore. Forest Park." He clasped the proffered hand.

"Your parents?"

"Still there, in the house I was raised in."

"And someday you will be, too."

"Los Angeles is in my blood. I'm home," he said with confidence.

"Susan will take it from here." Chaka interrupted the standoff.

Susan wore five-inch heels that made her look like a seven-foot-tall amazon. The CD dressed in the finest fashions a six-figure income would allow and highlighted it all with what had to be a very expensive hair stylist and makeup artist. Susan was straight out of Vogue and clearly loved the image, which she had worked so hard to perfect.

"Good morning, Kublai, good to see you again."

Khan smiled, but was unsure if they had met before.

"We are proud of the work. It takes the insights that Malcolm has already spoken of and brings them to life with movement and sound. Let's look at them."

The screen showed close-up profiles of young Black men with concerned looks on their faces. The voiceover began over the vintage Earth Wind and Fire song, *Lift Your Head to the Sky*.

"Do you feel that living your life day to day is a waste? That there is little meaning you can look up for? Then look to The House of Jeremiah. At our temple, you will find a reason to know just who you really are. How being with people who think like you can make life itself more fulfilling."

The images transitioned to men and women smiling and laughing together. The music swelled as the voiceover continued.

"Become a part of something much bigger than yourself. Become a supporter of The House of Jeremiah. It's not just a place of worship. It's a new way of life."

The screens faded to silent black. The executives sat silent for a few moments, waiting.

"I have just one thought," Khan said finally, "that might help sell it to my board."

The team listened intently.

"Can we add some mocha babies to the scenes to go with the people smiling and laughing?"

Kublai Khan looked directly at Chaka for her response.

She smiled like a woman who knew she'd won. "Of course we can."

"I assume you and the team are ready to fly to Detroit next week to meet with my board if needed?"

"I look forward to hearing when that can happen."

"Perfect. Chaka, let's talk in the morning."

Chaka nodded to Susan to walk their guest out of the agency. Going down the elevator Susan broke the awkward silence.

"You don't remember me do you?"

Kublai smiled and glanced at her warmly.

"We met at Ahmed's birthday party two years ago when I was his sponsor. He's a fine young man. We still stay in touch," she said with both a sense of pride and grace.

"I guess my memory isn't what it used to be," he said ruefully. "But you're in luck Ahmed's driving me today."

. . . .

Outside the agency, the minister spotted the limo at the curb and briskly walked toward it with Susan a step behind him. Ahmed stood by the shiny grill of the sedan, arguing with a parking valet.

"Get outta my face, girl. I'll make you leak like a faucet if you don't check yourself!" Ahmed arched his back, stiffened his neck and shoulders, and smiled sternly to camouflage the rage clearly growing inside him.

"You're just a chicken shit ex-banger who can't read parking signs. Move the fucking car," she said, close enough to Ahmed's face for him to smell whatever she'd had for breakfast.

The minister worried for the valet. He had seen that look before. Ahmed was about to blow.

"Breathe, my brother," Khan said as he grabbed his driver's clenched fists from behind and pressed out each finger slowly until his palm was open. Susan stepped in between him and the attendant. Ahmed's neck and shoulders relaxed as the minister turned his attention to the defiant attendant.

"Young lady, please excuse my driver's rudeness. He's been up all night with a sick child. We'll be out of your way momentarily."

The attendant quickly stepped off, staring with contempt at Ahmed.

"Punk-ass chump," she said by way of a parting shot.

Khan guided Ahmed back to the driver's door before he could respond. They both got in leaving Susan standing by the window. She gestured for Ahmed to give her a call and waved goodbye to the minister. Inside the car, Khan broke the stirring silence.

"Anger is a black man's kryptonite," he said as Ahmed started the car and pulled out into traffic. "People will use it to disturb your balance. Never let them." He watched the colors of the street signs change from white to blue.

"I know," Ahmed snapped. "That faggot thought she could punk me. I had to show her that I could hurt her…bad."

"And then what?"

"I'm no punk."

"So?"

"She was in my face."

"Use your head, not your heart."

Ahmed lowered his head and took a deep, cleansing breath as the stoplight turned green.

"Yes, sir. I apologize."

"And one day, you might even apologize to her," Khan added. Then he frowned. "Is there a special way you're taking me to the airport?"

"No, just the fastest," Ahmed said and then added, "All city streets. No muss, no fuss."

"Looks like I will make my flight thanks to you."

"No problem. That's what I'm here for."

Inside the terminal, VIP service made getting through security quick and friendly. Along the way, Khan said hello to the bellmen and TSA team members he encountered. In record time, he was sitting in his first-class seat, sipping spring water.

While the engines droned toward Detroit, Khan thought about how attractive Chaka was beautiful in an African-queen kind of way. Charming and powerful. She had become the hard-driving ad executive that she had declared herself to be. He had always known she could do anything she set her mind to. Advertising wasn't a model of diversity, so by rising to the top of the game, Chaka had proved she had gumption and remarkable spirit.

She was the one.

7

Making Plans

Laguna Beach, California, was the perfect symbol of all that was right with America: beautiful beaches, five-star hotels, and exceptional weather. Nestled by the Pacific Ocean in southern Orange County, yet far enough to miss the stench of diversity and cross-cultural anxiety of Los Angeles.

Kublai Khan had assembled an international brain trust for a private meeting at a five-star seaside resort.

Representatives of The World Energy Church of Seoul, the Sygen Wei Sect of Shanghai, and the La Raza Pentecostal Church of Brownsville, Texas were there to discuss how they could capitalize on the growing multicultural population trends in the US. The minister prepared by having pre-meetings with his guests. He met Reverend Caldera for dinner the night before at the resort's Argentinian steakhouse. The men sat in a private room where the scent of smoky apple and cherry wood accented the air and a side of lamb roasted slowly on a rotisserie in an open-hearth fireplace. They enjoyed a bottle of Bordeaux and a pair of rib eyes.

Reverend Caldera had brown hair and showed signs of needing less food and more exercise but maintained a ruggedly handsome face even when a fitness gym should be in his future. He spoke with a strong baritone voice and exaggerated Mexican accent. Reverend Caldera then took a healthy gulp of wine and cut into his bleeding beef while Kublai Khan pushed for an alliance.

"Together we can unite black and brown. Hispanics will be the majority in ten years," Kublai Khan said as he nursed his wine and carved a tidy piece of a medium-rare steak.

"Five," Caldera said as the meat juices pressed against the inside of his mouth.

"Pardon me. Five it is," the minister said as he thought how arrogant Caldera was being. "The fact is that a plan like mine will benefit you more than me. I want us to go into the meeting tomorrow with a united front."

"What about Wei and Hung? Do we need them?"

"This is a black, brown, and yellow coalition. They're crucial."

"What's my role?"

"Just follow my lead and agree with the projections."

"Done."

The two men shook on it and finished dinner without dessert.

After he returned to his suite, Kublai Khan spoke with Reverend Hung on the phone. Hung wasn't easy.

"I have no reason to support your plan. How much will this cost?"

The reverend seemed anxious as his voice came out of the speakerphone. Khan glanced at the plan summary and listened to the tide crash against the rugged shore just off his patio.

"The money is just a tool. The budget is just a start. Just bring an open mind."

That night, as Kublai Khan said his prayers, he sensed his own impatience and asked for divine guidance. As his head pressed against his pillow, he imagined Hung's face smiling at him approvingly.

At breakfast the following morning, he shared tea with Master Wei and also asked for his buy-in. Wei was a small slightly built man whose pale white flowing robes appeared to make him float from place to place. Looking straight out of central casting the Master had a silver white beard that flowed to his chest and appeared to sparkle. Wei listened and did not speak beyond pleasantries. Kublai Khan waited for the recalcitrant waiter to finish clearing the table. Finally.

"There must be something you want from me?"

Wei thought intently and said, "No."

"We can help with immigration, given the majority of your flock is in China?"

"Nothing," Wei said as he placed his linen napkin gently on the table and folded it into a perfect square and then stood up. His three manservants were already halfway across the restaurant from where they sat to attend to Master Wei's departure.

"Thanks for tea, Minister Khan. I will see you when time allows."

Both men bowed deeply, and then the minister was alone at the table, wondering if this was the only man he knew who wanted nothing from him.

• • • •

Les began the morning discussion with a quick review of the Mocha Girls strategic premise.

"Let me tell you a story about Rebecca and Tamara."

Les sipped a perfect cappuccino and sensed everyone was relaxed and listening with curiosity.

"Each woman was eighteen years old, and they both lived in the land of Jacob. Their lives were different. Rebecca was a noble-woman. Tamara was a slave. Becky loved to dance and Tamara survived washing and cleaning for her mistress. Each girl met a guy and had sex. After their encounters, Rebecca went back to dancing, while Tamara became pregnant and had a child named Sarah."

Reverend Hung moved nervously in his seat. Khan watched in his peripheral vision.

"Tamara has three more girls, Joan, Cassandra, and Mary, who each had three more girls. In future generations, the women beget more girls at a similar rate. Rebecca stayed childless until well into her twenties and had her first and only daughter, Diane, who went childless throughout her short life. In two generations, the rate of births was seven to one."

Master Wei sipped on his green tea, slowly turning his cup counterclockwise a quarter turn with every sip.

"Were the slaves Asian?" he inquired.

"How do you know this?" Caldera asked, pointing a pencil for emphasis.

Kublai Khan spoke. "Let him continue."

Les took off his metal-rimmed glasses for added emphasis.

"Remember Cassandra? She was sold to an African warlord and had twelve children. Her seven girls had an average of six females apiece through captivity."

The men in the room tried to do the math in their heads and saw the future.

"Generations passed and women kept having babies. Now three out of four babies born today in America are black, Hispanic, or Asian. My point is that women of color have more babies than White girls do."

"Are White women less fertile?" asked Hung as he fingered his half-eaten croissant.

"Yes. But there's more. The most fertile females are mixed race. Mocha Girls."

Les paused for reactions from the group.

"Our plan is to make Mocha Girls with African seed and take over America," Kublai Khan added.

After a few seconds, Master Wei spoke.

"It's not my role to question or criticize what you are planning, Honorable Minister. I do speak for the followers of Qi-gong. I will meditate on this matter before I give you my final decision."

Reverend Hung Sung Suk said, "I think your plan has promise. The key is the Mocha Girls. Taking care of them will take money and influence."

"It's the fathers who will spawn this transformation. In a matter of one generation we can produce thousands of impregnated females," Kublai Khan said.

"Childhood development will be a cooperative effort of our churches?"

Minister Caldera slowly sipped his black tea. "The idea here is the creation of a new category of racial differences that would trump the idea of whiteness," he said. Then he frowned. "I think your plan is flawed. The idea of blending into a racial hybrid will hurt our church."

Kublai Khan felt the double-cross.

Caldera smiled through his teeth and said, "I respect your position, Reverend. But we decline to participate at this time."

"The numbers point to an increase in mixed-race Hispanics that don't see themselves as Latinos," Les warned. "The change will impact your flock first. Better you join us now than need us later."

"Our flock will only get stronger," Caldera said as he stood and began his goodbyes.

"Thanks for coming and hearing me out," Khan said politely. "I won't take no as your final decision. We will talk."

Master Wei also his good wishes and left the room. Hung Sung Suk and his followers remained.

"Is Los Angeles the best place to start?" Hung said.

"It has the highest birthrates among all woman, and that's because of the mixed-race females," Kublai Khan reported.

"My female faithful are mostly Korean."

"That's the beauty of this plan," Les put in. "The growth of mixed-race people can come from any and all racial mixtures. It creates an arithmetic anomaly."

"Anomaly. How so?" Hung asked.

Les fetched a stack of computer reports from his briefcase and spread them out in front of Hung. His enthusiasm gave his voice a squeaky pitch and hastened delivery.

"The beauty is in the statistics. One birth. One person. One race. When you add the mixed-race factor, every birth compounds the federal birthrate by twenty percent."

"I see," Hung said defensively, leaning back in his seat to escape the rabid demographer.

"This is why the plan will work. The growth will be faster than the government can control. Blacks will become the fastest-growing population because this plan is all about fucking and having babies," Les pontificated.

"Let's talk about the marriages and birthing camps during lunch," Kublai Khan said.

"My church will develop the principles and values for living a sacred life on earth and yours will build the ideals and directions for political action. Each day the couples will learn to live faithfully. Then they will be returned to the communities," Hung advised. "It all starts with marriages. I am prepared to bring two thousand women a month to be joined in a holy ceremony with the men of The House of Jeremiah."

"My men will be there," the minister said.

At lunch, Kublai Khan enjoyed the sense of victory. He picked at a spinach salad and admired Hung's appetite for a luscious hamburger with all the trimmings.

"I have read about something called the one-drop rule. Does it affect our work?" Hung asked, putting his sandwich down and eating a spoonful of macaroni salad.

"It requires anyone who has any Black ancestry to be considered Black," Khan said. "Americans still abide by the one-drop rule."

"Then I could be Black?" Hung said.

"No, it only relates to Black people that look Black. If you're light enough, you can pass for White."

"So all of our babies will be Black?"

"Precisely. That is where the political power comes from."

Hung smiled.

8

Meeting Adjourned

Chaka took off her red-soled three-inch high heels while sitting in her silver Aeron chair while her Gucci one shoulder blue silk shantung dress snugly crept up her toned shapely legs and, in a continuously sweeping motion, put on her white jeweled Jimmy Choos. It was a quarter to six—and as everyone in the office knew, she had to make a stunning appearance at the Advertising Leader of the Year event at the Beverly Wilshire Hotel. Hoshiko "Star" Mathews, an art director, stood in the doorway, watching and stroking her furry friend with opal eyes.

"Got time to see the Nova rough cut?" Mathews asked as she cradled a well-behaved cat in her arms. The brown shorthaired female was smart adult feline who seemed to be ambivalent to most people and paid respect and reverence to those who fed her or catered to her.

"No way, Star," Chaka replied, clearly using Mathews' nickname to soften the refusal. "Can't risk it today. I'm hosting the VIP reception in less than an hour so just send me a link." She stood up and looked into the full-length mirror behind her office door. She looked flawless.

"It's better we do this now," Mathews pressed. She let her voice go lower and harder than usual. Chaka might be the boss, but shit needed to be done.

"This isn't a negotiation. Send me the link," Chaka said as she grabbed her champagne Margot clutch and pushed past Star in the doorway.

"Done deal." Mathews surrendered and slowed her roll while she walked down the red-carpeted hallway toward the creative department. She dropped her "ticked" tabby coated cat and let it stroll under her worktable and corner a red-rubber chewing toy. Susan Morgan, her boss, was putting the final touches on an art board as Star slipped her hands into the pockets of her artfully torn designer jeans and gave a status report.

"I'm sending Chaka a link to review tonight," she said while her Abyssinian played at her feet.

The tiny bells in the ball jingled as Cleo nudged it with her small wet nose.

"Sixty seconds? You couldn't get Chaka to stop for a freakin' minute?" Susan didn't look up from her work, "Girl, you got to learn how to make people do what you want them to. Even the CEO."

"I know. I'm sorry," Star said.

"Don't apologize. Just get it done." Susan finally looked up, right into Star's brown eyes, and arched an unimpressed eyebrow.

• • • •

Chaka headed to the Santa Monica Freeway in her chauffeured black Lincoln. She relaxed in the plush rear seat and listened to *The Chronic*. There was precious little time for her to relax and enjoy music and smoke a joint. Her "All Eyes on Me" ringtone announced a call from the honorable Kublai Khan.

"So how's my girl?" he asked.

"Let's keep it a hundred," Chaka said. "How was your flight, honorable minister?"

"When will I see you?" he asked, ignoring the question.

"At ten."

"Fantastic. I'll order in Chinese with some of those spicy noodles you like."

"Sweetheart, I mean ten in the morning. Tonight I'm staying at the Hilton. Can't do a rendezvous tonight." Chaka smiled as she said the last sentence, hoping it would ease Khan's disappointment. "Let's keep the good old days in a box for now."

Khan gave a huff of disappointment. "Then I will see you at the office tomorrow with Reverend Hung," he conceded.

"What's he like?" Chaka asked.

"He's a man of God in a blue pin-striped suit and huge diamond pinky ring," Kublai Khan said.

"See you in the morning, muscles."

"Goodnight, booty girl," he said, and she heard the fond smile in his voice.

Chaka restarted the CD and drifted back into an imaginary musical wonderland. The Lincoln sedan driver Andrew made a right on Wilshire Boulevard in Beverly Hills. She could almost taste the spicy noodles that she wasn't going to have tonight.

· · · ·

Kublai Khan wore a black suit with epaulets. On his left wrist was an inconspicuous Patek Philippe watch and a twenty-four-karat gold three-string elephant-hair bracelet. Hung sported a fresh haircut, shave, and manicure. His fingers shone with clear polish. A security team roamed the halls and two enormous black Cadillac Escalades were parked at the curb.

Malcolm Gilmore explained the revised campaign platform.

"When we first accepted this assignment, our agency had a few well-constructed notions about race and ethnicity and how that might impact the campaign mission of making interracial couples more acceptable."

Hung and the minister settled back in seats and relaxed around their hot beverages and began to focus on their laptops before turning their attending back to front of room as Malcolm spoke.

"After a few dozen focus groups and hundreds of shopping-mall intercepts, we trashed the first strategy and started over," he said, and tossed the report binders into a compact recycling bin in the rear corner of the room.

WHAM!

One of Reverend Hung's security men burst into the room with one hand on his concealed weapon and the other on his hip underneath his suit coat. Hung and Khan appeared surprised but in control of their emotions. The effect dissipated immediately. Gilmore continued.

"Why, in the early twentieth century, did some churches in America have a pinewood slab with a comb on a string outside the entry door?"

Silence.

"It was a signal that those whose skin wasn't as light as the pinewood or who couldn't rake a comb effortlessly through their hair were not welcomed in the sanctuary."

Hung and his representatives seem to focus intensively on the slave history while Khan displayed the lack of interest.

"Did you know that this country once practiced a social rule that children of mixed race would be considered the race that was the least privileged? And yet, now we can make interracial dating fashionable." Gilmore held a brown paper bag up, silently comparing its color to his darker skin.

"Are you saying we don't have to do anything to speed up the creation of MRCs and mocha babies?" Kublai Khan asked.

Malcolm was ready.

"Of course we have to lead the way. But the Forum marriages will be a beautiful event that'll make those babies a prized social possession. It will no longer be an accessory exclusive to celebrities like Kanye and Kim. Mocha babies are for everyone."

"We must find a way to show the positive economic impact that recently immigrated women have on the nation," Hung said.

"We will create a social media site that will give mixed-race women all over the world an opportunity to express their fears, tears, and hopes for the future." Chaka said.

Both men smiled.

After the meeting, when the team said goodbye to Hung, Chaka noticed Kublai Khan dismissing his security detail. Her team made a beeline for the elevators. Chaka said about a zillion "good works" and "goodbyes" and then turned to Kublai Khan, who had a shit-eating grin on his face. They were alone standing in the elevator foray. As they embraced, he cupped her Chaka's butt gently and tenderly kissed her.

He whispered, "Are we alone?"

"Does it matter?" she asked as she pushed his hand up.

"Of course we are," she said.

. . . .

Without a word, Chaka led Khan up the staircase toward her penthouse office. Her black double-knit business suit with white trim accented the way her hips joined with her narrow waist. The passion he felt was increased by his reptilian brain instincts when he gazed at the mid-waist juncture of her body. Chaka paused on the stairs for a moment to squeeze the minister's Johnson through his trousers.

"We're alone, but you still have to wait to get to my office."

"I may take you right here."

By the time they reached the top of the stairs, the minister had his strong fingers searching up Chaka's skirt. Khan pushed his forefingers past her panties, and caressed her vulva. Chaka jumped with surprise as he pressed her up against the wall at the top of the stairs. Her pearl necklace snapped on impact, its stones scattering on the polished plaster floor and cascading down the stairs like bouncing white rubber balls.

Kublai Khan thrust his penis against her and gathered her skirt above the silk half-slip that clung to her toned thighs. He pulled her panties down around her heels, exposing her unshaven labia. The frenzy of his actions made Chaka freeze, remembering.

"Give me a chance to breathe," she gasped.

"I'm the one who needs oxygen," the minister barked as he shed his pants.

He kissed her deeply and enjoined her tongue with his. She bit it firmly but gently. The quest of his hands excited her. The deeper they went, the more she pressed up against them. But she couldn't help thinking of a butcher prodding a piece of meat, too. And she wasn't a roast.

She resisted as he jostled her jacket off and flung it to the floor, followed by her skirt, slip, and panties. Her sheer blouse revealed her swollen nipples. He fumbled with the buttons and one of them popped free. He flung it into the mailroom.

"I can't get your clothes off fast enough," Kublai Khan said. He stood fully naked from the waist down, and she was down to only her half-open blouse and bra.

And suddenly she was back against a wall at a fraternity rush party. She could smell the apple wine and gin on his breath and feel the muscles in his arms rolling against her waist. She could almost hear the muffled, long-gone sounds of Motown from beyond the door of his bedroom.

She never had gotten the cum stains out of her shirt, and she never had decided just where the blame lay.

She pushed back and elbowed Kublai Khan in the stomach. He bent at the waist and gasped for air.

"Muscles. I won't let you do this again," she said.

He went stiff, stubborn, and stupefied.

"What are you talking about?" he demanded. "That was a hundred years ago."

"It wasn't that long ago," Chaka replied, the knowledge swelling within her, "and today it would've been called rape."

"I was drunk and stupid."

"You were out of control." Chaka stepped away, bending down to pick up her jacket and underwear.

Khan huffed.

"You can still catch your men in the lobby," she said without looking at him. "I'm going to lock up and head home. Good night, Kublai."

The honorable minister was already halfway down the stairs when Chaka pulled up her skirt and buttoned her shirt as she stared into darkness.

9

Born to Drive

Kimberly tried not to think of Juarez. She told herself that it wasn't her fault that she was a *hija natural* and her new relatives weren't ready to deal with her.

In the States Kim did her best to get back to *life* as she once knew it. A party would be the best medicine. Kim dressed for the night out and talked to her mother while pushing the conversation around to boys, fashion, and even pushed her luck about using the family car.

"I like the way this skirt fits you. I bet Timmy Pearson will love it," said Rachel as she held the slinky skirt on a hanger up for inspection.

"I haven't seen Tim in weeks," Kim reminded her. "It's great that the party is at his house, but it's no big deal."

Rachel took a white cotton top out of the closet and put it on the bed.

"He seems like a great guy, and his mother says he likes you."

Kim put a purple velvet vest on the bed next to the top. "I think he's nice, but I'm not really into him." She peered into the bedroom mirror and dabbed on her blush.

"Who's picking you up tonight?"

"Mom, I was thinking...." Kim turned back with her most earnest expression. "Can I have the car tonight?"

Rachel narrowed her eyes. "No drinking. And, no boys."

"It's just Julie and Natalie." Kim glanced back at the mirror, looking for any blemish or flaw in her makeup. "Honest."

· · · ·

"Ehmagawd," Kim moaned as she pointed the car at Toluca Lake. "Hermando and his guys? They were totally hot! Not so much like the guys here. Way more men than boys."

"I'm dying right now," said Julie, putting on the last touches of lip-gloss as her compact shook with the motion of the Hollywood Freeway. She wore her designer jeans and off the shoulder black peasant top she had been saving since the holidays. She felt skinny, beautiful, and ready to play.

"Don't even say you have no pictures," Natalie put in from the back seat, in between posting and texting with her phone. Her dark computer glasses helped frame her narrow face and muted features. She kept track of her social-media post while making sure her friends knew she was heading to a sick party without them.

"Did you get a hookup?" Julie asked.

"Seriously?" Kim scoffed. "I wasn't there for that. I was there to learn more about my dad's family. Didn't learn much. Other than that they're frickin' rich." She shook her head, trying to push away a fuzzy scrap of dream that wouldn't leave her alone. Something about drool…. "Hey, what about the party tonight? Who's going be there?"

"Everybody. It's the last party before college, and it's at Tim's crib," said Julie, putting the final strokes to her bottle-blond hair.

"Tim and I will finally get together," Kimberly predicted. "It's happening."

"I can't even tell you how awesome it is to be going tonight. I don't think any of my other friends are," said Natalie.

"Tim is funny, cool, and everyone knows him from lacrosse. Maybe he'll finally win a game tomorrow," Kim said as she exited the freeway.

She found parking in a side street. The girls gave a final check to their makeup and the way their heels fit as they started the short walk to the party.

"Now, you guys stay calm. Don't embarrass me. I want him to see how good I look," Kim said.

They walked through the door, saw a three-level maze of teen exhilaration, and paused in the living room to watch an active game of truth or dare. In the dining room, the party was sick with drinking and dancing. In the family room, gamers played Detroit Ratz killing gangsters and cops in the hundreds. The girls drifted over to the lying game, where Perry Randolph used his teeth to take the athletic sock off another guy. He spat it out in disgust and then looked up and saw Kim.

"Kim? Awesome. How was Mexico?"

"It was cool. Have you seen Tim? Just want to say hi."

"Kim and Tim. What a match. The dude is somewhere chilling," he said and turned back to the giggling crowd around him.

Kim and the girls walked through the crowd like fish swimming upstream. They navigated the thick throng of hyped dancers gyrating and swaying to pulsating gangster rap. She moved by a table stocked with cold cuts and a cheese plate, snatching up a piece of celery as she looked for Timothy. A chubby black guy with body odor started gyrating mimicked pressing his hips against her behind.

"Hey, shorty. Bring that fine ass over here so I can feel it."

Kim moved away from him, closer to Julie and Natalie.

The song faded, and another tune erupted from the speaker system. One dance was enough.

"Let's keep moving," said Kim, and then glanced through a window and spotted Tim's sandy-brown hair.

Tim was standing outside, a red plastic cup in hand, loitering by the shimmering blue swimming pool. He and his crew circled a keg of beer cooling in an ice chest on the manicured lawn. Kimberly kept her distance as Tim noticed her and nodded his approval.

"Kim, you look smokin'," Tim called as he took another drink from his cup. Kim smiled broadly and started moving toward him.

"Thanks. Great party," Kim said. She inched closer to where Tim held court. With a flick of her auburn hair, she was close enough to see the peach fuzz of his adolescent chin. Without another glance, Tim put his arm around Sheila Edwards from algebra class. Sheila cozied up underneath him as if she belonged there and flashed a small smile in Kim's direction. Kim took a step back and hugged her scarlet clutch bag hopelessly.

"I don't get it," Tim said, returning to the conversation. "There's more of us than them, so why can't the spics leave us alone and stay in Mexico? Throw them out."

Kim's mouth fell open in surprise. Then something on Tim's chest caught her eye.

"What's that you're wearing?" she asked as she leaned in for a closer look.

He wore a parody t-shirt that had a buxom Latina in a sombrero smiling above the "*Tapa Teen Ho*" logo printed across his ample chest. Kimberly lost it.

"I can't believe you are wearing such a lame tee. What's up with that?"

"What do you mean? It's just how I roll." Tim pushed his chest out, displaying his attire, and waited for a howl from his boys.

"It's their land. And that tee tells me you're dumber than you look," Kim said with passionate disdain.

"I get it. You're the new JEWNIC in town. Your mom screwed a Mexican newsboy while out of her fucking mind on weed, and then she pooted you out. Even your girlfriends laughed at you going to there to find your roots," he said, and swigged another cold one.

The gaggle of boys roared with laughter. Before Kim could find a suitable comeback, tears welled up in her eyes, and her legs lost their tensile strength.

"How rude! A JEWNIC—is that a real word?"

No answer from Tim and his boys. She stalked off.

In the kitchen, she confronted Julie and Natalie.

"Is that what you guys are calling me behind my back?" The tears rolled down her reddened face.

"Not me," Julie said.

"So, people are calling me a JEWNIC?"

"Don't let it bother you. We're your friends and didn't want to tell you what those idiots were saying," Julie said, putting an arm around Kim's shoulders.

"And I thought he and I…." Kim whispered, and buried her face in Julie's neck with a muffled sob.

Natalie gave Kim a bottle of ice-cold water. Kim took a sip and thought of other boys. The ones she thought would be right for her. The laughter outside faded, but the sting of prejudice lingered.

"I am ready to get out of here. Are you guys coming?" she said.

"Now? The party's just getting started." Natalie pleaded.

"I'm leaving, so you guys need to find a way home."

Kim grabbed her purse and headed for the front door.

"Don't worry about us; just get home safely," Julie called.

Before Kim pulled away from the curb in her mom's Honda, she paused. She knew better than to rush home emotionally wrecked. Kim went to the trunk. Inside was a dark-skinned mannequin with a cheap black Afro wig flowing from underneath a Chicago White Sox baseball cap. He wore a team jacket with the words *Safety Man* across his chest.

She picked him up by the torso and positioned him on the passenger side. It wasn't long before she was back on the road and remembered the sadness she felt from the racist who was once going to be her boyfriend.

"A JEWNIC?" she said to herself.

As she caught the on-ramp of the Hollywood Freeway, she thought about the future. She knew the people who were an inseparable part of her high-school life wouldn't be a part of her next few years. She spoke calmly to Safety Man.

"I don't care about money or being admired for the job I have. I want to be loved and led to happiness. Is that too much to ask?"

Safety Man stared into space and listened.

"Is that too much to ask? Really? He must love me and lead me."

Kim began to think of a new possibility. She would be whatever she wanted to be.

Kim tuned her radio to her favorite station and heard the thump of a familiar pop rock song. Juanita's favorite. The hook fit perfectly with her new attitude.

I'm perfect in a new way,

You get no big breaks

I'm going to find a new turn

I am a star shinning bright

My light gleams at night

I'm in love with myself

Turning over a new way right

I am a star shinning bright

When the second chorus hit, Kimberly was singing at the top of her lungs while Safety Man sat at the ready.

Once home Kimberly went straight to Rachel's bedroom, where she found her mom reading the latest Patrick Dungy thriller about the lost cities of Neptune and the fiery deserts of Jupiter.

"What's wrong?" Rachel asked, looking up. "It's still early."

"Nothing. I'm fine. Just got bored."

"Really?"

"I just want someone to love and share happiness with," Kim said as she flopped down on the bed and stared at Rachel, "I want a real family."

Mom closed her book and looked at Kimberly's clear eyes.

"What will you do until Mr. Amazing shows up?"

"Whatever. He will find me. You watch," she said while fingering the tiny pills on the white bedspread.

"Love won't pay the rent."

"You'll see. I just have to do me and he'll show up."

Kim sprang from the bed and headed for her room with a strut in her step. Before the boy of her dreams could show up, she needed to get her life together.

10

Retail Therapy

Inside the Meet in Paris bistro in Culver City, the minister enjoyed the grilled wild salmon and Chaka devoured the mussels a la Madrid, along with a glass of a white Bordeaux, which she had come to crave. Somewhere around coffee, the conversation turned personal.

"How're the girls?" the minister asked while slowly turning his cappuccino cup counterclockwise in its china saucer, ignoring the coffee inside.

"They're both well. Cantara thinks she's going to be the next Mo'ne Davis and Fanny will be the first Black girl from her school to compete in the National Science Decathlon."

"They're amazing," Kublai Khan said and pursed his lips.

The best moments of his childhood had been spent in Briggs Stadium. He fondly remembered climbing the steel stairs to the right field seats in the upper deck. There his father acted more like a kid than a military-police vet or a hard-nosed auto mechanic. Together they'd spent hours watching, listening to, and playing baseball—at least, until a stubborn ankle injury had made a little boy's dream vanish like the dry ice that kept his rum raisin ice cream frozen until the seventh-inning stretch.

He remembered dreams. He wouldn't tell Chaka what he thought of them.

"Are you satisfied with the logistics for the weddings?" he asked, straightening his glasses on the bridge of his nose.

"The numbers are better than expected. Thanks to the thousands of men coming from The House and Reverend Hung's bride projections, it's all on point."

"That's more than six thousand marriages and nearly five thousand births in less than a year?" he asked.

"The latest status report will provide the details," said Chaka as she played with her silver Burberry New Classic bracelet watch. "The plan is to work with the operational crew at The Forum to manage everything, from the lanyards to a gold corsage on every bride. I got this, honorable minister." She smirked up at him and reached for the silver tray that contained the lunch bill. "My treat."

She placed a black bankcard on the tray and passed it to a nearby waitress.

"You know, The House owes us a million or two," she continued, "and we're about to pay for another round of media that makes five million more. It's time we got paid." She leaned forward on her elbows and stared into the minister's eyes.

Kublai Khan gave her a diplomatic nod.

"Of course," he said. "I will look into the matter. There must still be some loud...I mean...I will...look into the situation...I mean...I promise to have you a check by Friday...end of business." He gave up on trying to speak and looked up toward the ceiling fan. This woman put a spell on him.

Chaka smiled.

"Thanks. The money is just fuel for the engine. We got to keep it humming." She leaned back, pumping her shoulders and arms in a circular motion like pistons in a racecar. Her eyes sparkled with excitement.

"Good. I'll check in with you about the money when I get back to Detroit. Thanks for lunch." Khan said as he looked into his wallet and resorted his cash so each bill fitted neatly underneath the spring bar that held the ones, fives, tens, twenties, and hundreds in ascending order. He tried not to think about Chaka's smile.

Kublai Khan paused on his way out to thank the bistro's owner for his hospitality and promise to dine there again soon. He felt eyes on him as he took Chaka's arm and they paraded out, wearing their designer clothes and sable skin like priceless accessories. Outside, the aggressive daytime paparazzi snapped pictures; anyone with their kind of presence had to be worth money to the tabloids. Ahmed pushed through the crowd, giving them a lane to the town car, and they were gone.

· · · ·

Kim came to love the stories of biracial women on mochagirls. com. She made herself an account within a week of discovering it and posted journal entries several times a week. Then she posted an entry on Valentine's Day.

"This is just like any other day, except for the fear I have that it could become my future. Being alone without someone in my life to lead me. Maybe one day I'll find the guy who likes to walk through

farmers' markets, or eat hot dogs and pretzels at The Grove before taking in a good zombie flick. I don't think that is too much to ask. Someone who will love me and lead me into happiness."

She was startled when a comment from a new user popped up.

"Hot dogs and zombie flicks? That sounds like a great Saturday night. It's not too much to ask for, it's just enough."

The screen name was HipHop4ever.

She sent a private message: a smiley face, followed by a "Hi, I'm Kim."

She got a smile back. "I'm Ahmed."

Over the next few months, they wrote about classic horror films and finding the world's best bratwurst in Los Angeles. Soon they were exchanging texts about seeing each other in real life.

"There's a chance that seeing you would be a good thing, but I don't want to spoil things by showing my ugly side," Kim wrote. "I can be a real witch sometimes."

"Wait until you meet Nana Rey. She's a piece of work. So what happens when you're witchy?"

Kim shook her head and typed, "I let my mouth get my butt in trouble."

"So tell me about your butt? Round? Flat or Just enough?"

Kim chuckled and made her decision. "That's silly. You can decide for yourself."

"When?"

"What about shoe shopping? Tonight?"

Kim bit her lip as the system lagged, but the answer popped up.

"I'd love to. Shoes are my jam!"

"How bout boots at Nordstrom's at The Grove?"

"I may be a simple guy, but I have great taste in women's shoes."

"Is this a date?" Kim held her breath.

"I guess so."

"Then it's a date. Meet you by the fountain at eight."

. . . .

It was a summer evening at The Grove. The restaurants were bustling with shoppers of all ethnic groups and income demos. The street vendors peddled their wares with reckless abandon: oversized sunglasses, cheesy baseball caps, and rubberized smartphone cases. Well-washed and perfumed women guided bugaboo strollers with their precious cargo strapped carefully inside. The classic four-tiered fountain trickled water into pools of large, colorful koi fish below.

Kim waited by the ice-cream stand in the center of the outdoor plaza and noticed that the movie theater was featuring a horror film she wanted to see. She knew that shoe shopping plus a hot dog and a movie was too much for a first date. Ahmed's profile image looked like the athletes she remembered from high school—he was muscular with dark brown skin and kept his hair and mustache closely trimmed. She guessed he might be on the shorter side.

Kim turned around to watch a young Hispanic couple with a bigheaded boy waddling toward her. Then she saw Ahmed, walking just to the child's left. He smiled broadly, and when he met her eyes, he started walking faster.

He was carrying a bouquet of freshly cut flowers. They looked at each other up close for the first time. Ahmed reached in for a friendly peck on the cheek and a polite hug. Not too much to ask for from a girl that he was talking to, texting, and emailing for four months. She pecked back.

"Hello, Kimberly. I'm Ahmed Reynolds, your personal shopper."

It was a good opening.

"Hello, Mr. Reynolds. It's so great to meet you. They say you're a shoe and boot specialist?"

"Yes, I am. I'm looking forward to showing you the best of our collection."

Kimberly broke the pretense with a laugh. "Okay, Ahmed, enough shop talk. You look just like your pictures. But wouldn't it be weirder if you didn't?"

"I could have sent you a picture of Denzel instead," he pointed out. "Now that would be weird."

They stood nose-to-nose, holding hands unconsciously. Kim thought it was the best start ever to a first date. She turned toward the stores and gently released her hand from his.

"Shall we get started at Nordstrom's?" Ahmed asked as he led her down a path where pricey stores surrounded a tiny patch of greenery in the asphalt-and-glass wonderland. He kept eye contact gently, invaded her space, and leaned close enough to smell her scent. Not in a creepy way, Kim thought—just like he enjoyed her presence.

"Follow me, Ms. Solberg. I know just the right pair to start our search."

They listened to the sounds of popular music spilling over the courtyard as they headed off on an arduous search for boots. They boarded the burgundy passenger tram that circled the shopping center and farmers' market. Ahmed held out his hand to help Kimberly up the steps of the train. They moved past shoppers who walked, ate, drank, and licked their way through the commercial paradise. Kimberly felt a cool breeze as she nuzzled up under Ahmed's arm. His hold was gentle but firm, like her life depended on it. Kimberly felt she was in the right space with the perfect guy.

Kimberly watched the people moving about and noticed the train was heading west.

"Are we going in the right direction? Isn't Nordstrom's that way?" Kim said as she pointed behind the tram, toward the bright signage of the department store.

"Oh?" Ahmed started and then sat back in his seat, his face cheeks darkening with a blush-moistened from perspiration. "Look at that. My bad."

"No bad. It's all good," Kim said, and she stood up and pulled Ahmed off the tram behind her. In two steps, they were running and laughing in the right direction.

11

Scheming at Coffee Klatch

Saturday mornings were busy times in the McGowan home. Matilda had ballet practice while Tammy played shortstop for the Sting Rays in the Huntington Beach peewee baseball league. Tyler and Marie Ann usually separated their errands in order to make Saturdays work. Today would be different. Marie Ann had a meeting with her niece, Star Mathews, to talk through the Gardena Cherry Blossom Beauty Pageant situation; Tyler had Tammy; and Mama Sakamoto would go to ballet class with Matilda.

The McGowan girls were five and seven years old, and Matilda was the youngest. Tammy took after her mother with black hair and almond eyes and a slight build while her sister's sandy hair and fair skin looked more like her dad's, her build sturdy and athletic. They often were not taken for sisters.

As Marie Ann drove from Huntington Beach, she thought of growing up as a teenager in Gardena, getting straight A's, and being a math and science scholar. Her SAT's had been in the top two percent of her graduating class, and she'd wanted to be a criminal behavioral scientist working for the FBI at Quantico. Marie Ann had been the captain of her basketball team, despite all her accomplishments, being "Queen of the Gardena Beauty Pageant" was what gave her family the most pride and recognition. She wanted Star to continue the tradition and didn't care how she got her there.

Marie Ann played with her car FM radio, looking for the local public radio station. The news was full of the crisis in public schools: inner-city teachers and administrators cheating on student test scores.

"The problem here," a commentator was saying as she tuned in, "is that these teachers are more interested in covering up their own mistakes than they are in helping our kids."

"You idiot!" Marie Ann snapped at the radio. "The problem isn't the teachers. Take the pressure off us so we can teach the children, not just test them." Her long, slender fingers clenched the steering wheel as if it were the speaker's neck. She hunched over the wheel, her right foot pressing firmly on the accelerator.

"No jail time. Fix the system." She took the Torrance Avenue exit and headed west toward Gardena. At Starbucks she found a space in the rear of the parking lot. She shut off her engine, closed her eyes, and let her hands rest in her lap.

She pulled the air in through her nose and pushed it out over her ruby-red lipstick.

O h o o o o o o o o o o o o o o o o o ... ...
Wheeeeeeww.................Ohooooooooo.....................Wheeeeeeew

Ten times was enough for her shoulders to fall and the muscles of her upper back to relax. Marie Ann saw muted lights flash and circle across the backs of her eyelids. She imagined being in a green pasture with Jersey cows wandering about, munching mouthfuls of grass as the morning sun warmed them. Apple trees appeared with playful squirrels jumping from limb to limb.

"Kenzo marami. Kenzo marami," Marie Ann recited in low, steady tones that made the meaningless words sound like a prayer.

"Kenzo marami. Kenzo marami."

She thought of the idiot radio commentator before going back to the pasture. Her thoughts drifted from images of the past to current concerns like completing her grocery list, sending her lesson plans to Principal Jefferson, and wondering if anyone was watching her meditate in her Chevy Impala.

"Kenzo marami. Kenzo marami."

The chatter of her mind slowed as she allowed her mantra to fill her soul, and let the thoughts pass through her like the air she breathed in and out.

Ohoooooooooooooooooo............   Wheeeeeeeeeeeeeeeeeeew.
Ohooooooooooooooooo.......................Wheeeeeeeeeeeeeeeew.

Feeling calm and centered, Marie Ann opened her eyes and focused on the leaves of the sago palm tree in front of her car. The glossy dark-green fronds feathered from the center of the plant, and their majestic fan shape glistened in the sunshine. She watched a pair of hummingbirds hover and dance around the foliage before darting upward out of sight.

．．．．

The coffee shop smelled of burnt beans with whiffs of cinnamon and vanilla and the sweetness of baked goods. The line was neat and singular as Marie Ann moved toward the counter to buy a nonfat caramel latte from the listless attendant, who shouted orders to a barista, who moved like a mime doing a routine for an adoring crowd. Budding screenwriters working on future film favorites, students hiding from their parents, and retirees getting the caffeine they craved to finish their morning walk, occupied the tables.

Star—she would always be Star to Marie Ann—was sitting at a table by the window. Like Marie Ann, she was five-feet-four-inches tall, with a little-boy figure and long black hair. Their differences were subtle; Marie Ann's skin was pale, which the family had always blamed on her father's blood, while Star's nose was slightly broader and her skin more the color of coffee with plenty of half-and-half.

Marie Ann spoke to Star in English as she sat down. They shared little Japanese between them.

"How are you?" Marie Ann said.

Star had a Grande Cappuccino fresh from the way-too-cool barista, who was now doing a land-office business. She sipped at it and eyed Marie Ann's cup.

"I hope they got your drink right. I know how much you love a perfect latte."

Marie Ann took a small sip of her own. "I've killed a few dozen baristas who didn't have a clue how to make my drink. But this one made a lovely one."

Star nodded and then bit her lip and set her cup down. "Auntie Marie," she began, "I appreciate you standing up for me with the pageant, but it was hardly necessary. I've decided not to participate this year."

"Why not?" Marie Ann asked, folding her arms in front of her.

"Mom says the judges don't want women who look like me in the competition. And it's almost impossible for a non-Japanese-speaker to get past the first round."

Marie Ann studied her niece thoughtfully. "Tell me, honey, the car loan I gave you last month is due. Can you pay me something on it?"

Star's shoulders slumped and her voice went up an octave. She loved her new BMW.

"No, Auntie, I'm tight right now. Maybe next month."

"What if you work the debt off by babysitting the girls?"

Star took another sip and then glanced around the coffee shop, clearly seeking a distraction. She jumped up and purposefully walked over to two young men in fatigues at a nearby table, bowed deeply from the waist, and thanked them for their service. The soldiers blinked at her, frozen with their hands locked around coffee cups. Star saluted, smiled politely, and returned to her seat. Marie Ann saw the men cringe when Star stepped away. The salute was too much, but Star returned to her seat grinning.

"Sorry about that, but we have the Army account and my boss wants us to thank soldiers we see for their service. It's a good thing." Star peeled the paper off her blueberry muffin, picked off pieces, and nibbled them like a polite rabbit.

"No problem," Marie Ann said coolly, not losing track. "I'll deduct a hundred dollars a session. In ten jobs, your debt will be paid."

"That would be great. You would do that for me?"

"Sure, Star. Let's win this thing."

"What if you could become the Queen?" she asked.

"I would consider it an honor," Star said, loud enough to have two patrons at different tables turn their heads her way curiously.

"Being a Japanese girl with a black father in the pageant would fight racism for all of us," Marie Ann pointed out.

"I care more about the family than fighting for a good cause," Star said, and coughed politely.

"What else would you like to get from the experience?"

"To express that in my heart I am Japanese and not just mixed." Tears welled up in Star's eyes, and she wiped them into a napkin.

Marie Ann pushed for resolution. "This is the way for you to honor your family and your father. I promise to be there for you all the way. You can do this."

Star finished wiping and blew her nose into the well-worn napkin.

"Bring it on. I'll do it."

Marie Ann shrieked and jumped from her seat, spilling her perfect drink. Star rose to her feet, and the women hugged excitedly while the other patrons looked on.

A Starbucks attendant rushed to clean up the spill while the ladies left the store, talking enthusiastically about Star's chances.

12

The Call to Service

The corner of Seven Mile Road and Livernois Avenue was awash in reinvigorated retail energy. People shopped at high-fashion shoe stores owned by men and women who talked, looked, and smelled like them. The storeowners sold clothing at a discount and kept the chain stores at bay in the suburban townships far from the inner city. Motown music anointed worthy speaker systems while children walked with their attentive parents along the boulevards in search of vegetables and fruits to accent their evening meal. The farmer's market and neighborhood redevelopment was a gift from the House of Jeremiah community temple, where Minister Kublai Khan was speaking that day.

Dressed in his customary black double-breasted military-style suit, complete with epaulets, Khan stood silently behind the pulpit. He finished the outfit with an emerald-green silk tie and a tailored white Italian-cuffed shirt. Beautiful bouquets of white and crimson dahlias, yellow water lilies, and gorgeous pink peonies flowers were placed at the foot of the stage. After the warm introduction by a church elder and the rousing applause that followed, he stood at the pulpit quietly, sipping at a crystal goblet of spring water. Left alone in front of thirty-seven-hundred church patrons, Kublai Khan gently caressed the microphone and waited for the assemblage to settle. They quieted swiftly, as if by instinct. Khan smiled.

"I come to you today," he boomed, "soaked in Yahweh's love and grace and seeking that he bless each and every one of us. I also come back to this city…my home…to share with you a blessed opportunity to meet our mission to fortify our political power in America." He used the white linen doily under the chalice to wipe condensation from its base.

"I dream that Black folks will be seen as equals in this land our kin were taken to. Instead, I have watched us get fewer opportunities and none without the harassment and brutality of the armed forces that trespass in our communities." He paused to drink from the vessel and watch the heads of his all-male choir nodding tacit approval. From corners of the church, he could hear followers muttering encouragement.

"Amen."

"Preach, my brother."

"I had a vision last night of a new day," he continued. "One where our growing community can't be stifled through forced abortion, sterility, and incarceration." Polite applause rippled up from women in the congregation. Other women, sitting in the nurse-and-missionary section, dressed in white uniforms with white stockings and shoes, watched his every move.

"The future I see includes having our seed incubated in the fertile wombs of our Asian sisters. I envision a mixed race of people that will be, in essence, Black."

Kublai Khan held up the goblet and waved off a child attendant bringing a pitcher to refill it.

"And to do so, we'll need our men to be free to populate the earth as they did in the Book of Genesis. It will be through our dominion of the Earth that a new world will be fathered—a more just Babylon. A Babylon that is ruled by Black people in a shared vision with other people of color, without the yoke of the White man."

He saw the faces of the women freeze in surprise. Some shifted on the wooden benches as the lumber squealed in pressurized delight.

Men in the congregation stared forward and tried to read their women's reactions in their peripheral vision. The women merely stared.

Khan continued as if his proposal were the most ordinary thing in the world. "Our women must allow our men to perform this biological role without fear that they will lose their love and families. And to the men, those of you who are between eighteen and thirty-four, we offer you a chance to join us. Trust me, sistas, the compensation you'll receive will pay handsomely for your sacrifice." He opened to a bookmarked page in his King James Bible.

"In Leviticus 18, our Lord describes unlawful sexual relations in great detail. Nowhere does he describe fornication with an acceptable virgin as unlawful. It also states in Deuteronomy chapter 22, verses 28 and 29, that compensation for fathering is acceptable." He glanced up. "Single men will be paid too, once they are screened for STDs and psychological issues by our medical staff."

The room was perfectly silent.

"So we must set aside social stigmas and ego, and let us remember that when Job met the challenges of a vengeful god, he did it with kindness and humanity." His voice rose, his words coming in rapid-fire cadence. "We know we all are brothas and sistas of Job, and we must find our own path back to the city of Babylon!"

He punched the air. Some courageous men rose to their feet while the missionary society joined them and applauded.

"We want you, and you and you and you to trust us," Khan called as more parishioners rose to their feet. "We will provide housing among our people and take great care of you. Your families will be made aware of your growth and development. You will be gone from them for no more than sixty days to insure impregnation in our birthing center." The applause grew louder. "Join us on this journey to a new prosperity and a new world of opportunity. It is just the beginning, one that will lead to a better community. Join us in the rise of a new Babylon!"

Kublai Khan stood before the congregation with his arms stretched out, palms up at his sides, and slowly walked down the center aisle of the assembly with a gentle smile affixed on his lips. On cue, Bishop Anderson's son Beau took to his feet and met the minister in midstride. As planned, two men from opposite sides of the church stood up and slowly walked to the altar. Then another, and another, until a steady stream of men was flowing to the front of the church. Kublai Khan smiled as Ahmed joined the following.

"My men. You are glorious. Together we're gonna be victorious," he said jubilantly.

The church erupted with applause. The honorable minister Kublai Khan stood among the church ministers as they encircled him while kneeling at his feet. Still holding the golden goblet, he chanted to the men who left their pews to be closer to him.

"The search for our place in the sun has come

To be last among the people we shun

Or first in the face of our Lord the Christ

That rules over the world he paid the price

Of death, then salvation, he became the Prince

For all the peace that believers have had hence

Of Kings we shout his holy spawn

Our seed will forge the return to Babylon!"

13

The Six-Hundred-Year-Old Man

Hung Suk and Kublai Khan walked through at the Forum in the final day of preparation before the first mass wedding.

"My princesses are devoted to the church and will follow my teachings throughout their lives," Hung said as the men walked across the stage where the men and women would be coupled and married to strangers. They were pleased that 987 Korean brides were to be joined with the men of The House of Jeremiah on the weekend.

"My men understand that their mates will remain loyal believers in you," Khan assured him. "They have also signed away their paternal rights."

The men stepped off the platform and began to walk slowly up the stairs of the old sports arena toward the loge level. They imagined how the future would go.

"In Washington, are there those who know this plan of ours?" Hung asked.

"Yes, some people of power know, but few believe that Black power is true power," Kublai Khan said.

"If that's true, then Korean power will also increase?"

"Yes. The chaos that will result in self-identification of the Census should stimulate more of our mixed-race children to see themselves as Korean. Ultimately, this will be up to God's plan." The minister puffed his chest as they reached the higher level gracefully.

The men walked through the common areas and found themselves standing by the long stainless steel snack bar, where they were handed hot-dog samples. Kublai Khan unwrapped his dog and took a bite.

"All beef. Enjoy. The vendors will also be selling whole-wheat pretzels and veggie juices instead of soda," he said between bits.

"Thanks, but no thanks," Hung said as he handed the warm package to one of his attendants. He pulled the tail of his jacket back, exposing his shirt-draped stomach and pressed the fabric against his skin so Kublai Khan could get a clear look at his trim physique. "How old do you think I am?"

Kublai Khan knew a trap when he heard one, and didn't bite. "You look great" was all he said. "Just how old are you?"

"In this incarnation? I'm six hundred years old," Hung said matter-of-factly.

"Really?" Kublai Khan replied. Well, at least now he knew the head of the Korean church was batshit crazy.

"As the deity of the faith, I tell you this," Hung said. "Our women aren't marrying your men. They are enjoining with me, their savior and salvation."

"Is that right," Khan said mildly. It wasn't a question.

The two men stepped outside the historic venue, where their security teams waited by a row of black luxury SUVs.

"What steps have you taken to ensure pregnancy?" Kublai Khan asked as he tossed the half-uneaten hot dog into a nearby trashcan. "My men need to return home in the first trimester. The birthing center can handle a maximum of a thousand pregnancies."

"The princesses have been tested many times before being selected to make the long trip. Their wombs will be fertile," Hung said. "What about your men?"

"They don't shoot blanks, if that's what you're asking," Kublai Khan said with some surprise.

"Then we will have what we want. Bastard children that will do our work," Hung said as he reached his car.

"In America, we don't call them bastards. We call them Black," Kublai Khan emphasized while standing still for full effect.

"Race isn't my concern," Hung said, stepping close enough for Khan to smell his aftershave. Then the men of god stepped into their vehicles, parked side-by-side.

"You're starting to sound more like a master than a partner," the minister said from his seat, his door still open. The engines started in unison.

Minister Hung replied, just loudly enough to be heard over the engine noises, "Mastering love on earth makes me more of partner than you'll ever know, my brother."

14

Making Things Right

Ahmed knew that it was a better idea to tell Kim about the Forum Princess Brides and his role in the baby daddy drama than to keep it secret but he had to come up with a good strategy to pull it off. That's why he returned to Kim's house with liquid lubrication in the form of discount Chablis. Two liters would be enough to make the conversation painless. He waited until the first glass was consumed to confess.

"I understand that the church is important, but don't cheat on me." Kimberly said as she poured a glass of wine from the white cardboard box on the coffee table and looked at Ahmed as her eyes begged for the right response.

"I owe The House my life," he said not finding the conviction he needed to convince Kim he was doing the right thing. Ahmed responded after first considering how defensive she was after finding out he was going to participate in the weddings. He knew that his future with Kim depended on his ability to be true to both his faith and his lady.

"I get that," Kimberly said and then added, "If you do this, we're done."

"This isn't about you or me; it's about serving Yahweh and the minister's vision for our community."

"Bullshit, you don't believe that. The whole thing is about knocking up those Asian girls," Kimberly said while taking a deep swallow of the cheap grocery store vintage.

"Okay. I won't do it," Ahmed said in more of a threat than a promise.

He felt trapped and manipulated by this agitated valley girl who didn't care about his church or his beliefs. He thought about how tough it would have been for "a shorty" to change his mind back in the day. Had he become pussy whipped? Or was he just giving his woman the room to share her opinion about their future together? His boys would say, "Show some balls, man!" Ahmed thought about what this situation could mean to his relationship with Kimberly as he stood up from the kitchen table and moved toward Kimberly.

She responded first.

"Cause I said so? No way, this has to be your idea, not mine."

"You can't tell me what to do and how to do it. I'm a grown ass man, and I'll do the right thing for me," Ahmed said.

"I'm just saying…."

"You just saying…. Right?"

"Having you in my life is all I really care about. Do you love me?"

Ahmed responded as only he could.

"Is that what this is about?"

"If you do…prove it," Kim challenged him with acute silence before anticipating the only answer that allows Ahmed to be the guy that can make her happy.

"I do love you and I promise to find a way out of the ceremony," he said while thinking about the choice he was making on the spot. It felt right and was consistent with his feeling for Kimberly and his faith in being the man that could find paradise.

"That's all I want. This is the start we've been looking for," she said, while standing nose to nose with him in the living room as the stale smell of box wine filled their nostrils. Kimberly touched Ahmed's hand, raised it to her chest, and gently placed it by her heart. Tears welled.

They kissed deeply and their bodies melded into one. Ahmed gently unzipped Kim's jeans and placed his hands into her panties. He felt her moisture and became more aroused. As they both pushed and pressed against each other, their tongues gently caressed and roamed their mouths as if looking for precious jewels in their bicuspids. They released their embrace as Ahmed stopped and looked at Kimberly lovingly.

"We don't have to do this," Ahmed said while trying to convince himself he really meant it.

Kim looked at him endearingly and grabbed him by the hand.

"Let me show you how I keep my bedroom. I bet it's messier than yours."

They walked hand in hand down the darkened hallway into her bedroom. When it was just steps away Ahmed confessed.

"My room is always a mess. Yours can't be as bad."

Kim giggled as they stepped into the closet she called a bedroom. In minutes the clothes, underwear, socks, and shoes that cluttered her room belonged to both of them.

15

At the Crack of Stupid

Ted Katey, the Forum event director took control of the 6:00 a.m. meeting by first introducing the representatives of both churches as well as the engagement team from Gibbons & Italia. The small banquet room and bar could hold 500 people but today there were a select 150 professionals drinking strong, hot coffee and waiting for the briefing to be over so they could get back to the work at hand. In the interest of time Ted asked each task supervisor to give a twenty-second status report.

"Okay folks, we are expecting a full house today. Let's start with ticket sales."

Ted focused his attention on the corpulent bottle blonde women sitting half way down the horseshoe table on his right. Molly Anderson from the ticket office wore a heavy knitted gray sweater to fend off the frozen blast of air coming from an overactive air conditioning system. The team members unfamiliar with the frigid conditions of the Forum were dressed in LA street clothes, shivered, and prayed for a short meeting.

"We've got about 16,500 tickets sold when I checked this morning at ten. Based on all projections we will have enough walk-ups to fill us up to 17,505," said Molly while fingering a thin-line black Sharpie.

"Let's talk about the 987 couples that are really the stars of the show today," Ted said as he turned his attention to members of the agency team. Francis Jordan, the head of engagement spoke on cue.

"We have ten luxury touring buses bringing in the women from the World Energy Church Sanctuary on Wilshire Blvd. We will transport them in fifteen-minute intervals so that we can finish their hair and make-up in the locker rooms before seating them on the floor in their designated seats up to an hour before the ceremony."

"The men will arrive fully dressed and ready to be seated ninety minutes before the ceremony. If all goes well the couples will have a brief period to get better acquainted before the ceremony starts."

"Good. So what happens after the service?" Katey said as he examined the men and women forcing themselves to not only appear focused and attentive but to stay alert.

"We will transport the new couples back to area hotels for their wedding night. Each couple will have an assigned bus and their overnight bags will be placed in the proper vehicles before the ceremony is completed. Our ushers will lead them out to the buses once the ceremony is over. The next day they will be transported to Atascadero."

"Sounds complicated."

Jordan clarified the logistics.

"We got this. Our team has briefed the couples in their language of origin. Our team speaks eleven languages and has professional experience in these types of people moments. The couples are clear about what's going to happen," Jordan continued.

"Okay, then we are good to go," Katey concluded before moving on.

"What about catering?"

"We understand that all the snacks for the couples will be provided before they leave for the Forum," said Lorenzo Salazar the robust heap of a man wearing a white chef's jacket.

"We also have vegetarian meals for the guests from both churches. Let's not forget the typical hot dogs, sodas, and hamburgers. All available at a price approved by the churches."

"It's the American way. Now let's hear from security," Katey said while looking at the two large men in well-fitted pale-blue police uniforms sitting in the middle of the table.

"We've set our coverage of the event at normal manpower levels. We've also asked the Inglewood police for a dozen black and whites to keep the perimeters secured, especially in the event of protesters. They have complied," said Sargent Kramer.

"Have you briefed the security teams of both churches?"

"We certainly have. They're submitting to all of our security protocols, including no police firearms inside the house unless requested," Kramer said.

"Good. How about the parking lot?" Ted said while focusing on the skinny wisp of a woman in a beige parking attendant uniform.

"We're all ready to go. Including our VIP list and preferred parking permits."

"What about inside hospitality?"

Ted turned to Baxter, the usher supervisor.

"We're two hundred strong and are ready to go."

"Great. Looks like we are all primed and ready for the event. Take the time, have another piece of Danish for the road, and prepare to have your teams in place before noon. Let's make today a memorable experience for all who attend and let's have fun doing it. This meeting is over."

. . . .

As the supervisors dispersed to their appointed duties, the agency team took the time to huddle. Jordan wanted to make sure everyone at G & I was locked and loaded for the rapid-fire events of the day. She stood on the Forum steps with a bullhorn even though she knew her voice would carry in the still morning air but wanted her team of white collar part-time workers and employees to know she had the bite of a drill sergeant. She was thick, aggressive and spoke from the bottom of her stomach to add more bass to her tinny voice.

"People the pros at the Forum know how to handle sports fans, music lovers, and rock stars. Our job is to handle church people. They're different. How come only forty percent of church people go to heaven?" she asked her team. Their silence indicated just how little such a bad riddle meant to her peons at half-pass-stupid in the morning.

"Anymore and that would be hell," she said chuckling.

"In thirty minutes the brides will be starting their day and we've got to watch them every step of the way. We can't have runners or any of these girls missing when the ceremony starts. That goes for the dudes too. The red team should get over there now and check out the escape routes. The blue team should stay here and prepare for crowd control. The green team head back to the agency for further instructions," she commanded.

"Now! You lousy excuse for professionals. Move your asses," she shouted into the megaphone, "People let's shake and bake."

Within seconds Jordan was left standing alone on the steps of the Forum pondering how funny she would be doing standup on Hollywood Boulevard.

16

Brides and Grooms

The World Energy Church on Wilshire Boulevard was awash with activity. Outside lines of white tour buses snaked around the corner of the church so when one bus loaded up with brides dressed in single strap embroidered white gowns another loaded up. The young women wore elbow-length white gloves and were crowned with faux diamond tiaras nestled in their long black hair uplifted for the occasion. The steady progression of brides from a distance resembled the movement and cadence of Chinese New Year dragon dancers.

Inside an early bus sat Ji-Woo Cho and Soyun Kang. Together they spent the hours before the ceremony playing with their smart phones and trying to anticipate what their love for Reverend Hung was leading to. Both the young ladies were eighteen and had just arrived from Seoul ninety days ago looking for a better life. Ji-Woo was trained as a cook and waitress, and Soyun was a high-school graduate without family and had been living on the streets before finding the World Energy Church.

"I believe everything the holy master says, especially his principles of marriage," said Ji-Woo while taking a Payday candy bar out of her small sequined white purse. She chewed each peanut carefully and left the caramel center intact for later.

"Hung says just to obey and trust that the Holy Spirit will give our union awesome power," Soyun said while checking out a Korean Music site where she could download her favorite K-pop hit.

"I hope my baby looks like Reverend Hung," Ji-Woo said, "he is so handsome, and if it's a boy he may lead our church one day."

"Girl….The fathers of our children are going to be black."

"Sure, I know. But that doesn't mean they can't look like the Master. He's all powerful."

"Yes. I am his servant, but it's not natural for our children to look like him. That would be so weird," Soyun said while their bus moved down Normandie and turn right onto Sixth Ave toward Inglewood.

"Black men are so addicted to sex. My mother tell me that black G.I.'s wanted it so bad that they raped virgins during the war," Ji-Woo said while she used her smart phone to look at baby clothes and selected a bright-orange stripped onesie for her shopping cart.

"Yes. I know the stories. I never met a black man, but I hope mine is just plain sexy," Soyun said with anticipation.

· · · ·

Down La Brea past The Forum on Prairie Avenue was the Inglewood Temple of The House of Jeremiah. The grooms were dressed in black tuxedos with red and white embroidered scarfs with the moon and flames symbol of The House. At the bottom of each end of the scarfs were the initials "HOJ" displayed in a typeface that was strikingly similar to that of the Freemasons secret society. The men were handsome in their white bow ties and shirts, and they were cleanly shaven with immaculate haircuts and highly shined shoes. All 987 men were politely sitting in the Temple hall and were receiving personal tribute from the honorable minister.

The minister walked among them. On occasion he would adjust a bow tie while whispering individual encouragement to the men. The grooms came from as far away as Fort Lauderdale, Florida, and Portland, Maine. The candidates wore solemn expressions that ranged from looks made by stoic monks in a sacred progression and mischievous man-children putting on their best faces for the grownups. The stale air of the sanctuary gave off an odor of sanctity and dated beliefs that struggled against the fragrance of drug store cologne and bargain basement-scented shower gel.

Ahmed arrived at the temple late. After spending the night with Kim, he thought that if he missed the bus to the temple that morning no one would notice and he would have found the coward's way out of the ceremony. Instead he got a follow-up call from his faith coach who made a swing by Nana Rey's house to pick him up. He still had hope that he would find a way out. Inside the church, he heard a familiar voice behind him.

"Hey, homes. Where you from?" said Walter "Tubo" Washington as he flashed the sign of a cupped right hand and his left hand index finger against his thumb and forefinger. He was tall and attenuated, and he flashed a mischievous grin. His dark mocha skin reflected the morning sunlight and added depth and richness.

"Whoa. Easy. I didn't know you were down with the Temple?" Ahmed said knowing the answer before his old set leader answered.

"Naw Tubo. I'm just down for the ladies....All right?" he said.

He then tried to squeeze through the door.

"Can't do it. I might get in trouble with the minister," he said as he put his right hand up to block Walter gently as he stepped into the temple.

He wanted to make Walter the temple security's problem not his. As Ahmed walked into the sanctuary, Walter grabbed the back of his jacket, pulled him backward beyond the door, and spun him around and got in his face.

"Son, you owe me. Remember I'm the reason you got out without getting wet," Walter said showing his teeth and flexing his chest.

"Slow down, dawg," Ahmed said with hesitation and a flaring sensation of fear.

Walter saw a security guard approaching him, stepped away from the door, and walked down the side path leading to the downstairs' kitchen entrance.

Once in the sanctuary, Ahmed knelt at the altar to pray. He asked for strength to do what was best. Ahmed's rose strong and focused on finding a way out. After altar call an auxiliary minister spoke of the details of their transfer to the Forum.

"Brothers, we will have grouped you by teams of four. If you have any questions, please see the ushers at the end of the aisles. We have 987 brides ready to be married. May Yahweh provide you all with the blessings of faith. We will be starting from the rear of the temple to load the buses."

Kublai Khan stepped to the microphone. Instead of standing straight in front of the microphone, he leaned over the podium and embraced it in his right arm and spoke to the men in the softest of tones.

"Brothers, you are joining me on a holy mission that will strengthen our church and the community. Your acts of courage will unite us and the new children you will bring into this world will help us grow the new Babylon."

Kublai Khan gathered himself and stood before the podium. His powerful presence engulfed the room. His voice began to deepen in tone as it grew more thunderous in volume.

"Yours is the promise of a new world, one where Yahweh's faith is in black men as the true seed of his likeliness. It is up to you to bring pride and respect to all you meet and to live your lives in true measure of the Lord. You are the men of the new world. Take this awesome responsibility with great care and allegiance. Go forth now and bring into this world a new mixed-race generation. Bless you all."

As the men rose to their feet in applause, Ahmed noticed Walter by the sanctuary door with his face pressed up against the glass. This time he got up and met Walter at the door while the attention was on the minister.

"Easy, you still here?" Ahmed said. Before Walter could walk in, Ahmed went chest to chest with the thug dressed in a cheap black suit with black Air Jordan Retro 6 athletic shoes.

"What's the plan?" Easy said in a loud whisper, "I'm just trying to get some strange."

"Here's the play, you step off and take your weak ass game back down the drain you come from," Ahmed said with bold certainty.

"Cool…. You win," he said as Walter flashed a scoundrel's set of teeth.

Ahmed watched Easy turn his back as to walk away and said, "Hold on…follow me," as he led him into the back of the church. The minister was finishing the instructions when the men returned to Ahmed's place on the aisle.

"We will start from the rear. Let's move orderly and quickly," said the coach with his eyes on any young man who would start acting odd as the boarding process started.

Ahmed's row was near the middle of the sanctuary. He had only a few minutes so he slowly took off his scarf and offered it to Walter.

"Here wear this and take this card with your new lady's name of it and don't tell her your real name, use mine," Ahmed said remembering that besides Easy's love for the ladies, he wasn't the sharpest tack in the box. The card read Soyun Park—Seat # 362.

"I'm going to join a pod in the front. I'll just wait by the bus until they move up front," he said, getting up when he was instructed to and leading his row to the buses, but before he could slip away, he saw Kublai Khan walking toward him. They stood together at the door to the bus.

"It's good to see you. Power be to Yahweh." Kublai Khan said while hugging Ahmed with one arm and cupping their right hands with thumbs enjoined.

"Thank you, honorable minister," he said while climbing aboard the transport in front of Walter.

"I thought you were going to wait for another group?" Walter said as the two sat together in the air-conditioned tour buses that played videos of one of the honorable minister's sermons on black pride and community service.

"No problem. I'll hang with you for a minute," Ahmed said.

On the bus he texted his brother Franklin:

"Can you meet me at the forum? Need you."

Soon he had the answer he needed.

"I'm good. What's up?"

"Meet me on the Loge level with clothes. Got to get out of here."

"Of course. You're Okay?"

"I'm cool. See you in twenty minutes."

"Copy that."

· · · ·

The bus unloaded at the east end of the forum and a small cadre of ushers led the men to their seats. They entered a tunnel leading to the open arena when Ahmed moved toward a restroom located near a concession stand. A tall and meaty Temple Security guard approached him suspiciously. Ahmed spoke first.

"What's up?"

"Young man, where are you going?"

"I need to take a leak. I'll be a minute."

"Just piss fast," the guard said as Ahmed went into the rest room and the guard continued down the corridor on the lookout for runners.

Ahmed nodded and headed into the john. Once inside he used his cell phone to text Franklin.

"Where are you?" he texted while standing on a toilet in a rear stall. He waited for two long minutes before he heard the notification of a new text.

"I'm in the west loge headed to the restroom."

"I'm in the east. Keep going," Ahmed texted knowing that if his brother just kept walking around the circular arena he would make it to the east side in five precious minutes.

"Keep walking west? That makes no sense."

Was he kidding?

"Go to the west restroom. I'll be there in five. Hold tight."

Franklin was not the most sure-footed person to pull off a caper like this but a fuck up or two was standard practice for Franklin. Ahmed just needed to get him to hold tight.

The arena was now busy with activity. The families of the grooms were arriving filled with pride and excitement. Many of them carried small bouquets for the brides and cheap cigars for the anxious grooms who used the occasion to celebrate their personal financial bonanza as ceremonial husbands and fathers without legal obligation. The commotion in the building gave Ahmed the cover to begin making his way to the other end of the auditorium until he reached the House of Jeremiah Information kiosk. Handing out brochures was Maria Salvador, a former high-school classmate.

"Ahmed! I didn't know you were in the ceremony. You look all handsome in your tuxedo. Nervous?" she asked as he barely stopped to say hello, she asked while looking for another non-believer to give a brochure to.

"I'm keeping it a hundred. Just had to go to the bathroom," Ahmed said as he gave her a gospel hug. He looked to the left and saw the sign for the East Loge Men's room but in front of it was a security barrier set up to separate the backstage area from the rest of the arena. He stopped hugging Maria and knew he had headed back the other way.

"I hear the Minister wants the ceremony on time, so you better get moving. Give me your phone," she said as he handed her his phone. Maria put her digits into it and handed it back to him.

"Call me," Maria said with a smile as she puckered her lipstick-less lips in a mock kiss.

Ahmed smiled and started walking quickly but deliberately counter-clockwise. Once out of sight of Maria, he broke out in a full stride run. He passed several ushers and HOJ coaches that saw him running back to his seat like the loyal solider he was known to be. His sprint made him feel good, not only was he getting some needed exercise, he was feeling the added tension and stress peel off his body like a pair of flannel pajamas. He reached the West Loge rest room in record time. Inside he saw his brother and couldn't help bursting into laughter. Franklin wore the sweat suit he had for Ahmed over his clothes. He looked like he had gained twenty pounds.

Together they posted up in two side-by-side stalls and began disrobing.

"Laugh all you want, but it's your ass that is the fool. I can't believe you were actually going through with this weird marriage deal," as he peeled off the sweat suit and tossed it over the stall wall to Ahmed.

"We better get going, before they notice you're missing."

"You're right. I appreciate you saving my ass. I just wasn't ready to commit to the idea of not being with Kim. Now let's get out of here."

The brothers headed for the exit, and Ahmed threw his tuxedo into the restroom trashcan.

They quickly climbed into Franklin's Chevy Tahoe and headed away from the ceremony. Soon they were driving down Manchester Boulevard away from the Forum.

"You must be really sprung on this shorty. I've never seen you so twisted. You know she's a white girl, right?" Franklin said.

"You got jokes? I didn't want to lose her."

"So what are you going to do if the honorable minister finds out you punked him because of a blue-eyed devil?"

"You don't even know her."

"Don't need to. Caucasoid are all the same. Sleep with them and lose your soul."

"It ain't like that. Kimberly is my lady," Ahmed said while thinking that maybe he is pushing too hard.

"You need to meet her."

"Yeah. And your minister is going to give you marriage counseling," Franklin joked as he turned west on Imperial Highway toward Watts.

Franklin handed his brother a joint and directed him to a "short dog" of Bourbon he kept under the passenger seat.

"Now let's get fucked up."

17

Blessed Assurance

A stir took over the arena as men in flowing white tunics took the stage. They circled each other and in unison approached the ceremony drums already on the stage. Suddenly the arena was filled with the sounds of thunder. A bevy of exotic female Korean dancers joined them on stage, swayed, and pranced to the pulsating rhythms.

As the troupe finished their dance, the arena settled again, the Reverend Hung Suk, and minister Kublai Khan came on to the stage from opposite sides of the stage and met in a manly embrace in the middle. Reverend Hung Suk was the first to speak.

He was dressed in an immaculate flowing gray gown laced in gold and accentuated with gold bracelets and necklaces. Around his neck was a jeweled large black cross of onyx and gold.

"This sacred ceremony is poised to celebrate and unite our churches in a new and significant way," Hung said while standing motionless at center stage.

The audience was filled with members of The World Energy Church who were bused and flown in from their churches in America and South Korea. The men wore black business suits with white tieless shirts buttoned at the neck and the women were dressed in simple white dresses down below the knee and modest black pumps and cotton white socks.

"Our task today will be to join these couples in a World Energy Church ritual that will forever join them in God," Hung said as he thanked Kublai Khan for the permission to commune with the many followers in the audience. He looked at the princesses in adoration. They wore veils that added an air of mystery. On their right wrists were exquisite orchid bouquets that were laced in white silk. They sat in silence. From time to time, the curious ones would steal a peek and the lucky ones exchanged smiles of approval from their groom sitting next to them.

Kublai Khan took a sip of water from one of the matching Waterford crystal goblets on the dais and nodded his gracious appreciation. The audience applauded warmly while raising to their feet in a standing ovation. After approving smiles from the parents and shy grins between the brides and grooms, they returned to their seats and the ceremony continued.

"This world requires our honest motives and true conviction. It starts with love, of me, thy God, and our children," Hung said while Walter grew impatient.

He imagined Soyun had well-toned sturdy legs under her floor-length gown and inched his hand toward its edge while bending over in a gesture that looked like he was tying his shoes. He gently touched her bare ankle and tried to inch up ever so slightly. Her bare legs had a hint of hair stubble that excited him. She didn't flinch and moved her leg closer to Easy. He also liked her pudgy nose, short black hair, and large round face.

"This world requires our honest motives and true conviction. It starts with love of me, thy God and our children," Hung said.

"With the power of World Energy and the spirit of Chi, I now proclaim you man and wife. Now please kiss your new bride and go forth and with the grace of our God and savior."

The couples rose to their feet and once they were standing together, the men slowly removed their veils and leaned in for a slow gentle kiss as they had been instructed to do. The newly married men and women smiled at each other and held hands as they waited to be ushered out of the ceremony. Side by side, they walked to the end of the aisles where they were guided out of the arena and onto the buses awaiting.

Together Soyun and Walter stood hand in hand waiting quietly to board the bus. He started a conversation with his bride.

"Can a brother get a kiss, sweet cakes?" Walter asked as Soyun's eyes lit up and widened. He just leaned in and kissed her firmly on her waiting lips. Their tongues met as he gently massaged her teeth and gums. Soyun's head moved forward and Walter pressed hard against her lips. Before he lost his control, Walter relinquished the ground he had conquered and the couple boarded a bus.

"You Ahmed?" Soyun asked when they reached their seats.

"Just call me Easy," Walter said.

"Eee…Zee?"

"That's cool. Very cool," he said finding seats in the back where they could get back to business.

The event was a success and six more of these mass weddings were being planned over the next three months. Chaka instructed her event planners to look for a larger venue in Los Angeles. The Staples Center was already on their radar.

18

The Sakamoto Sanctuary

Marie Ann loved that the two-acre nursery that was purchased by the Sakamoto family just after the Great Depression had become more of a collective hobby than a business. Today she worked the blooming plants while Star read a schedule for the upcoming beauty pageant and Grandma Sakamoto watched approvingly from her worn wooden armchair at the head of the aisle.

"The invitations are being delivered this weekend, and I have a good feeling," Marie Ann said while using a pale-green water hose on the Paeonia plants' delicate light purple flowers. "Have you started culture classes?"

"Yes, and I'm still not sure why these classes make any difference."

"They will help show how Japanese you are," Marie Ann replied.

"You mean as a half breed I don't have a shot?" Star retorted.

"Being Japanese isn't about genes," Mama Sakamoto cut in. "It's about what people think of us and the power we have to change their minds." She took a sip of piping-hot tea from her stainless steel thermos cup.

"Grandma, who are these people?" Star asked, the invitation forgotten as she stood up and turned to face her grandmother.

"White people have ignored, murdered, and imprisoned our people just because of the way we look, think, and pray. It's been a crime that is silent but still very deadly," Grandma said, gazing at the two younger women with eyes rich in decades of survival and suffering. "Our family endured the camps and found a way to keep our nursery, even when the government sought to steal it from us in the name of patriotism. We can change the world, but we must choose to change it."

The fragrance of flowers mingled with the warm, moist air, and the heady scent of dirt and fertilizer filled the silence after she spoke. Marie Ann trimmed dead leaves from the Camellia stenosis and placed the clippings in a brown trash container in the service cart at her side.

"So what does the schedule look like?" she asked, deliberately changing the subject.

"Looks like the talent competition, kimono, and evening-gown events will be my strongest. Not to mention the bathing-suit contest. I don't need the cultural classes." The sunlight filtered through the glass roof panes, reflecting off her black hair and making her skin shine.

"Yes, you do," Marie Ann corrected. "And when you reach the semis, all that will matter is that you perform the best."

"Having a queen in the family is better than going at it alone," Star admitted, moving a step closer to her aunt. "You're my secret weapon, *Oba-san*." She pressed her hands together as if in prayer, and slowly bowed.

Marie Ann returned the gesture. "*Hoshiko-san*, we are with you all the way."

19

And So It Begins

Star took her seat next to the other students in the tea-ceremony class. They sat *seiza*-style with their legs folded directly underneath their thighs, resting their butts on their heels. The students all had practiced how to turn their ankles outward and their feet rested in a slight "V" shape. Dressed in street clothes, the women wore black *tabi* socks and sat on tatami straw mats. They watched as the instructor, dressed in an orange flower-printed kimono, entered the room, carrying a gleaming silver tray. She moved with grace and genteel motion to the end of the room where the students sat in a single row in front of her. The *Chanoyusha* knelt, rested the tray on the mat next to the water kettle, and then spoke in a soft, clear voice.

"The tea ceremony is more to be respected than practiced. I will teach you the movements and meanings to understand the Way of Tea, and how to do it both traditionally and informally." She looked at each student in turn.

The instructor was deliberate in every motion she took. She first removed the *chakin*, a small rectangular white linen napkin, from her kimono and folded it meticulously into a triangle. Then she took the tea scoop and cleaned it against the *chakin*. With the slightest of motions, she placed a tea whisk in front of her. She did the same with the tea bowl. She then cleaned them both and returned the *chakin* to her kimono.

She took the powdered tea from a small container and spooned it into the large, thick ceramic bowl, and added hot water from the kettle with a bamboo cup. The grace and style of her presentation was a perfect example of the *hakobi* style of ceremony. Next she vigorously whisked the thick tea. Then she once again placed the *chakin* back in her kimono, sank to her knees as a final gesture, and sat gracefully on the mat.

"That was the *kakobi temae*," she announced. "It is a good example of the traditional tea ceremony. Any questions, ladies?"

Star raised her hand with a few other students. The instructor chose her.

"Isn't there a second meal after the service?"

"No, not really, but in many *temaes*, there are more confections served called *higashi*. However, this class is designed to teach you only the basics. You may move on to a more advanced temae later, if you choose."

Seiko, a brown-haired girl with blond highlights, raised her hand.

"What if you don't have the right tools?" she asked, glancing sidelong at other students to gauge their reactions.

"The use of different household tools like a ladle and cake whisk instead of the traditional tools is really okay. It is the spirit that matters. Now, let us practice."

After class, Marie Ann picked up Star outside the center.

"Wow, you did it! Was it that bad?" Marie Ann asked as she directed the car toward the freeway.

"Okay, it didn't suck," Star admitted, "but that's an hour of my life I will never get back."

"What did you learn?" Marie Ann asked, checking her rear-view mirror.

"Stupid stuff like how to use a cake whisk to stir powdered tea. Even *Seiko* was there. You know how ugly she is."

Marie Ann smirked. "I see the competition's started. Don't worry about Seiko. Focus on girls like Christina Yakimira and Tori Kita. They're the ones to beat."

The women were on their way to Huntington Beach. Star was staying for dinner and to talk more about the pageant, now only four weeks away. Marie Ann turned her Honda onto the cul-de-sac and pulled into the driveway as Star began shifting subtly in her seat. Marie Ann smiled to herself. The girl was getting more excited by the minute.

"Judge Ernie is very tough. He has very traditional ideas about Japanese women," Marie Ann warned. "Who knows? Maybe he was one in a past life. Or maybe he dresses like one when his wife's away."

The ladies laughed.

"Whatever the deal is, make sure you treat him with respect and speak to his traditional views in the interviews."

"Judge Ernie-san," Star squeaked in a mockery of a Japanese schoolgirl's voice. "I'm so very honored and humbled to meet you! May I get you a cup of tea, esteemed one?"

They laughed again.

"Maybe you can use that voice in the talent portion?" Marie Ann asked as she pulled her parking brake.

"Don't really know yet. Of course, I could sing."

"Yes, sing and play the piano. That would be awesome."

They got out of the car and walked up the brick walkway that led to the front door. Matilda and Tammy greeted them at the door. Matilda was nearly five and talkative. They both were study-leg healthy, while Tammy used her seven-year-old maturity to compete against the cuteness of the baby girl that Matilda used to get most everything she wanted.

The girls were bursting with energy as they ganged up on their favorite cousin Star.

"Star! We want to go to the movies this Saturday. Mommy—can we?"

The girls in unison tugged on Star's pant legs.

"Ladies, I know how glad you are to see Cousin Star, but let us get in the door and then we can talk about it."

With that, the girls rushed into the kitchen to assault Ty their attentive father. Ty enjoyed getting home early from his plumbing gig to get dinner started. His broad shoulders decried the hundreds of hours he spend as a competitive surfer before getting married to Marie Ann.

"Daddy, can we *pleeeeeeeaaaase…*."

"Let's take a couple of deep breaths, and then we can set the table for dinner," Ty said.

Star sniffed appreciatively. "Ty, whatever that is, it smells delicious."

Star threw her purse and jacket on the couch and made her own counterattack with the girls. She first grabbed Matilda by the back and kissed her neck incessantly while with her free arm twirled Tammy onto the sofa and gently sat on her. She had made what she called a Star sandwich. The laughter and screams were joyous. Marie Ann went into the kitchen and gave the dutiful cook a great big kiss as they embraced tenderly.

"You are the world's best husband. What's for dinner?"

Marie Ann opened the wok on the well-worn electric stove.

"Stir fry, yeah? When did you have time?"

Marie Ann liberated a lonely shrimp and devoured it while opening up a nice Pinot Noir. Then Ty noticed the shellfish heist.

"Hey. Not until dinner."

He took two wooden spoons and made them crossed swords against the shrimp thief. He playfully crossed them in his wife's face.

"I will protect these jewels with my life," he said in jest, before responding to Star's question.

"Time? …It takes about twenty minutes once you defrost the shrimp. All the fixings were in the garage refrigerator. Hey! No more for you."

"Dinner is served."

As everyone gathered at the table, the cook began the dinner conversation.

"How did it go in your tea-ceremony class?"

"Cool enough," Star said.

Ty pressed further for a sense of interest in the competition.

"Are you ready for this?" he asked honestly and then added, "I saw your mom and auntie go through it; it's no joke."

"Star is down. Just in her quiet way. They have no idea what's going to hit them," she said as she finished off the lonely shrimp still left on the plate.

The girls were spent and could feel bedtime was near.

"Okay girls, it's bedtime. Let's get dressed for sleepy time." Mom commanded.

After dinner, Star put the girls to bed, leaving Marie Ann to wash the dishes. Ty stepped out to the patio and smoked a joint, one of the few vices he had allowed to persist since his drug-hazed surfer days. About halfway in, Star stepped out from behind the glass patio door.

"Can a sister get a hit?" Star asked, stepping closer to the wafting smoke, reaching out with her slender fingers.

"So you think it's safe letting your sister girl out?" he replied, but he reached into his green plumber's shirt, just above the Root N Toot logo, and pulled out another doobie. Star shook her head at the offer and took the one he was smoking. She held it between her thumb and forefinger and sucked deeply on the slender fag, marking it with ruby-red lipstick prints.

"You're still keeping up with this bad habit?" Ty asked.

"Just don't tell your wife. I'm sure she'll scold me and tell me how it's going to ruin my chances in her beloved pageant."

"Doesn't sound like a lady down for the cause. You sure you're up for this, cuz?"

"Yeah, I'm down." Star took another pull. "Just getting used to the cultural classes and all the training I'm going to have to put up with."

"Lotta work. Is it worth it?"

"You know it's every little Gardena girl's dream to be a part of the festival. I'm a Sakamoto girl through and through, with just a hint of blackness for flavor. Of course this sister is down." She handed the smoke back to Ty put her hands on her hips, and struck a pose like a dancer finishing at center stage.

"I know you talk a good game, but can you handle the heart-break?" He wondered aloud.

"Believe me, son, I can handle it. I'm gonna ace the talent portion, and you know I got lots of personality and beauty. I'm Halle Berry meets Yukie Nakama. Yes. I'm keeping it a hundred." Star struck a cheesecake pose and flipped her short skirt up in a naughty gesture.

"Now you're talking, cuz. You're cray-cray enough to win this thing." Ty ground the smoke out in a green glass ashtray, and then reached into his pocket, lit up a square, and handed one to Star. They bumped fists, hugged, and finished their smokes before Marie Ann finished the dishes.

After dinner, Marie Ann and Star practiced possible interview questions.

"Tell me about your father?" Marie Ann asked, arranging her face into Judge Ernie's scowl.

"My dad is a Black business professional from a sharecropping family in Holly Springs, Mississippi, and that is pretty much it from his side of the family," Star said bluntly.

"You're not even trying. Give me an answer that shows how important he is."

Star groaned under her breath. "What do you want me to say? Unless I somehow find out he comes from African royalty, this is hopeless. I'm doomed." She covered her face with cupped hands in mock despair.

"What are you ashamed of?" Marie Ann asked.

"Nothing. He's my dad. I love him."

"Then scream it from the rooftops," Marie Ann ordered. "Tell me know much you love him."

"I love my dad," Star replied. "He is amazing and powerful." She rolled her eyes.

"I said, stand up and scream it!" Marie Ann grabbed her wrists and stood up, pulling Star up with her. "Tell me about your father!"

Star snapped, "My dad is one of the most amazing men I know. He always finds time to enjoy us and cares what we do!" The words rang in the kitchen, and she grinned with sudden inspiration. "He even taught me how to shoot a jump shot."

"You got to say it like you mean it," Marie Ann urged. "It's not what you say, it's how."

"I love my dad."

"Louder."

"I *love* my *dad!*"

"Say it like you're making Judge Ernie's head explode!"

"*I love my dad!*" Star cried, and thrust her fists into the air.

Marie Ann whooped and cheered. "All right! Now you're going to nail those interviews!" She laughed and clapped her hands together. "Just focus on growing up Japanese and the values you've learned along the way to becoming the woman you are."

. . . .

All throughout Gardena, young women were crying in their diet sodas because their hopes for the competition had been dashed. Empathetic volunteers' hand-delivered letters to the lucky contestants, along with bouquets of flowers, brilliantly colored Mylar balloons, and free hugs, all as the parents watched proudly. It all happened with blistering speed.

That Saturday morning was a nervous time for the Sakamoto family. Every member of the family was sitting near the phone, waiting for the fateful call. Marie Ann was beside herself as she fried eggs for the girls. She burned them and then switched to cereal. She tried to wash clothes, but forgot to add the detergent.

"I would ask you to mow the lawn," Ty teased, "but I think it's just too dangerous. The girls need a mother."

"Not helping!" Marie Ann yanked open a cupboard door and belatedly grabbed the laundry soap.

"Hey." Ty closed the door for her and drew her upright for a kiss. "On the real side," he said gently, "why don't you just sit down by the phone and wait for the call? You know it's going to be a good one. Star will get the letter. We can count on it."

She was just trying to summon up her sternest look when the phone rang.

Marie Ann lunged for the phone, tripping over the Saturday-morning clutter of toys and laundry. She fell in a heap on the green baroque sofa in the living room and grabbed the receiver.

"*Oba-san*?" Star's voice was soft, hesitant.

Marie Ann's heart sank. *No.*

"I made it!" the younger woman shrieked.

Marie Ann could hear the cheers of her sister and Star's father in the background. She gasped for air. When she could speak again, she swallowed the scolding she wanted to give her mischievous niece and said, "We're so proud of you. So when does the competition start?"

"Next week. I have to report to the grand ballroom of the Shibui Resort and Convention Center with my group for interviews." Star sounded like she was reading off the letter. She probably hadn't put it down since she'd opened it, Marie Ann reflected. "Then, after a photo session, we'll perform for the talent portion of the festival."

"So what song are you going to play for the talent competition?"

"I think 'Body and Soul.' More like Sarah Vaughn's rendition than Louie Armstrong's. I got it nailed."

"That's fantastic. I know you're going to blow them away," Marie Ann said as she stood up and began to pace the neatly appointed living room.

"You bet. Then I got to show up in a kimono." Star sighed. "You know I just have too much booty for an Asian girl. I'm still working on the walking, but Mom says that aside from the butt thing, I got a good chance to score well on grace and style."

"You can win this thing," Marie Ann assured her. "In about a week, the pageant will be over and all that will be left are the dinners, networking, and parades. I know you're going to become the next queen. I just know it."

"From your mouth to God's ears," Star replied.

20

Make It Yours

When Star reached the Shibui Resort and Convention Center, she became infected with the excitement. Colorful balloons and streamers accented the high-school band ensemble while the cheer squad gave the air of an athletic event. Through the swirling crowd, Star saw many of the contestants saying goodbye to their proud parents, family members, and sponsors. The Sakamoto family was out in force.

Marie Ann led an entourage that included a representative from the Kobayashi Tool Company, whom she'd recruited as Star's key sponsor. Together they stood in quiet support as Star said goodbye before she would head to the third-floor holding area to be with her group.

"Thanks for coming down to give me a great sendoff," Star said as she embraced her mother and Grandma Sakamoto, and saved Auntie Marie for last.

"You're going to do so very well," Marie Ann whispered in her ear. "Just stay positive and be yourself."

With tears in her eyes, Star turned quickly toward the elevators and smiled as the door slowly closed. Everyone in the entourage shouted support in unison.

"Baby, just be the woman you say you are," her father called.

"Show them what we're made of!" Cousin Shelley shouted.

Her mother put in, "Remember to call me when you have your first break!"

Star waved one last time as the door closed. She felt her tension ease. There was only the pageant now, only one object for her focus. She would see everyone again that evening at the sponsors' dinner, and again for the kimono and talent phases of the competition, but for now, she was on her own.

Once she reached the holding area, the security teams spotted her identification lanyard and directed her to join the others. Inside the small conference room, she noticed that her group was ten ladies about her age. Some were a bit younger but they all were out of high school and no older than twenty-five. Across the room, she noticed Tori Kita, a neighborhood girl she had known all through elementary school, but drifted apart after high school. There was no breakup or beef, just different friends doing different things.

"Tori, is that you?"

"Star Mathews. How long has it been? It's so good to see you again."

The girls hugged politely with Star's enthusiasm for the reunion simmering just below the surface.

"I didn't know you were going to be in the pageant. But, since your mom and your aunt had been court members it not that surprising," Tori said without hesitation.

"Yes, it's a family thing. Is this your first year?" Star asked as they stood together in the back of the room and the other contestants milled about.

"Yes and no. Last year I came out but didn't make it past the quarterfinals. I thought I would give it one more try," Tori said while her left hand stroked her shoulder-length hair.

"I hope the judges take mercy on me. I bet you make it to the finals this year. You are more of what the judges are looking for than me," Star said modestly.

Tori stood five feet tall and had a beautiful head of ebony hair. Her skin was a milky white but with softness and clarity. Her slender frame accentuated by well-toned legs and thighs provided the right optical concession for her small breasts and slender shoulders.

"That's just not true. Every girl has a chance to win, including you. Good luck and I hope we can be friends again when the pageant is over, whoever wins. Okay?"

"Sure we can. I like that," Star said feeling awkward for talking with so little confidence. She wished she could take back those words of self-effacing disregard for her chances in the pageant.

The girls embraced a second time, exchanged phone numbers, and made plans to go to a baseball game. The room was filling with other competitors. The encounter with Tori and Star were repeated a dozen times with other ladies. The vibe was warm and respectful with a quiet sense of expectation. Star noticed another person she knew. It's Christina Yakimira Winslow. She walked straight toward Star in a stylish beige outfit complete with a Louis Vuitton shoulder bag.

"Hello girl. Good to see you. I didn't know you went in for these kinds of community activities. Don't you live outside of Gardena?" Christina said with an arm's length hug and air kiss.

Christina was five feet eight inches tall, slender, with long brunette hair, and alabaster skin. Her almond-shaped eyes provided confirmation of her Japanese heritage although her Anglo features made her more "hapa" than pure breed. This was her year to shine, and Christina was not going to let a newcomer like Star get in her way.

"Never left. I guess this is your third competition? My auntie told me you were in again. Good luck in the competition."

The girls politely shook hands.

"I see you know Tori. We were together last year," Christina said with a roving eye looking around the room like she was sizing up the competitors one by one.

"We're old friends and will be using this time together to catch up and stay friends again," Tori said putting her arm around Star.

They smiled widely at Christina just as the loud drone of magnified sound pierced the friendly buzz in the room.

"Attention. Ladies. Please have a seat near the platform. The meeting will start in two minutes," the stern female voice announced.

Her diminutive stature made the six-inch microphone she cradled in her hands seem like a weapon of mass destruction. The room settled, and she spoke with a sufficiently amplified voice.

"I'm Grace Tanaka, the Chief Administrator of the Gardena Cherry Blossom Pageant. For the next five days, I will be your mother, your minister, and above all, your teacher as it relates to our pageant."

"During the days ahead it will be my job to make your experience rewarding. In order for me to do that, we must make some time to go over the pageant's conduct and values guidelines. The full details of these guidelines are in your orientation pacts."

As Ms. Tanaka slowly walked across the twelve-foot platform she made eye contact with every contestant in the room and watched each of them nervously smile.

"Repeat the conduct oath after me," she blurted into the megaphone.

"I promise to represent the moral and conduct standards of the Gardena Cherry Blossom Pageant…. I will respect and obey the pageant official…. I will only be seen with authorized men during pageant hours of competition…," said Ms. Tanaka who took a pause in the oath.

The contestants seemed amused at the mention of unauthorized men and with the inference that the wrong escort would be a serious infraction and could led to poor scores or ultimate elimination from the pageant. Tanaka finished the oath.

"…I will not consume alcoholic beverages during my involvement with the pageant and I will do my best to represent my family, my heritage, and our ancestors with charm, grace, and good humor," she finished.

"Any questions?" Tanaka asked.

Tori wanted to know what makes an unauthorized man. Tanaka gave her a rote answer.

"The key word here is men; the safest way to handle this guideline is to avoid men unless you have been instructed to allow a man to escort you during public appearance. All other men are not allowed except for immediate family members."

Tanaka's explanation was crystal clear, and Star knew she could follow the oath. She then turned to other more important matters.

"Is there any advice you can give me about the interviews? Will there be tough questions?" she asked.

"Depends on how you approach them. There're just three basic questions. Ones about your heritage are the trickiest. Just don't give them any answer that doesn't let your Japanese shine," Tanaka said with uncommon honesty and support.

She answered another question about interview questions.

"The easy questions are about personality. They have ways of trying to get you to reveal non-traditional attitudes and behaviors. Don't be too honest and keep your secrets safe. Then the last group is the 'got cha' questions that reveal how well you know Japanese culture. The questions will be specific and will require a direct answer. If you don't know the answer...fake it," she said like this coaching session was ready to come to an abrupt end.

"Is there a way to fake the interviews?" Star asked as Tori pinched her leg in the best high-school study hall form.

"Not really. If you don't know the answers today, you can't fool the whole panel. These second-level interviews are the important ones. They will determine who will make it to the quarterfinals and separate the likely winners from the others who are here without a chance to win the competition," Tanaka said.

"Thanks for being so attentive. Make the competition your own and know that you can only do your best and none of you have a score card," she said as she excused the ladies to go to interviews.

21

Chocolate Fury

The time of Star's interview was 2:30 p.m. sharp in the *Wabi Parlor*. As her group entered the room she noticed the table in the center of the room with five chairs and microphones perched on black metal stands leading to an amplified speaker system. In front of the table was one lonely seat with a table in front of it. It was clear that the feeling of isolation was intended to make the interview authoritative and a bit of an interrogation.

In seconds after entering the room, Star watched five judges walk into the room from behind a rear black curtain and took their seats. At the center of the table was a stern-looking man in his late sixties—Judge Ernie Morita. As he adjusted the mike in front of him, the other judges took their seats at the table. At the end of the table was the veteran newscaster on the local cable station WAZM, Peggy Yakamuri. Next to her was Jerry Akita, a popular film director who had just returned from Japan where he filmed a documentary about the Bento box industry. On the other side of Judge Ernie was Ester Kito, a fashion expert who was best known for being a taste master among the eighteen to thirty-four aged "fashionistas."

As they sat at the table, smiling Star smiled back. Finally Judge Ernie spoke.

"Welcome to the secondary interviews of the pageant. I'm Judge Ernie Morita, and we are the panel for Group B. I assume you're Hoshiko Mathews?" he announced with a stern look that reminded her of her recent trip to traffic court where she tried and failed to beat a moving citation.

"Yes, I am."

"Then let's get started with a few easy questions. First tell us about your family?" he said.

"We've lived in Gardena since my grandma moved here in the forties. My mother was a queen of the pageant as well as my aunt Marie Ann Sakamoto."

"Tell us about your father, Ms. Mathews."

Star paused for a moment and thought the judge was not asking a question he did not already know the answer to. So she went with the truth.

"My father's from South Central Los Angeles and met my mother at USC where they both were students. They graduated together and married right out of college. My dad's an attorney in Orange County, and my mom is a general manager of an insurance company. I have a brother Tom and a sister Marge."

The Judge smiled stiffly and looked at Peggy Yakamuri for the next question.

"Did the background and culture of your father help prepare you for this competition?"

"I'm not sure I understand the question?" Star asked for clarity.

"Would you like me to repeat it?"

"No. I will respond to it now."

Star had prepared for this question or ones like it for days. She knew that having a father from South Central that knew little about Japanese culture could have been a weakness. The help he had been as a father who lived with his family was certainly important to her but she knew that that wasn't what the question was designed to reveal. The key question would codify her mix race heritage.

"My father was always there for us. He even taught me how to play basketball. But, the most important thing about my father was how he showed us his great respect for Japanese values and traditions. He even converted to Buddhism and learned with his children the way of meditation and selfless contemplation. My father is wise and the most Japanese man I know," Star said with a flair for the drama of the moment.

"Thank you, Ms. Mathews," Judge Ernie said with a small smile that started in the right corner on his small mouth and extended slowly across his face.

When Star left the interview room, she felt pretty good about how she had done. From the minute she was outside of the room, a pageant attendant approached her with new instructions.

"Ms. Mathews, let's go to the dressing room so we can select a nice outfit for the photo session you have in twenty minutes." the guide said while walking briskly down the hallway.

The ladies reached the fifth-floor lobby and had no doubt where the dressing room was located. The noise coming from the conference room sounded more like the symphony of caged birds cheerfully chirping as they found rows of garment racks in all the proper sizes of the slim and even slimmer pageant contestants. As Hoshiki found the size two rack, she saw just how long the lines were in the size zero racks while the smell of floral, spice, and citrus fragrances worn by the ladies battled each other for dominance.

The standard garment was a short draped one-shoulder number made of silk and chiffon by a respected Japanese designer. The choices she could make were the color of black or white and the shoes and stockings that were available in the dressing room. An assortment of personal undergarments had been sent to their rooms earlier that day.

The ladies had time to try on the dresses and shoes behind the partitions in the ballroom and then once they were satisfied they needed to dash to their rooms to get dressed and have a brief but necessary cosmetic tune up prior to the photo session.

Star made the fashion transition in record time and spent little time worrying about how she looked in the dress. Short was her favorite style since it allowed her to show off her tanned athletic legs. As she walked past the signs directing her photo session, her makeup was perfect and she felt like a winner, even if she had to wear that silly sash with "Kobayashi Motor Tools" on it.

Inside the photo session, it was buzzing with the excitement of vanity. Each young lady felt the lights, wardrobe, and assistants were there just for them. As they listened to the instructions being given to them by the assistants, each contestant took their position around a standing chart that fanned out in a semicircle around an opening where the judges and pageant officials would be standing. At this point in the competition, everyone was a winner.

In the midst of the feminine pulchritude present at the session stood Joe Yoshida, a smallish man with a head of black hair that draped to this shoulders. The energy of his mannerisms appeared in stark contrast with the exaggerated gyrations of the ladies of the competition. Their nervous anxiety could only be quelled by the verbal commands of Mr. Yoshida.

At first, the high-voltage lights washed out the shadows of the studio. He wanted them turned down a few degrees. Then, the first row of contestants were to be rearranged in ascending order of height. Next, was the row of stand-ins for the pageant officials who would attend the photo session at precisely the time that Mr. Yoshida needed them to. To the indiscernible eye, it was chaos theory at its best, but to one of Hollywood's best photographers it was reminiscent of a complex symphony of musical instruments. He performed the job like the conductor of an orchestra, with swagger and artistic flair.

Christina and Star stood together in the second row of the contestants. As Yoshida peered through the lens of his coveted, Nikon D900 DSLR camera, he was ready for a few test shots.

"Want some chocolate?" Christina said while offering a shiny tin of candies wrapped in pastel colors.

"Thanks so much. My nerves are shot," she said while sorting colors with her fingers and pulling out one orange-covered candy.

"Take a few more for later," Christina urged while pushing the tin closer to Star and her eager fingers.

Star put a handful of them in her purse and enjoyed the refreshing pause as she allowed the sweetness and moisture of the chocolate to bathe her palette. It was pleasant. She thought Christina wasn't so bad after all.

After the photo session, the girls were released to their handlers and grabbed a box lunch as they headed to their rooms to rest and prepare for the talent rehearsal before that evening's performance. Once in her room Star practiced on her Yamaha portable keyboard for her solo tonight. Her rendition of "Body & Soul" was smooth and melodic and in perfect key.

Suddenly she felt some sharp cramps and grabbed her stomach.

"Oh." She moaned as she bowed her head and put it on the portable piano console top.

Star assumed that something was disagreeing with her and that the feeling would pass so she patiently waited for the hurt to stop. She found a way to stagger to her purse on the bed and ransacked it for a battered roll of Tums. Star chewed the chalky tablets anticipating the pain would stop. The discomfort grew from the pit of her stomach to her upper bowel like a slow intestinal wave. She continued to practice until the next wave of muscular discomfort hit.

"Oh my gawd," Star exclaimed as she balled up in the fetal position on the bed and kicked off her shoes on the floor. The pain how was in full bloom and all she could do was hold on for convulsions to subside.

Star leaped from the bed and bolted into the bathroom pulling her stockings off and panties down as she landed on the throne. Her body revealed the unmistakable evidence of diarrhea. Star prayed while on the toilet that the effects of her misery would be down the drain before she had to be on stage singing her heart out.

Prayer would not be enough. She called Marie Ann while sitting on the toilet.

"I need your help, Auntie. I got the shits and need some Pepto-Bismol fast," she pleaded while clutching her stomach and bending over in intestinal discomfort.

Auntie needed little explanation and knew what had to be done.

"I'm on my way. I have a bottle in the medicine cabinet."

"I think the chocolates Christina gave me could have been Ex-Lax. I got the worst case of the runs. How could I be so dumb?"

"Don't worry, child. What goes around comes around. Keep your head in the game. You'll be awesome."

"Oh. My stomach hurts. This is not happening. I have to be on stage in an hour."

"I'm on the way."

On the toilet, Star slumped into a mass of disappointment and depression. Her physical appearance was exquisitely torpor. Her discharge of feces was draining much of the energy. The only good thing she could count on was the fact that the music and lyrics were ingrained in her and could be recited and performed with little consideration for thinking of feeling. Star had left the door ajar so Marie Ann could enter without her having to leave the bathroom.

"Look at this room. Don't you just love it? The pageant spares no expense to pamper the contestants," Marie Ann said sarcastically.

Star responded with the most disturbing of guttural sounds.

"How are you doing, honey? Are you ready to get going?"

Marie Ann reached into an ordinary brown paper bag and presented Star with the healing potion of bismuth sulfide. She swigged the pink substance in the eight-ounce bottle with the urgency and frenzy of a wino. The effects were almost immediate as the coral-colored liquid provided the coating she needed. In minutes Star had enough energy and freedom to leave the toilet. Inside she dressed for the talent show and as she put on her long slip, bra, and panties, she knew that if she had any chance to win she had to find the courage to accept the awful incident was really on her.

She felt the warmth of her rage grow in her belly but not as a receptacle of pity or remorse but one of strength. The pain in her bowels reminded her of the choice she must make to be vigilant and attentive or live the life of a victim. She could think and plan with a clear mind and isolate her physical discomfort so it remained remote and captive. As the blood pressure rose and her pulse rate quickened Star knew that her time had come. This was her new beginning and she was thankful for the privilege.

Fully dressed in front of the mirror, Aunt Marie Ann watched with pride and doubt.

"Do you think you can do this? You look a little feverish," she said concerned.

Star straightened up and posed as if she felt no pain; she was faking it and knew that no one was going to stop her now. Game on.

"Let's do this. I'm as ready as I'm going to be," she said as another spasm of pain pierced her stomach.

The ballroom for the talent show was filled to capacity. Back stage the beauties worked hard to prove to the audience that their individual showcase talent was unique and refreshing. All the girls wanted was not to be embarrassed by a faulty poetry reading or an off-balanced pirouette. The judges would rule based on the subjective judgment of each physical gyration or oratory articulation. At the end of each performance, the judges would compare the seven-minute acts secretly and then present a ranking with the top contenders moving forward in the competition.

The acts that proceeded Star were a mixture of baton twirling, poetry readings, and modern dance interpretation. The pageant organizers had exaggerated the nature of the talent segments when they promoted the claim that every participant had God-given talent. Most were awful. Then came Star.

She was dressed in a beautifully sequined black strapless gown her mother found in a second-hand dress shop. Star looked formidable as she walked on stage and sat before the black baby grand piano. The costume jewelry Star wore sparkled and didn't betray her. The dangling earrings provided great drama and formality to the occasion. As she began the ballad, it was apparent that Star was class of the competition.

Her slender fingers caressed the Kawai Grand Piano's keys with the perfect adagio tempo in the lower octave range to introduce the feeling of mournful mood of the beloved jazz standard. The audience leaned back in their padded audience concert seats to hear the accompanying lyrics. Her wondrous voice started the singing with a steady tone of luscious timbre.

"My heart is sad and lonely

For you I sigh

For you dear only

Why haven't you seen it?"

Star's polished ruby fingernail's manipulated the black and whites with purpose and discrimination while each finger met their marks deftly. Her face revealed a half smile that belied the pain in her gut, and with each moment Star commanded the body sensations to live on a different plane of reality than the one she played piano on. As she sang, the two realities merged into one.

"My heart is sad and lonely

For you I sigh

For you dear only

Why haven't you

Seen it?"

The audience enjoyed the hopelessness of the lyrics while remaining still in their chairs and so engaged by the performance that no one got up to empty their bladders or opened a piece of hard candy. Their silence provided a rich bed of solitude for her next stanza.

"I can't believe it

It's hard to conceive it

That you'd turn away romance

Are you pretending?"

Star's voice leaped and swooped from strong bass tones through baritone and into the soprano pitch range. Star used her voice like a remarkable instrument that bellowed and wailed with unsatisfied emotion. Women used the handkerchief they held at the ready to catch the moisture that rolled gently from their eyes. The strength of Star's hands pressed powerfully against the ivories and introduced the final verse with allegro.

"My life is a wreck

You're making

You know that I'm yours

For just the taking I'd gladly surrender

Body and Soul."

When Star ended the chorus, every eye in the room was on her. When she sang the last note, a last burst of pain in her stomach rose beyond her chest and rested in her throat. She drowned the pain in love for the performance.

The audience rose to their feet and erupted in a thunderous applause. Star stood by the piano soaking it all in and feeling pain free. As the audience took their seats, she walked offstage toward Marie Ann who bellowed with pride.

"I'm so proud. Listen. They love you." Marie Ann while stopping for a moment for Star to soak in the sustained applause.

"It meant so much to me to feel you here off stage," Star said with the sounds of lingering applause still making love to her ears.

Together the ladies left the ballroom and waited with the other contestants for the judicial ratings to be posted. When the ratings were made public the contestants crowded around the bulletin board to get a peek at their results. Star's extra height gave her some advantage to seeing the list, but it was posted lower than her height and was difficult to see. Star angled in two directions to attempt to see the list. All she could see were bobbing heads and anxious shoulders. The girls giggled with excitement and screamed aloud when they saw their names above the failure line. The losing girls bit their lips and breathed into her hands while wiping their tears. As the ladies up front began to thin out Star was finally in view of the results.

The surprise was not that she had the highest rating of the performance. It was that her overall rating was an 8.6. That was good enough for her to be the current leader of the pageant. In the kimono competition, Star had to create some distance between her and contestants like Tori and Christina.

22

The Kabayashi Connection

The hotel ballroom was decorated like a well-appointed high-school prom with banners and flowers and brightly colored balloons. The combination of beauty queens and corporate interests was an alchemy that was rich in energy and emotion. The girls enjoyed the feeling of power and honor brought about by the reputations and mystique of the corporations that fueled their community.

At the Kobayashi Tool Company table where Star was the guest of honor included Star's mother and father, Grandma Sakamoto, Marie Ann, and Tyler McGowan. Because of the success she was having, Herman Kobayashi, the executive vice president of the company was a surprise guest with his wife, Mona. Everyone was excited regarding the pageant standings and Star was taking the attention with surprise and gentle modesty. Mona addressed the obvious aspect of the contest during dinner.

"Tell us how excited you're in being a semifinalist. It must be quite a surprise as a first-year contestant."

"It's quite exciting. I think that all the support I have been provided by my family has been the key to our success. I hope that I will not disappoint them."

Grandma Sakamoto spoke for the family.

"Darling, that wouldn't be possible. You will always be our favorite beauty. We just knew you would do well."

"Thank you, Grandma. That means a lot to me."

Star's mom responded.

"We are terribly proud of Star. It was a nice surprise seeing her progress in the competition. It was more than we could have ever hoped for."

Marie Ann was bursting with pride and optimism, and she took this moment to express her competitive spirit.

"And now things get really exciting. As we go into the finals, there's so much pressure on the girls. It's our job to make things easier for Star."

Mr. Kobayashi stood with a glass of champagne and spoke for the company. As the guests at the Kobayashi Tools table rose their glasses to toast Star who watched the people of table seven stand and raise their glasses in honor.

"It is an honor for Kobayashi Tools to be Star's sponsor. Here's to her success and…."

Christina Winslow and a handsome young male escort approached the table to present herself as the belle of the ball.

"Hello, everyone. My name is Christina Winslow. Star and I are in the same group. Thank you all so much for coming to the dinner. Your support is very heart warming," she said while gesturing hugs and kisses to Marie Ann and her sister.

Star abruptly stood up to flank Christina and protect her home turf.

"Christina and I have been through the entire competition together. I'm confident that when the final court is assembled she will be joining me on it."

"I appreciate your support and look forward to completing and being together on the court. In the end we both will be winners," Christina volleyed with poise and style.

"We're both very fortunate to be in this position. Shouldn't you be getting back to your table? The program is about to start," Star offered impatiently.

"Tell us..." Marie Ann interjected, "did you see Star's jazz performance?"

Christina nodded.

"Star has taught us a lot about the great Japanese Jazz musicians like Aki Takase and Charlie Kosei. Tell us your favorites?" Before Cristina could answer, Marie Ann looked to Star.

"Who is that wonderful jazz saxophonist Kaori...?"

"You mean Kaori Kobayashi; she is the niece of my sponsor and a brilliant fusion flautist as well. Her album *Luv Sax* is terrific," Star said with an enthusiastic and purposeful glint in her eye.

"We're so very proud of her. She's playing in Paris this month," Mr. Kobayashi said proudly.

Winslow felt the attention slip away from her and stood motionless looking for the right moment to escape. Marie Ann wasn't done.

"Christina, I heard your poetry reading was...cute. By the way I loved the costume you wore. Did you make it yourself?" Marie Ann said while speaking in a soft tone that made the question even more revealing. Christina's face turned flush as she stepped away from the table without responding to the wicked suggestion.

"Good evening," said Christina as she grabbed the hand of her escort and fled on the faded green carpet separating the white linen tablecloths on the circular banquet tables.

The Kobayashi Tools table waited patiently until she was out of earshot. Marie Ann spoke her truth.

"That girl is not to be trusted. She's the one who gave Star the ex-lax. If I could, I would hurt her."

"That was cruel, Marie Ann. You shouldn't be heartless. She's just a young ambitious girl." Grandma said while moving the stray pea pods on her plate around to soak up the remaining steak juices on her plate before carrying them by chopsticks to her awaiting mouth.

"I got my eye on her now," Star said.

Mona and Herman were surprised how animated the Sakamoto clan became after the visit by Christina.

"I didn't know the competition was so intense," said Mona.

"I would think the pageant official should know about the incident." Herman advised.

"It doesn't happen all the time. The best thing we can do is act as if it never happened. This was just a childish prank that was thoughtless and a little cruel. It's nothing serious," Marie Ann said assuredly.

The Kobayashi Tools table guests picked at their desserts with little interest. The dinner program was completing the introduction of the pageant contestants and they were asked to stand at their tables while the audience gave polite applause. When the announcer got to Star, he paused for added suspense before revealing her combined rating before entering the final stage of the competition.

"Star Mathews is the first newcomer who has reached the semi-finals. Star's rating of 8.9 is the highest score of all the competitors," he said over the buzz of excitement that was building. Everyone wondered if a rookie like her could navigate the tension and challenges facing the woman who wanted to be honored as the Gardena Cherry Blossom Festival Pageant Queen.

As Star stood by her chair and accepted the recognition from the adorning crowd, she let their gratitude sweep over her as if she was underneath a powerful waterfall. The moment left her cleansed of the difficult events that she had experienced and refreshed with the emergence of a new energy and optimism for the next stage of her journey.

The woman who sat down in her seat of honor at the Kobayashi Tools Company was not the same girl who had risen from her chair a few short minutes before.

23

Blessed Assurance

Star's gown was a long, champagne-colored Fernando Villa V-neck sequined formal. It had beige piping to accent a fantail that caressed the floor. The back displayed an open crisscross matrix design that revealed her bare skin. The dress challenged the status quo and offered the pageant judges something new to consider. Star smiled to herself in the mirror as she examined her reflection. The dress was her armor, and she was going to win this particular battle.

Before the semifinalists were led on stage, they were put in line in the order of their current rating. When Star led the contestants onto the stage, their entrance would be greeted by wild applause and a blast of a teenage pop princess singing "Starlight Girls."

As the girls lined up, pageant stylists calmly went from woman to woman, adding final touches to their makeup, straightening meandering helm lines, and combing hair back into shape. Star stood motionless while a stylist used a small brush to stroke and tease the ends of her hair to accent the ever-so-tight circles that fell in playful swirls around her bare shoulders.

"It must be tough on a girl to have hair with so many curls… poor thing," Christina whispered to Tori.

Tori replied, "I think Star's hairdo is awesome. She reminds me of Ariana Miyamoto."

"Imagine that…a hafu as Ms. Japan? It'll never happen here." Christina pointedly spoke loud enough for Star to hear. With a quick turn, Star shot a sharp glance at Christina, put her index finger to her lips, and blew quietly.

"Shh! Ladies, we're about to go on," she said. "Let's be beautiful."

The stage manager gave the signal. The announcer said Star's name as she walked onstage.

She strode like a queen. From the way her hair was piled high on the top of her head to the sparkling custom jewels at her ears and throat, her presentation was flawless. Her confidence was a beacon of soft white light that illuminated her physical presence and lit the way to her spot next to Michael Watanabe, a local television sportscaster who stood prepared to ask the final questions of each semifinalist. Star waited patiently for the applause to cease before Watanabe spoke.

"Ms. Mathews, this is your first competition, and it says here that you are the leading contestant. What's your secret? How did you fit in so fast?"

Star gave him a practiced, infectious smile. "I don't have any special knowledge," she said. "But if there's a secret quality I have, it's my confidence and the belief that my inner spirit will shine through."

"There's some real excitement about your performance of 'Body and Soul.' Tell us, what was the inspiration for that selection?"

Star kept her thoughts off her face. Leave it to the pageant to bring up her jazz first. "My father. He introduced me to the music of great artists like Louis Armstrong, Sarah Vaughn, and Dizzy Gillespie. I fell in love with the music. 'Body and Soul' has always been my favorite."

"What did you learn from your mother's side of the family?"

Star's eyes darted past Watanabe and fixed on Grandma Sakamoto in the front row. The white-haired woman bobbed her head and gave her a wrinkly grin.

"I learned how to cook Japanese food and our family history from my grandma," Star answered. "She taught me how important it was to carry on the traditions that have made us strong."

The next question would be the last, and she braced herself. Watanabe knew what was coming, too; she could see it in the curve of his smile. A bit challenging…a little predatory.

"As a woman of mixed race, what are the challenges you face in the Japanese community?" he asked.

Star blinked. It wasn't the phrasing she expected, but she was prepared. "I'm sorry. Could you repeat the question?" she asked. It was a cheap play for time, she knew, but if Watanabe was going to bring up her race as a kicker question, she was going to make sure the audience knew she wasn't trying to deceive anybody. Pride was the point of this, and she would make them hear the question twice before they heard her reply.

"Sure. As a woman of mixed race, what are the challenges you face in the Japanese community?"

Star lifted her head high. "I am proud to be an African American woman," she announced. "But I'm proud of more than that. Perhaps the challenge I face is people having one perception of me without considering who I say I am. Tonight I am a proud Japanese woman."

The answer drew polite applause and gave pause to the judges as they wrote notes on the writing pads in front of them.

Watanabe thanked Star and she walked offstage with a smile and gait that proved she was still the beauty to beat. As she entered backstage left, Marie Ann greeted her with a tight embrace.

"Honey, you were magnificent. I don't think anyone could have done better."

"I stumbled on the last two questions." Star hugged her tighter.

"Oh, that's just in your mind. What I saw was a talented young woman with charisma and charm. You nailed it."

"I don't know, Auntie. I just don't know," Star said, wiping her moist hands against the soft textures of the antique linen handkerchief Marie Ann gave her. She looked into her aunt's eyes as if the power of her ambition could be transferred through a glance.

In the next moment, she saw a new possibility.

24

Seigi

The ladies left backstage and went to the holding area to be invited back on stage for the announcement of the finalists. Star drank herbal tea to settle her nerves. The bite of hunger in her stomach reminded her that she hadn't eaten all day. Each new contestant who entered the holding room from their evening-gown interviews took a moment to acknowledge Star. Christina stayed on the opposite side of the room.

When the last semifinalists walked into the room, Star leaned into the mirror to touch up her makeup. Then she stood up, assumed her regal posture, and headed back onstage.

Back in front of the adoring audience, Star felt like her feet rested on small clouds and floated from one step to the next. She took her position in a wide semicircle with Watanabe in the middle. As he spoke, the excitement blossomed in the auditorium.

"This is the moment we all have been waiting for," he intoned. "After a grueling five-day competition, we have eliminated thirty-four lovely ladies with tremendous charm and beauty representing the Gardena community. Now we have ten wonderful ladies, but five will make it to the court that will represent Gardena in the year ahead."

A hush fell over the auditorium.

"I'll name the five finalists who will comprise the Queen's court," Watanabe went on, "and then the Queen from the finalists. Let's start with the fifth member of the court. The lucky girl is…Chloe Ito."

Ito broke out in tears when she heard her name. The girls standing near her celebrated, hugging and air kissing while maintaining their composure.

"The fourth member of the Gardena Cherry Blossom Festival Court is Christina Winslow."

Christina gave a mocking look of surprise, pressing fingertips to her collarbones without causing one hair to fall out of place.

"The third member of the Queen's court will be Victoria Sato."

Victoria cried gently and hugged the other girls. Star smiled and applauded her, feeling her anticipation bubble up her spine. This was it. She was almost there. The court, and possibly the crown, was waiting.

"The second-to-last finalist of the pageant is Sherry Yamada."

Sherry folded over, holding her stomach, and then cupped her hands around her face. Star felt the hunger pains in her stomach turn into a rock of anxiety. Five of the girls left in the circle would be losers. Could one of them be her? That had seemed impossible until now, but with so few spots left, she was either the queen or a very high finisher. How much power did the judges have to overrule Ernie?

As Michael Watanabe took a beat before he spoke the last name on the list.

"The last member of this year's court is…Keiko Phillips."

The four other girls that weren't Keiko moved slowly, as if their feet were bogged down in wet cement, to encircle her and share in her excitement. Star was numb but joined them in homage to Keiko.

The leftovers were led offstage quickly.

Star found herself back at the holding room. The seconds she stood alone seemed like eons and the loneliness she felt pierced her heart with disappointment. Suddenly, her mother and Marie Ann were there, consoling her. A huge wave of resentment and anger came over Star, while Mother and Aunt held her up between them with their merciful arms.

"What happened, Mommy? Why didn't they put me on the court?" Star sobbed.

"Baby, we will find out what happened. I promise you," her mom said.

Mary Ann had another, more certain view of the situation.

"He did this. That bastard."

As Star wept, the sisters looked at each other with a determined stare.

"Sis, this is on me. I started this nightmare and I will see that we get justice," Marie Ann pledged. She cupped her sister's head tightly in her hands and touched their cheeks, their tears blending into a common grief.

"This hurts all of us very deeply," she whispered. "We want justice…Seigi."

"Seigi!" the other woman repeated.

Star continued weeping as Christina Winslow was crowned queen.

25

The Tea Ceremony

In the days after the pageant, Star let herself run on autopilot. She ate her grandmother's beautiful meals with appropriately grateful noises, replied to every question with superficial answers as if she were still onstage in the pageant. She was the mournful heroine in her own kabuki play.

Marie Ann was alive, brimming with rage. She had taken on the job of finding out what had really happened in the pageant. The first person on her list was Richard Ahira. She knew that the ballots were public records and she had to get his permission to view them. She met Richard in front of City Hall. Richard bought sandwiches from a street vendor and sat with Marie Ann in the courtyard.

"Richard, I'm not here to interrogate you. I just want to have lunch with a dear friend and talk," she said, pulling back the paper from her chicken-salad sandwich.

"I appreciate that. We all felt Hoshiko did a wonderful job in her first year," he said before taking a swig from his Diet Coke.

"Let's forget the pageant for a few hours." Marie Ann nibbled at her food and then glanced curiously at her old schoolmate.

"Please don't ask me to share the ballot with you," Ahira sighed. "It would be bad for the pageant."

"That's fine with me," she said.

Ahira rolled his eyes. "I'll tell you what. Unofficially, we're having a chat about what I think *may* have happened."

"Unofficially?" Marie Ann echoed.

"Yes. And I can tell you what I've heard. But this can't go any further."

"Okay. Tell me what happened."

"Well, I wasn't there, but here's what I know. She was nearly perfect going into the last event, but there was some rift among the judges. Her scores from one judge were consistently much lower than the others were. That mismatch created quite a discussion among the judges and officials."

"Then what happened?"

"Judge Ernie lost it. He started ranting about Hoshiko not being Japanese enough. She was not only leading, she was pulling away. Without Judge Ernie, she would be on the court."

"So, what was the score on his card?"

"It was 3.5, the lowest of the entire competition. When he was asked why he went on a tirade about Star being a hafu."

"We have heard his views about mixed-race contestants," Marie Ann said severely. "Why was it an issue at the end of the pageant?"

Ahira looked down into his cold beverage for guidance and then looked into Marie Ann's dark-brown eyes.

"It was her hair. The judge felt that her hair was not straight enough."

"Her hair?" Marie Ann frowned. "Her hair has a unique texture and a look I would be proud to have. You really think that was it?"

"Maybe next year it will be different," Ahira soothed. "Who knows? Judge Ernie may retire from the competition."

As if there were a chance in hell of that. As if it would fix anything. Marie Ann swallowed her rage, hid it behind a mask of calm.

"Thanks. All I wanted was the truth."

. . . .

The McGowan girls greeted their father with screams of laughter and shuffled to get a better look at the grocery bags he was carrying. Star stood nearby and seemed to enjoy the view of the girls' adoration. Tyler noticed Star in the kitchen and saw her smile. It was encouraging. He hadn't seen it since the competition.

"So how were the girls today?" he asked with little concern for the answer as he stacked the fresh fruit, vegetables, and other staples on the counter.

"Matilda wasn't a problem all day. Tammy was another thing. She was always hungry, and if I didn't feed her, she was cranky. After lunch, she was a delight." Star plucked a plum from the plastic grocery bag and bit into it unwashed.

"It's been a long time since I've seen that smile of yours," Tyler remarked.

"Funny. I didn't even know I was smiling."

The girls were in perpetual motion until Tyler ordered: "Upstairs. Get ready for ballet."

Matilda and Tammy turned on a dime and headed upstairs to put on their leotards. Star stayed in the kitchen, prepping an afternoon snack the girls would eat before dance class. Tyler stood by the kitchen door and continued to study her mood.

"What's next?" he asked.

Star finished putting the crackers on the everyday china with the fruit and cheese.

"Don't know. But I was thinking about modeling again. Maybe I'll take a few classes and put my portfolio together."

"That sounds cool. I've always thought your face should be on magazine covers."

Tyler stood close to Star while she put the cracker box into the cabinet's lower shelf. His crotch brushed her rear end, and in seconds, he was hard as a pipe. As she spun around, Ty stumbled and lunged in an attempt to kiss her. His mouth missed its mark and landed on the groove of her upper lip. Star kneed him in the groin.

"Stop it. You're married," she said.

"I just couldn't help myself. I'm so sorry," he said, and grabbed his balls through his blue work pants.

"Don't worry," Star said flatly. "It's okay. You just wanted to screw the loser."

"No. It isn't like that...I adore you." Ty tried to pull Star closer to him but kept his grip on her arm gentle. He didn't want her to punch him again.

"I can't handle this. Please leave me alone," she insisted. "This will never work."

The girls came romping downstairs, dressed for ballet class.

"I'm going to drop the girls off at ballet," he told her, feeling his face getting hot. "Then I'll run you back home. Marie Ann will pick them up."

Star merely nodded, her feet planted like the roots of trees as she stood her ground.

Tyler escaped while he could.

. . . .

Marie Ann was drawn to the nursery, where she spent an hour watering the plants in the third Quonset hut, collecting her thoughts about the pageant travesty. She feared the injustice would go unpunished, and could only blame herself for pushing Star into the competition. Marie Ann deliberately wandered to the back acreage, where the small trees grew. There she stood among the maples, magnolias, hawthorn, dogwood, and lilac. She enjoyed the patches of shade and bursts of color that fashioned a halo of brilliant light around her head while her body was awash in the shadows. Marie Ann kept walking until she found one of the tallest trees in the lot with deep-orange fruit.

Marie Ann picked a few of the deep-orange berries and put them in a small shoulder pouch she carried. As she gathered the fruit, she prayed.

"Please allow our pain to vanish and our love for each other to return in abundance."

She walked through the next few days in a dream.

. . . .

Tyler made it back in record time. There in the living room, Star was sitting by the minimal light of a small Tiffany lamp in the corner. The shadows in the room softened Tyler's mood and approach. Ty felt his heart racing and his groin swelling as he stood in front of his twenty-two-year-old niece. His mouth went dry and his voice rose to just below the squeal of a guilty teenage boy.

"Let me explain," he croaked. "I have been in love with you since we met. And I've kept my mouth shut for all these years."

"You pity me?" Star snarled. She stood up, pushing into his space, and then pounded his chest with her fists like a well-toned drum set.

"No way," Tyler insisted. "I saw that smile again and I knew you would be better. I really care for you." He inched closer to the scent of lilacs and cherry blossoms lurking just below her ears and neckline.

She stood straight, took a small step backward from Tyler, and lowered her eyes.

"I know, Uncle Ty."

Star looked up with a crooked smile and a twinkle in her smoky brown eyes. Tyler held her hands and kissed her forehead.

"Do you feel the same way for me?"

"I don't know. You're my uncle."

"How do you feel?" he asked again.

"I guess so. But, we can't."

Ty held her closer and kissed her forehead gently. Then she found his lips. They fell in a heated heap on the couch. Tyler knew that he had little time. He caressed her waist and rested his large hands on her behind.

"Ty…I do care about you," she admitted before kissing him lightly on the lips.

"You are so beautiful," he said as he pressed his mouth against hers and gently caressed her legs and thighs.

Tyler took his time and sought out every erogenous zone he could find with his hands, tongue, and pelvis. Her groans and quiet screams encouraged him and showed him the way to her pleasure. Afterward, they lay in their own juices, their bodies entangled.

"This is my fault," Star confessed.

"Don't be silly," Tyler told her. "I wanted this to happen. We are both adults and I think it's best we let this stay our secret." He pulled up his tighty-whitties and blue jeans simultaneously.

"Yes, we should keep this between us," she agreed while sitting naked on the edge of the couch.

They slowly put on their clothes, like ninth-graders who'd just had sex for the first time.

Then the purr of an engine from outside broke the spell.

"I want to see you again," Ty muttered as he hurried Star out the side door before Marie Ann could come in the front.

. . . .

Marie Ann Sakamoto McGowan stood in front of the full-length mirror and admired the special kimono she wore when she performed tea ceremonies as Queen. Her blue and red 1920s vintage kimono had embroidered water lilies and camellia blossoms on it, giving it great vibrancy and character.

From the top of her Shimada mage hairstyle to the bottom of her Zori sandals, Marie Ann was impeccably dressed. She was a model of Japanese perfection as she prepared to perform the tea ceremony. She had even reserved the finest teahouse in Gardena for the occasion. When Judge Ernie arrived at the teahouse, she greeted him with a respectful bow.

"Judge Ernie, how wonderful to see you again," she said. "Please come in." She interrupted her bow and stooped down to help him remove his shoes and put on black Zori.

"How thoughtful. I appreciate the invitation," he said, glancing into the inner room. "Have the other guests arrived?"

"No, Judge. I'm sorry, but the councilman sends his regrets and Herman Ito had a conflict. I hope it's not an imposition? It will just be you and I. Is that okay?"

"Of course. You and I have lots to catch up on."

"Wonderful. Then join me on the deck for a light snack," she said, leading the judge outside to the table set with a small meal.

"I have prepared a *kaiseki* with some of your favorites like *chasoba-zushi* and *kabocha*," she explained as she carried a serving tray into the room. All the small dishes were arranged in finely lacquered bowls, accompanied by sauces. As Ernie ate the green tea sushi and Japanese squash, they talked of the Sakamoto family.

"I have always wondered how your family kept the nursery through the internment," Ernie remarked, swallowing a bite of *Abako*. "How did you do it?"

"I'm sorry. It's a family secret." Marie Ann inclined her head gracefully.

"Well, it must be. No family I know kept their property. Your family did," he said.

"No, sir. Can't discuss. Forgive me."

Ernie narrowed his eyes, but gamely changed the subject. "Do you still work on the property?"

"Yes. I still care for the plants and trees. In fact, I have brought you a gift. Over there," she said, and gestured to a small plant, about two feet tall with a white ribbon tied around the brown clay pot.

"How thoughtful. I hope it doesn't require a lot of care. My green thumb has turned brown."

"No worries," she replied. "I can help." She began gathering up the dishes. "Please join me in the tea room."

The *Chaji* began with the judge sitting with his legs folded underneath him on a tatami floor while Marie Ann entered the room with the utensils for the temae. As she knelt in front of the judge, she deliberately cleaned each item. When the cleaning was complete, Marie Ann performed the other movements of the service.

She used a crucible and pestle to grind the green tea leaves into powder, and then added powered pine nuts. Her technique was flawless as she added hot water and used the whisk to mix the warm concoction. She turned the tea bowl in three-quarter rotations to reveal the beauty of the ceramic cup as she passed it to Judge Ernie to partake of the tea. He in turn rotated the bowl and took one slight small sip from the teacup, then another, and then one last large swallow to finish the tea before passing the empty cup back to Marie Ann. After, she silently cleaned the utensils and placed them on her tray. She stood up and left the tearoom, leaving him to his silent contemplation.

Marie Ann wasn't surprised when she returned to the tearoom twenty minutes later and saw Judge Ernie on the *tatami* in a fetal position. His wrenching convulsions caused his body to contort and twist on the floor. On his hands and face were large ganglia cysts the size of silver dollars. The judge opened his eyes and tried to speak. Marie Ann patiently stood over him as a body spasm ripped through him. The smell of feces and urine filled the room, and his mouth foamed with thick white slobber as he spoke.

"Ugh," he groaned. "What is wrong with me? Why…is this happening….Agh…."

"I understand," Marie Ann said respectfully as she looked across the room to the potted plant she had pointed to earlier. There was a soft sound at the door, and she glanced up to see Star standing in the doorway, dressed in her own flawless *yukata*. Here to bear witness, to the end of the Judge.

"…Help me…." Ernie rasped.

Marie Ann turned back to him, her smile a perfect mask. "I'm sorry. There's nothing I can do. This is strictly a family matter. Your malice is destroying our family."

"Ugh," he said, and his body went lax as he slipped into unconsciousness.

Marie Ann turned her back on Ernie and slowly strolled to the back of the tearoom where the room was bordered by small potted fruit trees. In the middle of the row was the plant with orange fruit. Star bent down and picked up the pot, cradling it in her arms while she and Marie Ann walked toward the man on the floor.

"Judge, do you know what my gift is?" Marie Ann asked the still-warm corpse.

Star gazed down at him, impassive.

"I guess you'll never know," Marie Ann said, and turned and walked out of the tearoom. Star followed gracefully at her heels, carrying the little strychnine tree in her arms as the late afternoon sun cast long shadows in the newly lifeless room.

TWO YEARS LATER

26

Chanting, Dancing, and Surveys

Dr. Alejandro Garza approached the microphone at the podium in the grand ballroom of the Mayflower Hotel in Washington, DC. His faculty assistant pointed an HD video camera at his head to broadcast the professor's words to the computers of thousands of Latino students across the nation. The professor peered over his brown horn-rimmed glasses at the cozy group of government professionals, and spoke instead to the young minds inside the camera.

"The biggest threat to our society is the US Census Bureau," Dr. Garza proclaimed.

The hotel audience stirred in the leatherette chairs. Garza continued, "Twenty years ago I predicted that people of color would control America, and now so-called Hispanics and Blacks are being duped into thinking that one day they too will be White."

He flashed a toothy smile at the Orion 53099 StarShot.

"When you look at my beautiful brown skin and thick black hair, you see a proud Latino," he announced. "Not a White man. No matter what the Census says I am," he added.

Garza was a sturdy two-hundred-twenty-five-pound former Ivy League rugby scrum half, and a Rhodes Scholar to boot. He wore a custom Nehru-style steel-gray sharkskin suit and proudly sported a Native American beaded necklace with a black leather medicine bag resting near his heart.

The camera focused tightly on the professor's head and shoulders, occasionally widening its shot to show his rapidly shifting hands. The professor's eyes were glazed as his gestures became more theatrical. In his mind, Garza summoned the ancient spirits of *la raza* as he closed his eyes for a glimpse of the future.

"People of color will lead the American culture for decades to come. And the government will be transformed into serving the legal rights and privileges of the poor, incarcerated, and illegal among us," he predicted and sipped from the plastic cup on the lectern. The three Hispanic female educators sitting in the front row to his right stared right through him as if they hadn't heard. The men next to them from the OMB took copious notes while one scrolled through a smartphone. On Wikipedia, no doubt, to learn more about the unusual speaker from California.

Professor Garza rolled inexorably toward his conclusion.

"The Census seeks to control the way we see ourselves. Being proud of our blackness, brownness, and yellowness means the end of the dominance of White people. Using racial categories that make us whiter is a desperate measure that we must resist. The spirit of our ancestors must prevail." He gazed around at the audience, which had totally failed to react. Satisfied with the video, at least, he straightened his papers, gathered them up, and walked off the stage.

From the far left corner of the platform, a dark-skinned man dressed in a light beige deerskin suit with a headdress and white face paint stepped onto the platform, beating a small drum while he chanted in Navajo.

Hozhoogo naashaa doo

Shitsiji hozhoogo naashaa doo

Shikeedee hozhoogo nassshaa doo

Shideigi hozhooogo naashaa doo

Taasltso shinaagoo hozhoogonaashaa doo

Hozho nahasdlii

The chanting man pulled a small glass flask from his waistband. The vessel was half-filled with a light-green fluid. He opened the flask, took in a mouthful, capped the bottle, and returned it to his belt. Then he spewed the fluid in a light mist over the audience as the people in the front rows sat motionless. The blessing mist had the smell and taste of peppermint. The shaman repeated his blessing, in English this time, for the benefit of the heathens.

"In beauty I walk

With beauty before me I walk

With beauty behind me I walk

With beauty above me I walk

With beauty around me I walk

It has become beauty again

It has become beauty again

It has become beauty again

It has become beauty again."

Then he left the room.

After the presentation, Garza took a few questions from the audience. One was about the threat mixed-race people were to the freedom of Black and Brown political power. The professor calmly addressed it.

"Blended-race people are confused. The politics of race weighs heavily on our perceptions of what it is to be Black or Brown in America. Blacks should be Black. Brown is Brown."

A Latino bureaucrat raised a hand. "Are you so sure," he asked, "that the Census is the threat you say it is?"

"The Census does not own our identity," Garza replied. "My work is to remind Latinos of our power and the power of our spirit world. This world is our world. Thank you." He nodded to polite applause, and his eyes strayed toward the camera as it continued to record.

After the speech, Dr. Garza held a live webcast backstage with Minister Khan. They stood side by side against a black curtain as Kublai Khan shared his views on mixed-race Black people and their sense of who they think they are.

"Being Black is about power," Khan said, looking into the camera and imagining college sophomores sitting cross-legged on their beds in shorts while peering into their PCs at him. He continued, "The fact is, the decision to be any color or race is not a choice but an obligation. The spirits of our ancestors are watching."

"What are you doing to educate these misguided individuals?" the professor asked.

"The world needs more than talk and homework; we need something vivid," Khan said.

"What does that mean?"

"Something very special," Kublai Khan replied.

The two men stood in silence as Garza closed his eyes and his lids fluttered rapidly. Then he said, "In the next two years, there will be a California miracle that will change how people think about Black people."

The minister stared at the professor with wide eyes and a ridged upper lip.

"Interesting," he said. "Your prediction. Not mine."

Dr. Garza looked blankly at the camera and signaled to his assistant to fade to black.

. . . .

In the Diversity Working Group, Les and Kublai Khan sat next to Reverend Roscoe Harper, an unsophisticated man of God with a high-school education who had learned his social graces from pimps and hustlers in the streets of Chicago. He was dressed in a green Adidas sweat suit and Air Jordans fresh out of the box. Harper wasted little time in trying to impress Khan.

"African Americans have historically been considered Black. The mixed-race distinction needs to be eliminated. Black is Black," Harper said, while standing up for greater emphasis.

"This is a new America, and as mixed-race folks become more educated, they will rise up," said Timothy Foresight, a well-known political operative from Virginia. He sat in the middle of the conference table, wearing a royal-blue business suit that that was more bargain basement than it was designer.

Kublai Khan was careful to meter his tone and volume to hide the hostility he had for the issue.

"Black people are an economic powerhouse. They need to know what's at stake before they mark the Census identity box," he rumbled.

"Sounds like you both are politicizing this issue?" Foresight said, staring at Khan and Harper.

"You have no interest in educating folks about race?" Foresight said from behind accusatory lips and wide eyes that appeared to frame the claim with contempt.

"I'm focused on something more urgent. Something powerful," Khan boasted.

"Blacks are ill advised to think of themselves as anything but Black," Reverend Harper suggested with his eyes on Kublai Khan. "We don't care if they're light, bright, and damn near White."

"You both are missing my point," Foresight replied. "Informed or not, it's their choice...not yours."

· · · ·

When the session was over, the minister left the conference to attend to church business with his Baltimore temple. Solomon and Harper discussed their interests during a dinner reception that evening in the Senator Hiram Revels office building on Capitol Hill.

In the cavernous rotunda, temporary chairs and tables were set up for the seventy-five people who were part of the working group. The business-suited participants were served by aging Black men in white jackets with silver serving trays, laden with pigs in blankets and crustless tuna sandwich quarters. Both men took advantage of the open bar.

"Foresight poses the problem Minister Kublai Khan is concerned about. What can be done to keep Black people in the boat?" Les asked, nursing a bourbon and Diet Coke.

"We need to rebuild the idea that blackness is about staying true to the tribe. The spirit of our ancestors demands it." Reverend Harper killed his drink and turned in the direction of the bartender before adding, "I would love to sit down with the minister."

"I'll set up a chat," Les said.

"That would be great." Harper handed his glass to the barkeep for a refill.

"Consider it done."

27

Chicken Dinners on Miracle Mile

Kimberly had just left the 99-cent store on Wilshire Boulevard, and with a few bags of ramen noodles, snacks, soaps, detergent, and other odds and ends, she made it past the tall office buildings and museums and headed south on Fairfax Avenue toward the small one-bedroom apartment she and Ahmed shared with their two-year-old daughter, Holiday.

Since moving in with Ahmed a little after she became pregnant, the young couple had worked hard to stay together. Ahmed went back to school to study accounting and later landed a job as a paid intern in a large accounting firm. They loved his work ethic, his no-nonsense demeanor during work hours, and his quiet loyalty to his girlfriend and child.

When Kim reached home, Ahmed was feeding Holiday a snack of cheese, crackers, and fruit. Kim put her plastic bags on the kitchen table, kissed Ahmed, and hugged her daughter.

"How's her appetite?"

"Fine. She's on the top of her game. How was the walk?"

"It was nice. The Ethiopians are out and playing Gebet'a. Maybe after dinner we can take Holly out for some fresh air."

"That's cool. I got a few numbers to run before tomorrow morning."

"Just do it before dinner. I'll stick a chicken in the oven and make those potatoes you like."

"Nice, I'll be done here in about an hour," Ahmed said and pulled out his briefcase and laid file folders on the well-worn sofa. While he was double-checking the numbers, Kim watched him from the corner of her eye.

"I saw a nice apartment today near Miracle Mile," she said casually, "and it's a two-bedroom. So...cute." She paused in her food preparation and walked into the living room to see Ahmed's face.

"How much? I'm scared to ask," he said, clearly trying to stay focused on the task at hand.

"Holiday would have her own bedroom, and it also has a dining room," Kimberly tempted.

"How much...?"

"Fifteen hundred dollars a month and they only want first and last," Kim pleaded.

"No way." Ahmed shook his head. "I told you, first we pay off the credit cards and then we look for a new place. Getting us out of the hole you dug with those nutty spending sprees is going to take some time. In a few months, I'll be up for a raise, and then things might get easier. Trust me."

"Okay. I get it. You know...I did see the prettiest sundress at Sears."

"Kimberly Solberg. Give me a break," Ahmed said in jest.

"Okay then. But maybe having a second bedroom would be good for Holiday and—"

"—and what?"

"—and maybe a new brother or sister?"

"What? ...How could that be?" Ahmed said clumsily.

"I don't know yet, but I wanted you to know I thought...." she trailed off and waited for a response.

Moments passed before he spoke. His ears burned at the tips and his mouth was suddenly parched.

"Do you really think you're pregnant this soon?" he asked at last.

"...You think this is too soon?" she asked. "The point is...I'm late and I'm never this late."

"I'm sorry...I didn't mean it...you surprised me," he said, trying to hold her arm tenderly before she pulled it away.

"I don't believe you," she said, and walked back to the kitchen.

"Believe me?" he called after her. "What about you? You sprang that on me...while I'm working."

"Yeah—but you never want to talk about moving," she said, and went back to the poultry.

"So are you pregnant or just trying to move?" Ahmed shouted as he stood up and dumped his accounting papers all over the floor. He appeared in the kitchen doorway as Kim set the oven to 350 degrees Fahrenheit. "Jesus...why are you so manipulative? Just be straight with me."

"Straight? That can't happen when you act like a king and not my boyfriend. You aren't the only one getting a paycheck. I work too." She shoved the bird into the oven.

"Being a waitress at a pancake house? Last time I checked, it was my job that pays the rent."

"Really, you're going to go there?"

"You better recognize, woman," he retorted.

"No, you'd better. We'll know soon enough…Daddy!" she snapped as she stood up.

Kim could feel something had changed in the apartment. The sounds were different now. No longer could she hear the tender voices of proud and loving parents. The voices were replaced with the tinkling of silverware during dinner, and then the scraping and clanking of dishware and the swooshing of the dishwater. Sounds of things, not sounds of life. Later, when she put Holly to bed the noises were even more muted, leaving the tiny apartment quiet when her little girl closed her eyes and went to sleep.

28

Boulevard Dust-Up

It was Friday night on Hollywood Boulevard and the atmosphere was electric. The excitement came from two energy sources that made the place famous. One was the rich and famous that raced about town in their high-priced cars and limousines, shopping, eating, or making a scene at restaurants and nightclubs nestled in the hills and valleys around Hollywood. The other energy source was the wannabes. They searched for the significant and beat their deflated chests when they saw someone special or, better yet, got a glance to prove that they existed on the same plane of reality.

Officers Creech and Fuller had just started duty at the Hollywood station and had completed their third hour of patrol. Things were slow for a Saturday night. A domestic disturbance and then a purse snatching led to a chase down Gower South to Sunset. The teenage suspect got lost, so the cops headed back to Hollywood Boulevard.

"Damndest thing...first I had him and then he was gone," Fuller lamented.

His stocky frame was built for racquetball and not for sprints. Fuller still panted in short, tight breaths and sweat stained his shirt around the shoulders and under his arms.

"You know the legs are the second things to go," Officer Creech said.

"Yeah…yeah…Cut the shit. Let's get back to patrol before something else jumps off. That boy ain't done. We'll see him again. Remember he's skinny, dark-skinned, and wearing a dark hoodie," Fuller said.

Fuller pointed the car toward the Kodak Theater while Creech looked out for any commotion.

· · · ·

Jeremy Talbert and Sidney Dennison were young wannabes. As they hung out on the corner of Hollywood and Ivar, they talked about what they could get into when there was no money for cover charges, drinks, or even cheap-ass souvenirs.

"Dawg. Let's find a good movie. I think there's a Bruce Willis joint down the street. Let's do that. That way I can get home by ten or my mom's gonna kill me," Jeremy pleaded.

"Son, you are acting like a White boy since you moved to the West Side. Bruce Willis? Really? You got to man up and show that you're Black enough to hang with me," Sidney said with a smile. "Let's sneak into a titty bar?" He saw Jeremy's expression and quickly added, "Psych. I got to be home by eleven. I'm with you on this."

"Dude…I thought you were just being a dick." Jeremy shook his head. "So what do you want to do next?"

"A movie? That's whack. Let's just keep walking and checking out the shorties on the boulevard. I'll be Wesley Snipes and you can be my White sidekick."

Jeremy was used to jokes about his skin color and how his sandy-brown hair matched nicely with his hazel eyes and slight physique.

"Dawg. This is like you were in grade school," Jeremy complained. "I thought junior high would make you more creative than that motherfucker?" He caught the surprised expression blossoming on Sidney's face and followed up with, "Is that Black enough for your ass?"

Sidney grabbed Jeremy by the neck of his hoodie and pulled it toward him. Jeremy resisted the tug, lost his balance, and gently scooted off the sidewalk. He grabbed Jeremy's pants leg. In seconds both boys were on the ground, wrestling.

"Let go of me," Jeremy laughed. "Before I do a slam and jam on you like the WWF!"

"No way. I'm going to ram your fucking head into the cement like you stole something," Sidney retorted, grinning himself. "You're going to start crying like a bitch."

. . . .

As the two teenagers' match mushroomed into a joyful frenzy and a few bored spectators stopped to witness the fray, Officer Fuller pulled his car to the curb.

"Hey, is that our guy? Check him out," he said.

Creech was the first out of the squad car and engaged the boys on the pavement between the stars of Billy Joel and Edward G. Robinson.

"Okay, you two. Separate and there won't be any trouble," Creech commanded as the boys kept on tussling good-naturedly. They ignored him, and he dropped down and slipped an arm around the darker boy's throat in a submission hold.

"Officer, please…we're just messing around. Give us a break," Sidney said while resisting the tight pull of Officer Creech's forearm around his neck.

With the patrol car parked cockeyed against the curb, a crowd began to form. Fuller danced around the front bumper and grabbed Jeremy by the seat of his pants as he tried to get away.

"Slow down, young man. Is this boy trying to hurt you?" he asked.

"No. Just let us go. We'll be straight. Honest," Jeremy pleaded as Fuller's right fist held on to his belt with the determination and control of a prizefighter. With the boys firmly in hand and wiggling in protest, the officers loaded them into the rear of the vehicle.

"So what's this beef all about?" Officer Fuller asked.

"We were just roughhousin," Jeremy complained. "No beef… please, Mr. Officer."

"No trippin' on the boulevard. My bad. I started it," Sidney confessed.

Fuller leaned over to whisper to Creech.

"I think this is our guy," he murmured.

"You think so?"

In handcuffs, Jeremy and Sidney soon were secured in the cruiser and taken to the station for questioning.

29

Spit and Baked Beans

Inside the station, Jeremy was separated from Sidney by a six-inch-thick gray stonewall and an automated security checkpoint. Jeremy sat for hours on a padded bench with his reddened wrist twisting and turning against the ridged edges of handcuffs secured to the railing in the waiting room. Police officers and station operatives hurried about while Sidney sat fifty yards away, down a startlingly bright hallway illuminated by overhead fluorescent lights fitted into the ten-foot ceilings in a six-by-six jail cell. Alone in the stark brightness, he sang.

"I'm not the man that can be chased into the other

Just a young nigga who would switch his skin for another

In a minute, or an hour...it's just not the color.

Or I would rub my face against the bathroom tissue... why bother?"

Jeremy knew the verse and recognized his friend's mood.

"Sidney! What's happening? Tell me something good," he called. Seconds passed, and all he heard was the shuffling of an unruly drunk going into the lockup, resisting the way the officers pulled and prodded him past the turnstile in the long hallway.

"Let me go. I got rights! Hey! I ain't done nothing," he yelled before the cops pushed him into a cell near Sidney and locked him in. "Hey! Somebody call me a laur' yer…you punk-ass cops!"

Jeremy looked up at the cops as they returned, wanting to ask about Sidney, when he heard the song start up again.

"Just fuck the man…screw him good

Each one steals our heart and soul

Take them out so we can make more…

Kill the man…Kill the fucking man."

"What's going on?" Jeremy called back to Sidney. A cold sweat materialized on his skin, and he twisted to yell after the departing cops. "Officer!…Officer! …Someone needs to check on my friend!"

Officer Fuller approached him with a grim and bloodless look.

"Boy, you got to keep quiet. If you do, you'll be out of here in about thirty minutes. Be patient." He rested a hand on Jeremy's leg reassuringly. Down the hall, the lights in the jail cells went dark and the intense hallway lights dimmed, throwing shadows along the secured corridor.

"But what about Sidney?" Jeremy asked.

Officer Fuller pulled his attention away from the bench and glanced down the shady hall, where he heard a sudden groan.

"Ugggghhhh. Uggggghhh…Ohhhhhh…Ugggghhhh."

Fuller rose and walked back into the jail without turning back to Jeremy.

"Hey!" Jeremy yelled after him. "Come on. Tell me something."

Fuller's fast walk became frantic footsteps, as he approached the cell of the drunk.

"Jesus Christ…did you have to get it all over the floor? That's what the fucking toilets are for, you moron…I got to find someone to clean this up. Are you done?" he demanded.

"I don't feel so good," the drunk said, his voice echoing into the jailhouse plumbing.

Fuller sighed and reached for his shoulder mic. "Get someone down to cell seven for a cleanup," he said into it.

"Ugggh…Ohhh…Ohhh…Aye…Aye…."

Jeremy could barely hear over the groans. He heard the ascending sounds of Fuller's footsteps.

"Remind me. Who is Sidney?" the cop asked as he put his leg up on the bench and ignored the moans coming from the sick drinker.

"You don't know? …He's the Black kid I came in with…. We were play-fighting on the street," Jeremy said in disbelief.

"Ohh…my purse-snatching suspect," Fuller said.

"Sidney's no thief," Jeremy pleaded. "I was with him all night, and he didn't steal anything!"

"I don't know. If I were you, I would stay calm," Fuller advised. "You'll be out of here before you know it. Just take care of yourself."

"I want to call my dad," Jeremy said.

"Young man. There's nothing more I can do. A detective will question him later. I think I can have you out of here in less than thirty." Fuller said, looking at his watch.

"I'm not leaving…not without my friend."

"Whatever. Good luck, kid—take my advice and stay off the boulevard." Fuller headed for the sergeant's desk.

From down the hall, Sidney's mournful voice pierced the air and then faded into the hermetically sealed void.

"Don't take me away from trouble

That lives inside my mind

I look for my freedom in the rubble

And among the troubling times

The dangers than touch my soul

Can't be freed with the harness of force

Get away from my face and free me

For I'm set driven on another course."

Later that night, Jeremy was released on his own recognizance and Sidney was found dead in his cell, hanging from a bed sheet tethered to an overhead light fixture.

• • • •

News of the Hollywood incident swept the nation. In Chicago, Reverend Harper booked a redeye to Los Angeles and was visiting with both Jeremy and the parents of Sidney Dennison by early Monday morning. At the Talbert home, he addressed Jeremy's parents.

"I'm Reverend Rufus Harper, from the Freedom Brigade. Our mission is to seek justice whenever we see racism. That's why we're here," he said, sipping at a sweet cup of coffee on the Talbert's burgundy floral loveseat.

"We welcome your support. We're just thankful Jeremy was unharmed," said Jeremy's father while holding hands on the matching sofa with the boy's mother.

"That's why we're here and thankful Jeremy's okay. I'd like to ask a few questions?"

"Of course. I know you suggested over the phone that we get ourselves an attorney, but unfortunately we can't afford one."

"Don't worry about that. One more question, Jeremy. Did you at any time fear for your life when you were in police custody?"

"No…? What do you mean?" Jeremy asked from the seat next to his father.

Reverend Harper tilted his head and studied Jeremy's face. "Do you think they treated you like a White boy?"

Jeremy took a deep breath that stretched his chest like a nervous rooster while he struggled to hold back tears and body palpitations. His torso shook from the pressure until he let the tears of grief run down his face.

"I miss my friend," he said, and shrugged off his father's attempt at a muscular hug.

"Take your time," Harper said as he took another sip of coffee. "Did they treat you differently than they treated Sidney?"

"They had him in a cell and sat me on a bench outside," Jeremy admitted.

"Did you think Sidney hung himself?" Harper continued.

"I don't know."

"There's no easy way to say this," Harper said. "Have you ever been taken for a White boy before?"

"When I'm with my friends, sometimes we get funny looks, but mostly when we're out of town. I get different looks."

Harper leaned back on the loveseat, nodding with satisfaction. "Our mission will be to get justice for Sidney, and I must control the conversation. Whatever you do from here, talk to the media only when I tell you to."

Jeremy looked at his father and waited for him to answer.

"We understand," the elder Talbert said. "Just as long as there's no lying or misrepresentation about anything, including the police treatment that night."

"Agreed. Now we are going to pay our respects to the Dennison family. Thanks for letting me talk with you this morning," Harper said, swallowing the last of his coffee. "Shall we pray?"

Without a word, the five of them and the two security men held hands in a circle, bowed their heads, and closed their eyes. Harper spoke.

"Heavenly father, we seek out justice for these two young men. Help us discover the truth behind what happened to your servant Sidney while in Hollywood last weekend. We will find a brighter day…. In your holy name, we pray. Amen."

With warm handshakes and gospel hugs, Reverend Harper and his security team got back into the black Cadillac Escalade and headed for South Los Angeles.

The Dennisons lived in a small two-bedroom apartment with two teenage boys. Mr. Dennison was a retired municipal bus driver. Reverend Harper found their home by the scores of neighbors that were mingling around the front door, paying their respects to the mourning parents.

Harper looked for a figure of command. He found several men with gang colors who were protecting the peace. He finally selected the biggest, blackest, baddest one among them, who glared at Harper. The brother stepped in front of Harper and his security man before they could reach the front door.

"So, what can we do for you, my brother?" the big man rumbled.

"I am Reverend Rufus Harper from the Freedom Brigade in Chicago," Harper announced, "and I have flown all night to pay my respects to the Dennison family and see what I can do to command justice."

"Aren't you the dude that's on Rev. Sharpton's News Hour?" the brother asked, squinting. "I liked what you had to say about economic empowerment and set-asides." He shook Harper's hand and stepped away from the door.

Harper trundled inside. A thin ebony man in a sleeveless undershirt and tattered blue jeans, smoking a Black and Mild cigarette, stood in the tiny living room. The room smelled of coffee and cheap bourbon. A heavy-set woman in hair rollers, a floral housecoat, and bedroom slippers sat in the kitchenette next to a half-empty box of Kleenex. Her eyes were swollen and bloodshot. Both parents looked up from their blank stares and acknowledged the Reverend's presence with nods. Mr. Dennison spoke slowly in low tones.

"You dat pastor from Chicago who's always trying to stir the pot and get justice for Black people. You here to find out who killed my boy?"

"Yes, sir. I am," Harper replied, drawing himself up to his full but unimpressive height. "The Freedom Brigade wants to say how sorry we are that your boy died." He doffed his baseball cap and cupped it gently in his hands.

"He didn't just die," Mr. Dennison spat. "Those bastard cops murdered him. So what are you doing to do about it?" He stubbed his smoke out on the Kool's cigarette ashtray on the coffee table.

Mrs. Dennison sobbed into her tissue and looked up at the reverend.

"Sidney was a good boy who never hurt anybody," she told him. "I want people to know he was God-fearing."

"I will do my very best," Harper promised. "Have you received a coroner's preliminary report?"

"No, but KJLH news said it was suicide," she said, reaching for a clean tissue. "I was washing clothes in the laundry mat when I heard it. No mama should hear her boy's dead on the radio." She sobbed again as Mr. Dennison came up behind her and rested his slender, strong hands on her shoulders.

"I will be talking with the Police Chief today to demand any information be released to you," Harper said. "We just want to help in what little way we can." He fingered a Bible in his right hand.

Mr. Dennison reached out and shook Harper's hand.

"You find what they did to my boy," he ordered.

"I promise you I will. But first, can I see Sidney's room?" Harper glanced down the short hallway that led off the kitchen.

"Sure. He's the one on the right. He shares it with his brother, Ray-Ray," Mama said.

Inside the bedroom, Harper walked between the twin beds and noticed the Raiders team poster on one side and the Rams poster on the other. Ray-Ray stood at the door, watching. He wore a blue and gold football jersey with the number 24 on it. He looked much older than his probable age, and appeared to have had life harder than most. He wore colors of the gang life and appeared overwrought and underfed.

"I bet Sidney was a Raider fan," Harper said, resting his hands on the small bookshelf at the edge of the bed.

"You'd be right. Reverend," Ray-Ray said. "What do you want?"

"I'm here to see Sidney gets the justice he deserves. Don't you want that?" Harper asked. He looked at the stack of papers piled up by the headboard.

"What are you looking for?" Ray-Ray asked as Harper turned some of the loose papers over for closer examination.

"Anything that would either help us or protect your brother's memory," Harper said.

"Can you make something disappear?" Ray-Ray asked.

"You mean something that needs to stay private?" Harper answered. "Of course."

"Then you should take this," Ray-Ray said, walking into the room. He stuck a hand between Sidney's mattress and his box spring and pulled out a small blue notebook.

"What's this?" Harper asked, taking the book.

"Sidney's notes. There's some pretty raw shit in here."

"Oh. I get it. Thanks," Harper said as he put the book in his coat pocket.

"Sidney and I got lots of riffs and joints about killing cops and being freedom fighters. Serious. Don't show it to Mom. I'm a rapper—want me to spit something?" Ray-Ray asked. He inched awkwardly over to stand by his small desk, adorned only with a laptop computer.

"No, son. Not the right moment. But I'll get back to you. Okay?" Harper said.

"That's cool. I know you're down with T-Bone and his crew. Maybe you can hook a brother up?" Ray-Ray asked as Harper left the room with the notebook.

Leaving Nickerson Gardens, Reverend Harper read Sidney's thoughts about the Los Angeles police and the Black community and his chaotic ramblings about a better world. Before the limo reached his hotel, it pulled up behind a drugstore, where Harper found an old commercial-grade baked-bean can, put the notebook inside, and poured lighter fluid on the yellow-lined pages. He watched the book go up in flames until the paper was ash.

"Dust to dust," he said to the curling black pieces of a dead boy's soul.

30

Professional Courtesy

When Chaka got the call from Kublai Khan, they hadn't seen each other in a while. Their schedules didn't mesh well even though their love for each other was still growing. Chaka felt her pulse kick up as she picked up the receiver.

"Hello, Minister. I almost forgot what your voice sounds like."

"Hello, my queen. Can you join me in Cairo next week? I will be there for a conference and I'd love to have you there as my companion."

Chaka felt her eyebrows go up. This wasn't sweet talk; Cairo was on his schedule and he wanted to be there with her.

"I'd love to," she said carefully. "It's just that on short notice I can't get the proper care for the girls. Maybe I'll go next time." She smiled to herself. "You didn't call me just to take me on an Egyptian adventure."

There was a chuckle on the other end of the line. "Truth. I'm calling you to extend a professional courtesy to a business associate of mine, Reverend Rufus Harper from Chicago. Can you clear your schedule today?"

"What's this about?"

"It's about the two Black boys who got arrested in Hollywood last weekend. The one Black kid was hung in his cell and the other was released. Some people think the cops thought the one they let go was White."

"I haven't seen any news reports on this," Chaka said with a frown. "You think the cops couldn't tell White from Black? And if the Black one looked White, he would be alive today?"

"That's part of the story. They need you to find a way to turn this into an opportunity."

Chaka tilted her head, intrigued. "You want me to create a media circus?"

"I wouldn't use those words. I think you can shine the proper light on the problem and help us acquire the maximum media coverage. The window of opportunity is closing very quickly."

"I get it, Minister," Chaka said coolly, "but we have to find a way to ignite the Black community. I will take the meeting this afternoon and will report back to you tomorrow."

"Thanks. I'll expect your call and your invoice."

"Goodbye, Minister Kublai Khan," Chaka said earnestly.

As Chaka went back to work, thinking about the Hollywood incident, ideas started churning in her head. The fear of every parent was real. The story had everything: the dangers of growing up a young Black boy, the arrest, and a child left isolated in a darkened cell. She could imagine little Sidney huddled in the cold dark with his sweatshirt hood shadowing his face.

What an image.

Before the meeting, the team reviewed the media and social media outlets for trend lines and looked at attitudinal studies for a sense of the social and political climate in America.

They were not in any way prepared.

. . . .

Chaka's first impression was that Harper was too pompous for his own good, even though he had a good grasp of the media problem. As the meeting began to break up, Harper insisted on summarizing yet again.

"Thanks for taking the time to meet with us," he said for the third time. "I appreciate how you and your team evaluated the situation and offered ways to move forward. I think that with the right preparation, we can have a City Hall protest rally that might shift perspectives in our favor."

"I'm glad you appreciate what my guys can do on short notice," Chaka replied, subtly gathering her papers into a neat stack. "But we need a hook. Imagine poor Sidney in his dark cell alone, with his hood up over his head. Turn the menace into pathos. How about the phrase Hollywood Hoodies?"

Harper's eyes grew to the size of saucers and a wide smile covered his face.

"The Hollywood Hoodies. I think that's terrific!" he exclaimed.

"Beautiful." Chaka smiled. "This has been a good start. In our next meeting, I would love to meet Jeremy."

Harper drew himself up. "Jeremy is a fine young man," he said proudly, "and his parents are there to protect and counsel him along the way. He is both articulate and photogenic. And his sadness for Sidney is very real."

"Does he look believable?"

"He's handsome, with brown-sandy hair and hazel-green eyes. He looks more like his mother, but it's possible that the police who arrested him thought the fight on the boulevard was a Black-White thing and not just two Black teenagers goofing around."

"Interesting. That'll feed the outrage. If Sidney was a light-eyed soul brother like Jeremy, the cops would have acted differently and Sidney would still be alive. It's a profiling case. Fascinating."

"My point exactly," said Harper. "It's all about perception."

"Perception," Chaka said, "is what we're here for."

. . . .

Outside, Reverend Harper spoke by phone to Kublai Khan.

"I think Chaka's team can assist us in getting the message out and possibly help us gain national attention. It's time we ignited people into action."

"Good," Kublai Khan agreed. "I have the contacts you need to reach the most committed activists. I'd start with the local chapter of The House of Jeremiah and its leader, Timothy Islam."

Harper nodded, even though he knew Khan couldn't see him. "I know him. He's got a powerful energy and he's devoted to the cause. When can we meet with him?"

There was the soft click of computer keys—Khan checking his schedule, Harper guessed. "He has an event at the temple today," Khan reported. "It's a clothing drive, so I'm sure the Freedom Brigade can afford a meaningful donation. We appreciate the gesture." There was a smile in his voice.

"Jesus has blessed us with a bounty. I will leave him with a check," Harper said.

Time was money, and power waited for no one.

31

City Country City

From the steps of Los Angeles City Hall, one could see the old Parker Center, the home of the Los Angeles Police Department. As the crowd of two hundred men, women, and children from South Los Angeles stood and shouted opposition to the death of Sidney Dennison, men in blue casually walked into the police headquarters without so much as a glance at the commotion.

A dozen police officers, mostly Black, stood around the perimeter and watched the proceedings. A cameraman captured the stoic faces of the officers and the growing agitation of the crowd for the web.

"Black lives matter!" shouted an elderly man in an orange, red, and purple dashiki with his fist held high in the air. Sprinkled throughout the assembly were signs and placards showing an angelic grade-school graduation photo of Sidney.

Reverend Harper stood at the makeshift podium and spoke into the microphone with the rolling cadence of a Southern Baptist minister. He knew that the camera was running, and he needed to make something happen.

"Brothers and sisters," he boomed, "I stand before you as a man with fire in his heart. It's been ignited because of the case of two young Blacks being arrested in Hollywood for simply roughhousing. The real tragedy wasn't the fact that they were arrested. It was that young Jeremy slept in his own bed that night, while Sidney was found hanging from his own hoodie in the morning."

The crowd erupted in whoops and yells and then quieted as Harper raised a hand in benediction.

"We will not stand for injustice," he continued. "Young Sidney Dennison should have gone home with Jeremy. Both boys wanted to enjoy the scene on the streets of Hollywood. They didn't realize they were dressed like the kind of troublemakers the police see all our boys to be, no matter what they're doing."

"No justice, no peace!" someone shouted from the middle of the crowd, and everyone took up the chant.

"No justice, no peace! No justice, no peace!"

Harper pressed on. "You don't have to take my word about what happened," he called, "because there's a witness to the Hollywood Hoodies incident with us today. Please give your attention to Jeremy Talbert."

Reverend Harper stepped away from the podium, trusting a sixteen-year-old boy to galvanize his listeners.

Jeremy stepped to the podium weakly. His first words were nearly inaudible.

"Hello. I'm Jeremy…Talbert," he mumbled, "and I'm…bbb… bbb…Black."

The crowd roared approval.

"Jeremy! …Jeremy! …Jeremy!"

Jeremy's voice wavered as he spoke, and his hesitation only spurred the crowd to get louder and louder. Every word he spoke was greeted with emphatic screams.

"Jeh-ruh-mee! Jeh-ruh-mee! JEH-RUH-MEE!"

"I want to speak for my friend Sidney," Jeremy pressed, "who died a few nights ago in a Hollywood police cell. I was there."

The camera caught the crowd swaying back and forth, as they tuned in to his emotional struggle.

"We both felt the cops shouldn't have arrested us," Jeremy went on, the microphone carrying his small voice over the heads of his listeners. "We...we...weren't hurting anyone. I tried to tell the officers that we were buds and we were just having a little fun hanging out on the boulevard...but they didn't listen. When they let me go, I was surprised Sidney wasn't right behind me."

Jeremy took a breath and paused for what seemed like a minute. The crowd fell suddenly quiet.

"Nothing I was going to say will bring Sidney back," he said as he looked up from the notes Harper had given him.

Silence, as perfect as the moon's.

"...I have white skin...some people say I'll never be treated like a real Black man." Jeremy looked down at his shoes, then up at the faces in front of him. "But what people think about me doesn't really mean anything. My Blackness is not on my skin. It's in my heart."

"Be Black!" a woman's voice called.

"Stay Black!" a man replied.

The crowd started jumping up and down in a frenzy, picking up the chant. "Be Black...stay Black...be Black...stay Black...be Black...stay Black!"

Jeremy stayed around for interviews after his speech, and used every opportunity to spin the story for reporters and bloggers alike.

Harper jumped in at the end of every conversation to say, "Use our hashtags—beblackstayblack and blacklikejeremy." The interviewers dutifully wrote everything down.

The viral videos were next.

The first video showed the bare head and shoulders of Justin Hennessey, an English actor, speaking into the camera while riding on a horse-drawn chariot racing through cobblestone streets in central London.

"I am Black like Jeremy," he intoned, in a perfect Eton accent.

Then the image morphed into Jessica Alba, dressed as a modern dancer at center stage, where she said, "I am Black like Jeremy,"

Then the image transformed to Hall of Famer Benito Maricon, the Cuban baseball star, who repeated, "I'm Black like Jeremy."

Next was Eva Morales, the movie star, dressed as a galactic storm trooper on the set of her most recent film. Then it was the Australian movie star Pleather Jackson, dressed in a tuxedo and holding a champagne glass, then the action film hero Justin Wong, dressed in a wetsuit and walking out of the Pacific Ocean. They all repeated, "I am Black like Jeremy," and the video finished with NeSha Langston, a Black reality TV star dressed in a gold lame two-piece. She too said, "I am Black like Jeremy," and then added, "Aren't you? Upload your video at BlacklikeJeremy.Com."

Within weeks, the website had two million hits and 150,000 videos had been uploaded. Anthropologists and academics alike joined Minister Kublai Khan in offering the hypothesis that if in America the single drop rule was the law of the land, and there were traces of African DNA in all human beings, then everyone in the nation was Black.

The discussion became manna for talk shows on radio and television, with a cadre of experts surfacing to defend the merits of racial and physical profiling.

· · · ·

"Welcome to Talk of the Town with our host, Cynthia Chambers. Today her guests are Reverend Rufus Harper from the Freedom Brigade and Pastor Tucker Dalton from the Christian Covenant Church. They will be discussing the topic. 'Who's Black?' Here's Cynthia."

Cynthia smiled blandly at the camera, her blonde hair shimmering under the lights. "Welcome to where we tackle the difficult issues. Today it's just—who are Black people, and what do they really want? My guest today is Reverend Rufus Harper, who has helped make Hollywood Hoodies a household phrase. Welcome Rev. With him today is a man who is no stranger to controversy himself, Pastor Tucker Dalton from the Christian Covenant Church in Chino, California. Welcome to both of you." She turned her smile on her guests. "Reverend Dalton, it's nice to have you with us today to discuss such a controversial subject."

"I appreciate your invitation to confront the terrible precedent Harper's people are creating here in Southern California," Dalton offered. He was sitting ramrod-straight in his blocky modernist chair, his suit and face a little too shiny under studio lighting.

"Well, let's get down to it, then. What is so wrong with what Reverend Harper's doing?"

"He and his outside agitators are stirring up the people of Los Angeles by taking a sad incident in Hollywood and making it into front-page news with that 'I am Black too' thing…" Dalton shook his head. "Disgusting."

Harper, seated beside him and comfortably filling his own space, made a harrumphing noise. "Yes, we've helped our people understand that they have a right to demand justice for Sidney Dennison. The people who agree with us are not going to let people like you," he glowered at Dalton, "tell us just who are. Not ever again."

"But Reverend," Cynthia interrupted, "I think Pastor Dalton is saying Black people are clearly people who look one way while others don't. Does your campaign try to blur the lines of race and ethnicity?"

Harper turned to her and gave her a polite, almost fatherly smile. "People are declaring for themselves what race they identify with," he said, "and being Black is no more about biology than it is about physical appearance. It's social. And people have seen that one of the victims that awful day in Hollywood is fighting against the social perceptions that he isn't Black. We're all Black like Jeremy." He looked sideways into camera two and added, "The idea of choosing who you really are resonates with all people."

"This is blasphemy," Dalton snarled. "God has blessed all of his children with the capacity to be different races and ethnic groups since the start of time. Confusing people with this kind of political manipulation is a selfish act. The members of the Christian Covenant Church won't stand for it!" He wiped his sweaty brow with a cotton handkerchief while the harsh stage lights warmed his partially bald head.

"Reverend Harper, what do you say to Pastor Dalton's accusation of manipulation?" Cynthia asked, reading from a small stack of notecards she held in her hands.

"I don't agree with Dalton," Harper said simply. "I think that people want the freedom to declare what race they identify with most. And Black is where it's at."

"When your people were still in caves and had tails, White people were navigating the oceans and establishing civilizations," Dalton growled as his face turned scarlet.

"You're a racist," Harper said, a hint of frost creeping into his tone, "and misinformed. Black people of Africa mastered the oceans and conquered much of Europe with cunning and bravery. Haven't you heard of Hannibal?"

"Our Lord and the laws of Nature have created the races to be different as any species," Dalton retorted. "Therefore, White people have to be, and are, superior to any other racial species on Earth."

"If that's true," Cynthia cut in, "how do you explain people like Jeremy Talbert, the survivor of the Hollywood Hoodies case? They look White but see themselves as Black." She held out a languid hand. "Doesn't that make race simply a personal thing?"

"I don't believe any of that psycho-babble," Dalton grumbled. "People like this Jeremy kid are biological abominations. People should look like the race they are. If they don't, they are strange and unnatural."

"So you think the millions of people in this country who are mixed-race are abnormal?" Harper interjected, struggling to hide his smirk.

"Don't put words in my mouth, I didn't say that," Dalton snapped. "White people must protect our society and way of life. White people must reject the idea that they can be another race."

"I urge Americans to help transform race and politics in America by defining themselves as Black," Harper proclaimed. A wicked gleam appeared in his eye. "Who knows? From where I'm sitting, I can see thick lips, curly hair, and broad nostrils. It looks to me like Pastor Dalton has a nigger in his woodpile."

Reverend Dalton's face turned the color of a robin's chest as he surged to his feet, overturning the coffee table in front of him. Harper scrambled back out of striking range and blundered into a nearby lighting stand, then rebounded, balling his fists in preparation for a fight.

But neither one threw a punch. The two men stood nose to nose, breathing heavily, and suddenly began hurling insults at each other. After a few seconds of ratings gold, Cynthia stepped in between them and pushed them apart like chest-beating boxers at a weigh-in.

"You psychotic bastard!" Reverend Harper roared, his cheeks and neck flushing dark. "I hope you...you burn in hell!"

"There isn't enough power in those monkey brains of you people to change our way of life!" spat Dalton as camera one zoomed in close on his rage.

"Black people have put up with the lies and deceit of people like you since slavery! No more, you ugly cracker!" Harper bellowed as he threw his arms around the preacher in a hostile bear hug.

As the studio assistants rushed in to separate the two men, Dalton twisted free and scrambled back while Reverend Harper calmly straightened his tie and readjusted his suit jacket. The camera cut back to the host, who remained calm and in control.

"Gentlemen," she said, arching an eyebrow. "What a show. I invite you both back to discuss this further. Thanks again for being on Talk of the Town."

. . . .

The #blacklikejeremy campaign became a problem for Washington and the administrators of the US Census. The African American working group was brought back together under an emergency provision to study the issue. The working group met in The Albert Hotel, on DuPont Circle. Kublai Khan was there remotely by speakerphone.

Quickly the conversation turned to the issue of self-identification. The fear was clear. An explosion in the "Other" racial category would damage the accuracy of the data. Reverend Foresight was quick to see the ramifications.

"The government must rely on the integrity of its people and adjust for the results of social change. This is a good thing."

"Anything that impedes one minority group over another is cause for grave concern. A Black citizen isn't a White one," Les asserted.

"We're already down the rabbit hole now," Reverend Harper insisted. "Race is now a choice. We better get used to it. And Black is what's happening."

"It's unfortunate that my people are choosing other categories than Hispanic to describe their race in the census," Dr. Garza remarked, and added, "and some of those are now becoming Black."

"Yes, that's regrettable," Kublai Khan agreed from the speaker in the middle of the conference table. "But the Black like Jeremy movement has transformed race in America." There was a short huff of breath, possibly a snort. "Get used to it."

. . . .

Les and Harper shared a car to Dulles Airport.

"Birth camps?" Harper blurted when Les told him the story. "Where Asian women are having Black babies?" He stared.

"Yes. That's the deal. A fully functional facility with a full staff of nurses and doctors," Les confirmed.

"The idea is just plain immoral. What was he thinking?"

"As simple as it sounds…he wants what you want," Les said with a shrug. "Power." He held his pale fist up for emphasis.

"Les, you know the minister can't keep a lid on those camps. Sooner or later, it's going to leak out. I suggest that he get their affairs in order—things like birth and marriage certificates as well as permits and medical records."

"I'm sure everything's in order. But the House of Jeremiah should prepare a press campaign soon to offset any negative public perception about the center," Les concluded. Outside the window, the Washington monument slid past, touched with blood and fire against a dusky sky. "But it shouldn't be an issue. It isn't against the law to provide medical benefits to underserved mothers, or to offer early childhood education."

"With all due respect, I don't know how the House and Minister Kublai Khan thought that controlled birth camps could impact the national census. Do you?" Harper asked.

"He and I talked extensively about it. The numbers are clear. If the camps closed tomorrow, California's Black population would still be changed forever."

"Even so, it would never make a difference in federal appropriations," Harper said.

"Don't doubt the numbers…unless you got something more reliable than White people calling themselves Black. The birth camps are worth supporting," Les said.

By the time, the men got to the airport the conversation had turned to sports, urban decay, private schools, and the high price of college tuition.

32

Freefoit

From the time Chaka retrieved her bags off the luggage car-
ousel at the Detroit Metropolitan Airport, she began to relax. The
Minister had taken care of everything, including a first-class round-
trip ticket and a driver. First stop was the evening sermon at the
House of Jeremiah temple on West Grand Boulevard, where the
minister delivered a spiritual message about self-determination and
community unity to two thousand followers packed into a remod-
eled movie theater.

The minister began his time alone with Chaka in the short
ride over to the House mansion. They sat together, holding hands
in silence as the driver sped through blocks of burned-out and
abandoned homes and closed storefronts in the red-soaked streets.
Sprinkled throughout the bleak scene were a few manicured lawns
and well-maintained homes demonstrating that a few people
remained. Chaka saw a red tricycle with a broken front wheel turned
over in the dirt where a lawn once grew.

"Where did the people go?" she asked, turning her eyes to the
rain-spotted windshield.

"They come to us broken and looking for hope. We will transform this city one family at a time," Kublai Khan replied.

"But where are the people going?" Chaka repeated. She turned and looked into the minister's eyes as he glanced down into his lap.

"Sometime they stay with their families—hotels…shelters," the minister admitted, stroking his thumb over the back of Chaka's hand. "Our job is to serve those who come."

"My cousin Marvin moved to Alabama…and they're fine."

"Living with cow dung on your shoes is never good," Kublai Khan said. "Some of us stay put."

"I left a decade ago. Still sore?"

"No—I get it. But there are people who stay in a city…. Those are the people Yahweh wants me to serve." He shook his head. "Hungry?"

"I can eat. What you have in mind?"

"Anything you want. Chateaubriand. Shrimp scampi. Paella."

She smiled. "Barbeque ribs and greens with ham hocks."

"Whatever. The least I can do is keep you satisfied," he said, and kissed her hand.

"Satisfaction is one thing," she said as he let her lower her hand again. "Truth is another."

"Truth about what?"

"About us. And the idea of sharing a life together."

"In time. Let's just relax," he said, and tapped on the glass to direct the driver to the corner of 8 Mile Road and Livernois. Chaka smiled at the familiar address.

"I read that George Clinton was in town," she said.

"I thought you might enjoy him. You know he's from Detroit?" he said.

"Clinton and the Fundadelics are the bomb! Now better than ever."

"Not a chance. But they're in my top five."

Chaka and Kublai Khan were taken to a table near the stage to enjoy Clinton's recorded work as men dressed in earth-tone sports coats and bright wide-collared leisure shirts sat with their hats in the laps, enjoying the company of polite women smoking menthol cigarettes. The restaurant lounge was near capacity as the people sipped on caramel-colored drinks and talked in anticipation of the performance. The minister and the ad pro joined the drone of polite chatter.

"Do you think White folks can play funk?" the minister asked.

"What do you mean by play?" Chaka replied while she sipped an Irish coffee.

"I mean play as well as Black people. Miles is on record for saying that there are chords that White people can't play. In fact, there is a musicologist out of Baltimore that says there is clinical evidence that indicates that White people's ears can't hear chords like the straight six and therefore they can't play as well as Black people," he explained. "I believe funk music is ingrained in the Black experience. Whites can't fathom its true meaning."

"So how do you explain Dave Brubeck?" Chaka challenged.

"He was passing. Brubeck was a Black man because he played like a brother." Khan hid his broad grin behind his Diet Coke.

Clinton and his all-stars stood onstage a moment later, soaking up the cheers of the audience before the drummer slowly turned the screws of his snare drum and gently tapped it with his drumstick.

The trumpeter blew short burst of air through his instrument and listened for a straight G. O'Neal channeled the gods as he made the sounds of angel laughter come from the back of the baby grand.

The trumpeter gave birth to memories of jazz with the sounds of every song ever written. The man who never removed his hat and sunglasses before the thunder struck took them both off in homage. The piano came alive and gave birth to the sounds of pleasant sadness.

The rows of small tables and hard chairs were the launching pads for earthbound creatures to be changed into bodiless beings that enjoyed the rhythms made by masters. The drummer's beat lifted the rising spirits while the poetry of the trio kept the mindful souls dancing.

Hearts and minds rose to the heavens and fell back to earth throughout the set, and would continue as long as there were jazz, funk, and The Baker's Keyboard Lounge.

. . . .

Kublai Khan and Chaka exchanged a tender kiss as the limo arrived at the gray brick mansion with old English turrets and tower windows. It was built by a nineteenth-century industrialist during the boom days of the motor city. The House of Jeremiah had owned the ten-acre complex for a decade. Kublai Khan maintained it as his primary residence where his seven children resided without their birth mothers. He had been married three times. Once he was elevated to the head minister of The House he vowed never to get married again unless he was certain it was Yahweh's will.

Chaka entered the mansion from the backyard car porch and was escorted discreetly to the master bedroom. Their relationship couldn't exist in the harsh light of the media. Chaka took to unpacking and then dressing for dinner. The Minister had business on the property to attend to so it would be just a few hours before they would be alone.

She chose a luscious rib eye for dinner, and the minister had a seafood stir-fry. The late-night supper included grilled asparagus and scallop potatoes with a small dinner salad. The wine was a remarkable Côtes du Rhône that Kublai Khan selected from his two-hundred-bottle wine cellar. Dessert was a fresh peach cobbler the staff had prepared for the occasion. Chaka had a nice port after dinner; the minister had sparkling water.

As Chaka sat in an oversized Victorian armchair, she was satiated and pleased with herself for choosing to be with Kublai Khan during the holy week. She was totally relaxed for the first time in months. Her thoughts turned to her girls.

"Cantara reads beautifully and hates soccer and Fanima's good at science but would rather play sports. Yes—I worry about them being productive—but their happiness is my biggest concern."

"Talk to a dog about being happy. It's a grave social disease only humans contract," Kublai Khan preached. "Your girls can only be productive."

"I just want that for them too." Chaka continued, "I'm their mother."

"You can't protect them from themselves," he said.

"Who protects your children?" she said as she finished arranging her dresses in the spacious closet.

"My girls learn to be powerful from the people who look, act, and feel like us. I spend time with the boys laying the bricks in their path for being a man. And yes…I have people who are with them through the day. Yours will become as remarkable like mine," he suggested. "What do you want from them?"

"They will go an HBCU...and pledge a sorority. I want them to know more about black history than what happens in February," Chaka insisted as she sat on the double-Queen-sized bed with the floral silk comforter.

"What about money?" he asked.

"I don't worry about money. It comes to me," Chaka said,

"I will carve a path for our kids that we all can follow," the Minister vowed.

"That's sweet...but I'm not another babies' mama like your others," Chaka said without hesitation.

"I'm sorry, of course you're not. I meant...," he said. "Everyone has a heart but in life it's right to get a start," he said while smiling and using his infectious dimples to deflect the truth Chaka heard in his declaration.

"I know. I know. That wasn't fair. I know you're a good father—but not every woman wants to hear what a man's going to do for her."

"I'm here for you. Any way you want it," he promised as he stood next to her with his hands holding her petite frame with his large wandering hands.

Chaka and Kublai Khan embraced and he disconnected her bra and she opened up his brown alligator belt as his pants slipped gently to the floor. As they kissed passionately, he hugged her tightly and forcibly pushed her onto the bed. She quickly bounced off the mattress and back into his arms.

"There you go again. I just don't get? Are you mad at me?" she said while pushing him in arm's length of her.

"No. What do you mean?" he said while unsurely dropping his arms to his side.

"You're so aggressive…" she said. "What's that? I hate this side of you. Where's this coming from?" she asked as she stepped away from the minister and sat in a chair across the room.

The minister stood alone in his underwear and felt vulnerable with the pointed questions. Her manner was rare and made his pulse quicken and caused his heart to pound in his chest.

"I…I…I'm sorry you feel that way…I love you." he said and approached Chaka is small deliberate steps. She raised her hand in a stopping motion.

"That's not the point…I believe that you love me but this is a problem you need to deal with—for real—before you and I start making plans," she said. "Get some help man."

Beads of perspiration rolled down the minister's brow. He thought of the many times Chaka had complained about rough sex and once thought it was just her way of saying she liked it.

"I'll deal with it," he promised.

"A trained professional—not one of your people." She said standing close to him with her hands on his broad shoulders.

"Okay I will," he surrendered and held her head in his powerful hands and pressed gently against her cheeks while she smiled.

She enjoyed his tender touch. His strong and anxious fingers felt like the finest linen brushing the small of her back with the brief whisk of cool moist air caressing her luscious thick lips and her broad but petite nose. Chaka's features highlighted her coarse, thick black hair. Her short and impeccable dread locks adorned her head like an exquisite crown befitting an African queen.

Later that night Chaka was gently waken by the sound of Kublai Khan hustling papers at his desk. He read from both the Quran and the Holy Bible. She watched intently as he sat in an African silk robe deep in thought. He scribbled down a note on the yellow-lined writing pad.

"Kublai…coming to bed?"

She knew he was never far from his thoughts and obligations. It was much easier to love the man than the devotee of the Lord.

"Yes, Chaka, but it's high holy days and I have to convince two thousand people to put away their weapons and pick up their rakes and shovels," he clarified without looking toward Chaka.

"Are you mad at me?" she asked.

"I need to prepare," he explained while looking up at her with enough sentiment to mask his true feelings.

Chaka also had an interest in putting in some community work of her own.

"I'm going with you to Southwest Detroit," she said.

"Of course. And we will stop by Sister Noble's café for breakfast," he said.

"I can smell the biscuits," she said.

"Miss Noble makes an amazing turkey sausage," the minister suggested.

"Bless your heart…still trying to get me off the swine. Can't help myself," she confessed.

As Chaka entertained gentle thoughts of a quiet and peaceful day with Kublai Khan she remembered just how important he was to the people of Detroit. In many ways the challenges that the troubled city endured was made just a bit easier by his strength and conviction.

Chaka wandered off to sleep in the Victorian mahogany bed and the minister sorted his papers and said evening prayers before resting his body and soul on yet another night that Yahweh gave.

33

Shower, Shave, and Service

The morning sun pierced the silk curtains of the bedroom and found Kublai Khan already up doing his morning physical regimen. It consisted of thirty minutes of military-grade calisthenics and twenty minutes of Tai chi. On alternate days, a trainer would join him in his fitness room for weight training and yoga. On this day, he returned to his bedroom to prepare for a full day of activities related to Holy Week.

He fell into step with an assistant as they both strode through the well-lit hallways and stairs of the old mansion. The young man handed him a phone message from the director of the birth center in California. The minister frowned at it as he climbed the staircase to the master bedroom where his queen was beginning to stir.

Chaka was just getting out of bed when Kublai Khan entered the room.

"What's wrong?" she asked immediately.

"Nothing we can't handle," he assured her. "It seems we are under investigation by the boys from ICE."

"What in heavens for?"

"Not sure yet. But it seems someone tipped them off about the birth center, and they're challenging our authority to keep them from inspecting it. I don't know enough right now. Our attorneys are working with them to clear this up before it hits the press." He stripped off his T-shirt and headed for the en-suite shower. "After today's message, I will be returning to Los Angeles."

"Of course," Chaka said as he leaned into the stall to turn on the water. "I'll pack for both of us while you stay focused on your message." There was the sound of wood sliding on wood—his sock drawer being pulled out, probably. She was a practical woman who believed in clean underwear above nearly all else.

Dammit, he needed that.

"Join me?" Kublai Khan called, standing in the bathroom buck naked.

There was a rustle from the doorway, and he turned to find her standing there, still in her nightgown, examining him. "Tempting," she said, and gave him a small, private smile. "But I think we should be cool until you see somebody." She turned and walked back into the bedroom. "I'll wait until you finish."

"Suit yourself," he muttered, and stepped into the steaming spray.

. . . .

The minister stood still before his congregation, collecting his thoughts before he spoke. He held the Holy Bible close to his chest, symbolically hiding the words in his heart. Dressed in a long, stylish black robe with gold and red embroidery, Kublai Khan represented the hope of the believers that the truth of God could be articulated by man and could forge the experiences of knowing her.

The Black faces in the pews were upturned as one. The air in the spacious sanctuary was heavy with expectant silence.

"I'm reminded," Kublai Khan said at last, "of the African village ruler on his deathbed who summoned his three sons to see him. The boys had been fighting over who was going to be the next king. The ruler handed the eldest boy a bunch of sticks and challenged him to make them so strong they could not be broken." He raised a handful of twigs he'd been keeping in his pulpit. "The king promised that whoever could fulfill his charge would rule when he was gone."

Out in the audience, some heads bobbed, and a few tilted in puzzlement.

"The young man studied the sticks and was stumped," Kublai Khan continued. "Then he said, 'Father, I am the strongest, but making the sticks themselves stronger than me…that's impossible.'"

More nods.

"The king said, 'Let your brother try,' and he looked at his middle son with pride. The second son put the bunch of dry sticks on the floor and studied them for an hour before stacking them on end, but they all fell down in a heap. He cried as he passed the sticks on to the youngest son."

A fifth-grade boy in the front row was so captivated by the story that he leaned forward to rest his elbows on his knees.

"The youngest boy pulled out a small pocketknife as his brothers laughed," Kublai Khan continued. "The boy used the knife to cut a strip of bark from one of the sticks." He drew a black silk ribbon from his pocket. "He then took the sticks and tied them together, and jumped and sat on the bundle without breaking even a single stick." With quick fingers, he wrapped and knotted his own bundle, and gripped it in both hands to show its strength.

"In Ecclesiastes chapter four, verse twelve, it says, 'A cord of three strands is not quickly torn apart.' It means that the power of collective work and responsibility starts with the knowledge that together we are stronger than we are separately." He lifted the tied bundle high above his head. "We who are many must become one."

Now most of the heads were bobbing. The boy sat up straight and stared at the bundle as if expecting it to deliver words of prophecy.

"This is why I propose a National Black Community Day," Kublai Khan continued, "when millions of our people will descend on the capital to stand in unity about our future. Doctors, corporate professionals, merchants, teachers, preachers, and mothers and fathers—everyone who makes our neighborhoods breathe with life. Brother Herman Crenshaw has agreed to lead this project and provide more details at the next steering committee meeting. Come and make a difference."

As the minister finished his message, an elder of the House took to the pulpit and instructed the congregation about the next daily message and the fact that Kublai Khan would not be at the Temple but in California on urgent church business. The news rippled through the pews and produced a visceral groan. The room settled down when it heard that the beloved Sister Helen was to be the guest speaker and acknowledged their approval with calm applause.

On the plane back to Los Angeles, Chaka relaxed, drinking a Bloody Mary while the minister sipped ginger ale and listened to old Motown hits on his phone as he wrote notes for his next sermon. Chaka interrupted just as Marvin Gaye finished flooding the minister's ear buds with a final, haunting note.

"Is Helen ready?" she asked calmly.

"Her eyes lit up when I told her," Kublai Khan replied, his own eyes still on his work. "These notes will help."

"It's fabulous you think so. It's the faithful I worry about." She sipped her cocktail.

"Sister Helen was the right choice. The women will be behind her."

"Some will. Other just like more bass in the pulpit," Chaka thought aloud.

"It's done."

"You ready for ICE—and their questions?"

"If it's Yahweh's will," the minister said, and he opened his Bible and looked for a passage that could help quell the fear and foreboding that lingered in his mind.

34

Stella and Little Boy

Unable to sleep after the ruckus at the news studio, Dalton sought out and obtained the makings for an old remedy his mama swore by—peach-tree-leaf tea, the juice of a fresh lemon and two jiggers of moonshine, sweetened to taste with honey. He sipped gently on the concoction in his tiny kitchen a while before he wandered out to the barn to tend to Sebastian, the rats, and reptiles. By three in the morning, he was settled in his armchair, watching a World War II documentary, and working on his third tea drink.

The knock at the door stirred him from a doze, and he heaved himself to his feet and shuffled over to answer the call. He cautiously pulled the door open to see who was on the other side, but froze when he heard the visitor's voice.

"Boy? You gonna take all night?"

Dalton froze in place.

"Just pull the god-darn door ajar and let an old woman in, whydontcha?" The voice was creaky, drawling, and familiar. "Ssshhhiiittt…. Rusty, you still scared of the dark?"

Dalton knew this was impossible. He had buried his mama at the Red Banks Community Cemetery back in Holly Springs two summers ago, after she lost a painful bout with cancer of the colon, but he did believe in miracles and Jesus did rise…so why couldn't Mom?

He opened the door wide to the white specter of the woman he had adored in life. She floated gracefully into the room, revealing no trace of the stiff limp she'd had most of her life thanks to a cantankerous mule. She glanced at him knowingly, without as much as a peck on the cheek for her baby boy.

"Son, I don't have long, so I'm not gonna pussyfoot around. You know I miss being here with you?" She stared straight through him.

He wanted to answer, but the cat had his tongue.

"First, don't worry about me," she ordered. "I sit on the right side of the Lord and my time there is joyous. All your people are here, except Cousin Herbert, praise God."

The pastor knew that he had put a little extra shine in the teacup, but that wouldn't call up the spirits, or so he thought. He could smell fresh peaches, like the ones she'd made cobbler with to go with the homemade ice cream at Sunday dinner.

Her face was soft as diffused moonlight and her cheeks and eyes shimmered with translucence as he looked into the deep slots of midnight where her eyes used to be. She wore a linen housecoat, just like the one she'd worn before sunrise when she fed the chickens and slopped the hogs. The threads of the cloth glowed like lightning bugs beaming from a mason jar, and revealed a space between the hem and floor where her legs should have been.

He found himself standing in the watermelon patch behind his parents' farmhouse when he was a child, holding the reddest, juiciest wedge of watermelon he had ever seen.

"Go ahead and taste it," his mother urged him. "It's a gift."

Dalton just stood there, speechless, with his eyes wide open.

"Boy, go on. Taste it."

He found the melon crunchy-cool, and the juice gently tickled the roof of his mouth with a taste sweeter than sugarcane.

"See? I told you. Eat it quick before it melts," she commanded, as the pale-green rind began to melt in his hands like an ice-cream cone in the middle of a summer's day. He lapped up the rest of the red meat of the melon before it dripped through his fingers.

"You found a nice girl?" she asked. "Not like that Mae Willy back in high school that got your pants all stiff?" She didn't wait for an answer. "Pitiful child. Listen up. I got something to say."

Dalton remembered growing up on a red clay dirt road and waiting for the school bus when the road was still moist from the morning dew and the heat from the hot sun had not yet turned the clay brown again. And he remembered Mae Willy. She had been a bright high-yellow Negro girl who had always saved a seat for him, until the bus driver had told his mom and he'd never heard the end of the stories about pitiful Mae Willy.

"Son, I saw you on that show. I don't know about all that race and Black and White stuff, but what I do know is you acted like the scared little boy you were when the kids called you 'tummy cakes the mummy shakes.'" She stared through him with empty holes for eyes. "Get over it. Just like on the playground, you got to git 'em back. Show them who's in charge. Remember what I taught you?" Mama Dalton's shadowy head grew to the size of a trailer truck, and beams of light poured out of the spaces where her eyes would be.

Mama, he thought, but the word wouldn't come out of his mouth.

The headlights in her eyes blinked low, like high beams switching off in the face of approaching traffic, and against the dimmer illumination, he noticed that her frosty braids were now dreadlocks, and moving oddly in the wind. What wind? he wondered. Then he saw that the braids were growing in length and twisting out in different directions, as if they were alive. The locks were serpents that gnawed on each other and twirled in the light, spiraling toward the sky.

"Kick 'em in the balls," his mother told him, "and when they fall, kick 'em some more until they fall to the ground like a bale of hay. If they be Black...don't stop...just don't stop. Ya hear me, boy? Don't you ever stop," she bellowed. And the king snake came out of the slit that was her mouth and wrapped himself around Dalton's torso and shoulders before opening its serpentine mouth to swallow Dalton and its own body whole.

In the instant before the darkness took him, Dalton could feel the steamy vapor drying on his eyebrows and upper lip. Then he noticed that his eyes were still closed, and he heard the sound of Little Boy exploding over Hiroshima.

. . . .

When the Pastor Dalton returned to the Christian Covenant Church after the Talk of the Town brawl, he was treated as a conquering hero. Before the Sunday service, he met members of his flock in the basement of the small church in Chino, California, where they were served a hot breakfast by the women's club.

Between the Jimmy Dean sausage and farm-fresh eggs, he spoke of the experience as if he'd gone behind enemy lines in a foreign land.

"The host of the show didn't tell me who the other guest was until just before we went on air." Dalton chewed as he spoke. "I thought it was going to be that loudmouth coon Kubba Con. Harper is such a cretin. When he defiled Mama's memory I had no choice but to treat him like the devil he is."

Clement Rodgers, an elder, asked, "Did you fight after the show?"

"Harper wanted to sue the show. We all agreed to put it behind us." Dalton swallowed a bite of his sausage biscuit, and coughed to make it go down.

After breakfast, Dalton went to the rear of the storefront church to pray before he entered the pulpit. Today he would preach to a few hundred believers who were beyond prayer. Dalton needed to give them hope and he found it through their fears and hostility against people who didn't look like them.

Today he wanted to find a Trim tab—a control point for a scheme of epic proportions. A gospel battle he had no chance of winning, but one that would leave his righteous and indignant imprint on race relations in America. As Dalton stood at the pulpit, he knew he needed to find the right leader, and he trusted that man was in the pews this Sunday morning. Today he sought a more graphic approach.

"Some of you know 'bout my little hobby," he began. "I raise mice and breed rats, and I keep snakes. Sure, I love the litter critters to death, but I do it with purpose. What if I crossbreed the white rats with the colored ones—generation after generation? Would there be any white ones left?" He looked around at his silent, rapt listeners. "I found the answer. Heck no. The white rats are the only ones you can count on to make whites. The others just keep pootin' out all kinds of colors."

His followers murmured assent to an obvious bit of wisdom.

"Rats can help us see the truth," Dalton went on. "That's why today—with God's help—we're going to do something about that."

He knew he could look into the eyes of Sister Martha Jenkins, who always sat in the right front center aisle and held her chubby arms around her two youngest grandbabies while her son Eugene and his second wife Wilandrea huddled at her right flank. Or he could just bellow accusations about the illegals that were violating American values at Brother Nate and his stepson, Timothy, who came to Bible study every Sunday morning and then stayed for service.

There were plenty of options. He had groomed his congregation well.

"Our problems started with the Blacks. They seek to extinguish the flame of our righteousness and steal the very air we breathe. Our success lies in our purity," Dalton preached as Jenny and Herman Kimble nodded agreement from the middle center pews.

"We must take our world back," he went on. "Not from the ones whose sexual habits bring unwanted children to the world—but from the mixed-breed babies they produce. These mongrel children are the garbage and filth of their parents. Together we can stop this scourge by destroying their seed." The pastor stepped off the twelve-inch riser and onto the cement slab floor of the church, and strolled over to stand behind a black-draped box.

"We must command the strength and guile of the serpent," he intoned. "Let it strike—strike—and strike again, until we have destroyed this threat to our species." Dalton pulled the drape off the box and revealed a wire cage holding a ten-foot pale white boa constrictor. He took a fat black and white mouse from underneath his robe and held it high above his head. Some men in the congregation stiffened their necks and raised their eyebrows, and the women uttered noises of disgust and held their hands over their mouths in horror.

"Don't be afraid of Stella—she loves to end them," he said as he dropped the squirming rodent into the cage. The overfed mouse raced onto the back of the boa, looking for some way out as the snake's body slowly pressed against the chicken-wire walls, leaving a square-patterned imprint on its ivory skin. Slowly, the coils closed in.

Before the dance ended, the pastor put the drape back over the cage.

"Let the church say—Amen."

Dalton noticed Master Sergeant Jimmy Blair, dressed in his usual faded desert fatigues, sitting in a rear row with his eyes closed, swaying back and forth. The pastor slowly walked down the aisle, stood before the soldier, and rested his hand on his shoulder.

"Brother Blair," he said, his voice ringing, "we recognize your sacrifice in the Gulf, and the Lord walks with you as you seek full employment in a job worthy of your talents and the return of your wife and kids."

Blair opened his eyes and stared up at Dalton in worshipful silence.

"So stand up," Dalton urged, "and join me a verse from 'On the Battlefield.' Hold my hand and sing with me." He wrapped his fingers around Blair's, stepped back, and pulled the bigger man to his feet. "Come on, soldier. We can praise God as he finds a way. Sing with me, son."

Blair took a deep breath, and their voices rose together.

I'm a soldier on the battlefield and I'm fighting

I promised him I would serve until I die,

I'm fighting

On this Christian journey I've had heartaches and pain, sunshine and rain,

But I'm fighting

I've been up and I've been down

But I'll never turn around

Because I'm fighting…

I'm on the battlefield for my Lord.

They both sang with Blair's voice ringing out, a true baritone, always on key and on beat. Chorally trained, Dalton thought; there was something almost sad about the image of the burly soldier as a long-ago choirboy.

"Let the church sing," he commanded.

The master sergeant sang the second stanza at the top of his lungs as tears began to run down his cheeks. When they finished, Dalton let the church settle and trusted that the next voice heard would be Blair's.

It was.

"I'm ready to be on the battlefield," Blair announced. "We've got to take back our rightful place in the free world. We've gotta be Christian soldiers. God bless our Pastor. God bless us all!"

Dalton smiled to the heavens.

More men bore witness and applauded Blair's declaration. Before the offering, the Christian Covenant Church begat the Christian Soldiers.

35

Burgers and Slim Jims

Master Sergeant Blair was a Wild Turkey man. He enjoyed the way the bourbon coated the uneven edges of the ice and pooled at the bottom of a highball glass, how it emitted the sweet vanilla tones and aromas of charred oak barrels, honey, blackberries, and crafted leather. And it didn't hurt that the high-proof alcohol took effect with speed and economy.

The dark and dank surroundings of Malarkey's offered refuge from the droning street sounds he tolerated in his room on the outskirts of Korea Town, where he spent most of his time when not in the pews or looking for day labor. Tonight, he swapped war stories with Carl and Mike Prather, his longtime war buddies, while they gorged themselves on greasy burgers, stale BLTs, and bottomless boilermakers.

"We were posted on a hundred-foot dune," Blair announced. "I scoped six sand niggas with automatic rifles at two hundred yards and first took out the jigs posted by the transports." He put his burger down on the oil-soaked napkin in the red plastic basket and then lifted an invisible rifle and peered through the scope. "My 50s tore through their bodies like butter. One by one I took 'em all out." He pulled the phantom trigger of his assault rifle six times.

From the corner of the bar, Chuck Berry's "Maybelline" began to play on the vintage Rock-Ola Encore jukebox.

"Damn, Jimmy. Is that when Snap lost it?" Mike said with wonder.

The classic rock-n-roll hit reminded the sergeant of his mulatto spotter—who hated his Black half more than Blair ever could, and often joked that the best thing about niggers was that at nightfall they all disappeared. When Snap heard the Chuck Berry ditty come up on somebody's iPod in combat, he would swivel his hips and shake his booty while howling, "Maybelline, why can't you be true?" Blair could see the wide brown eyes right in front of him, the coffee-colored fingers playing an air guitar, the white teeth grinning.

"Not really. But my boy did talk about his dreams that night," he said, slowly and deliberately.

"What did he say?" Michel asked.

"He was haunted. That's all. Stalking and sniping has a way of eating you out from the inside," Blair said.

"Snap ate his Beretta in Al Jahra," Carl told his brother.

"Why?" said Michael, his eyes little-brother eyes. The kid hadn't seen as much as the older one had, though in Blair's opinion he had still seen plenty.

"He couldn't stand the pain," Blair deadpanned.

"What about you?" Carl asked the sergeant.

"I'm not dead yet," Blair countered.

"What about dreams?" Carl inquired and took a swig of the sweet 100-proof bourbon.

"Sleep like a baby. Two hours at a time, and I always wake up crying."

The visions came up, unbidden: gaping head wounds that tore hair, bones, and sinew away from his targets' body parts. Legs separated, skulls exploded, and organs exposed and aerated in the burning sands.

Blair took a swig of bourbon and let it burn its way down his throat. One kind of pain could distract him from another.

The night was still young as Jimmy and the brothers Prather left Malarkey's for a liquor-store run to replenish their buzz of the bird at a discounted price. They stumbled into the parking lot, where a young Black teenager taking a Slim-Jim to the driver's window was vandalizing Carl's Chevy. Before the kid could retrieve his tool from inside the door molding, Blair was upon him.

"What the fuck…boy, I got your wretched ass," he said as a fist to the kid's stomach dropped him to his knees. "I should open you up like the bottom feeder you are," he growled, and brandished a six-inch folding knife pulled from a waist holster. The teenager was terrified enough to recover and sprint away from the drunken vets while Carl and Mike laughed at Blair losing his prey in the darkness.

"Look at that motherfucker go," Mike hooted. "Sergeant, your fish is gettin' away!"

Blair stood up and put his knife away.

"Come on, Blair. Were you really gonna gut the little bastard?" Carl said in disbelief.

"Thieves," Blair muttered. "Can't stand them."

"So what? The car is still here. Let's get some more of that dirty bird," Mike wheedled.

"Yeah, let's get out of here," Carl said as he used his key to open the Chevy sedan. Mike walked around the car to ride shotgun while Sergeant Blair sank into the back seat and thought about his last mission with Snap in Kuwait. The target had been a teenage suicide bomber. The exploding shell didn't care how old anybody was.

．．．．

The Christian Covenant Church of Chino was housed in a vacant building that had once been a twenty-thousand-square-foot Fox Brothers Foods grocery store. Behind a makeshift black curtain stood the leftover refrigeration units where the pot roast, pork chops, sausages, and porterhouse steaks once were kept. The smell of ammonia filled the space behind the curtain, as it was the duty of the congregation to use disinfectants daily in an effort to rid the sanctuary of all leftover food odors.

Personally, Blair thought it was appropriate that a house of the Lord smell a bit like a butcher shop. There was, after all, power in the blood.

Before the morning service, Dalton called Blair to his Spartan chambers to pick up flyers for the first Christian Soldiers' meeting.

"Brother Jimmy, thanks for helping us get the word out."

"Thank you, Reverend. I just want to be useful." Blair cradled the stack of flyers to his chest like he would hold a child.

"I want to share some of my thinking." Dalton sat back in his creaking office chair. "It involves Babylon and the people of Israel."

"I have read about that," Jimmy agreed.

"Good, Jimmy. Allow me to read from Revelations."

The reverend reached for the heavily worn Bible on the plastic coffee table.

"And the angel cried mightily, with a loud voice: 'Babylon the great is fallen. She has become a dwelling for demons and a haunt for every impure spirit,'" Dalton read.

Blair closed his eyes and meditated on the words until the pastor spoke again.

"I have seen the new Babylon. In my revelation, I saw The House of Jeremiah, led by their unholy devil of a leader known as Kublai Khan. He has forced thousands of women into bondage to produce scores of mixed-race babies. The brides of these nigger half-breeds are illegal aliens. They must be stopped."

Blair opened his eyes. "I am a soldier. Use me."

"Praise the Lord," the pastor said.

Alone before the service, Dalton went into his dressing area, where his gleaming brown cotton robe was hanging on the back of the door, still protected by the dry cleaner's plastic it had come in. With little effort, he slipped his arms into the gown and allowed it to drop to the floor over his shoulders. He took a long look at himself in the floor-length mirror attached to the bathroom door. He quickly raked a comb and brushed through his salt-and-pepper hair before making his way to the floor of the old grocery store and onto the riser, to his large hand-carved chair with red velvet cushions.

He turned to his audience, seated himself, smiled, and allowed the services to take their course, from the opening prayer by pastor-in-training Herman Gallagher to the social calendar by Sister Shirley Caruthers. After the collection, he made his way to the pulpit.

"Let us read our scripture for the day," he intoned. "Psalm 137 reads: 'Remember, O Lord, against the Edomites, the day of

Jerusalem's fall, how they said, and "Tear it down. Down to its foundations." O daughter of Babylon, you devastator. Happy shall they be who pay you back what you have done to us! Happy shall they be who take your little ones and dash them against the rock!'"

He looked up at his listeners, who were wrapped in total stillness and absolute focus.

"As the solders of the covenant and the only true protectors of the White species," he said, "it is our responsibility to destroy these sons and daughters of Babylon. We can manifest the Lord's will."

36

Skin Traffic on Ice

The Honorable Minister Kublai Khan entered the Homeland Security Investigations offices on Ocean Boulevard in Long Beach, California, and thought about the power of luck instead of the power of Yahweh. In the decades of running the operations of The House of Jeremiah, he had never been investigated or held in detention. It was a record he took great pride in.

The meeting was with Special Agent Michael Miller and was without attorneys. Kublai Khan knew the type, and recognized the man as he walked in. Miller was somewhere in his middle thirties, a small, wiry White man with an attentive face and dark hair so closely cropped to his skull that Kublai Khan wondered why the man didn't simply shave his head and be done with it. He wore a standard-issue dark-gray suit, but the bulge of the shoulder holster ruined the line. Kublai Khan nodded to himself. Miller presumably felt that he was wasting his skills at a desk job, and was probably looking for an interesting investigation where he could raise his profile in the department.

The agent drank strong black coffee while the minister sipped orange pekoe tea in the small cubicle meeting room. Ivory-colored panels blocked the ambient sunlight from the hall.

"Minister Kublai Khan, does your church own the property at 71250 Valle Road in Atascadero, California?" Miller asked.

"Yes, we do."

"There're problems," Miller said, and spread a sheaf of photos of young Korean women across the desk.

"What problems?"

"Who lives there?" Agent Miller asked without looking up.

"It's a birth clinic. Nothing more," Khan said. Best to keep his answers short until he knew what Miller was really looking for. "You said there were problems?"

"Do you know Jeong Myung and Eun Yang?" Miller asked, lifting his eyes to Kublai Khan's. His irises were pale blue, and he had a stare like a dead fish.

"No. Who are they?" Kublai Khan gripped the strap of his shoulder bag tightly, but met the agent's gaze.

"They're missing minors. Korean citizens. INS reports their last location is at your alleged clinic," Miller said. "There have been accusations of human trafficking. We expect your cooperation with our upcoming inspection."

"Of course," Kublai Khan said without hesitation. There was no other possible answer.

"If anything is out of order, we will be investigating your business and personal operations as well."

"I would expect nothing less."

. . . .

The minister left the federal building at a quick march and found his driver sitting at the curb along Ocean Boulevard. Once inside the black Lincoln town car, Kublai Khan called his business manager at the birth center. Flop sweat moistened his testicles and made the cup in his white cotton underpants sag as the man picked up.

"Brother Peterson," Kublai Khan growled. "The records of the women—where are they?"

"On the executive file server," Peterson replied.

"All of them?" Kublai Khan demanded. "We need to check and verify Jeong Myung and Eun Yang have never been there. I just left the ICE office and they're doing an investigation into missing kids, so you'd better move your ass. Do it now!" He punched the red icon and sat back against his seat, breathing heavily. Then he shook his head to clear it, and dialed Hung's private cell. Moisture gathered on his forehead and slowly rolled down his temples and into his well-groomed sideburns.

Hung was not nearly as accommodating as Peterson.

"The brides are mine. Don't worry," Hung insisted over the delicate clink of metal on china. Kublai Khan did the time-zone math; the man would just be finishing breakfast on a rooftop veranda. Couldn't even put down his fork for this.

"They suspect trafficking. Do I have a problem here?" the minister asked, listening carefully for any nuance or inflection in Hung's answer.

"Traffic? Ours is worse than yours," Hung said, laughing.

37

The Soldiers Go Marching

After a meal of pasta and gravy, Kim put Holiday to bed and Ahmed handled the dishes. Afterward, they sat in the living room sipping some Christian Brothers box wine and talking about the House of Jeremiah.

"I know you owe them, but this is a strange time to introduce Holly to the church. Why service this Sunday?" Kimberly asked.

"It's not strange. My family is in the House. I know what you think of Minister Kublai Khan," Ahmed said, sipping his white wine from a jelly glass.

"You know what I'm thinking?" Kim asked flatly. "So tell me, just how do I think?"

"You think the church hates Jewish people. They don't. That's what the news media wants you to believe."

Kim arched an eyebrow at him. "Your minister didn't say that Judaism was a dirty religion or that all White people are devils?"

"He regrets having used those words," Ahmed assured her.

"He never apologized."

"He's done so much good. We would have never met without the help of the House of Jeremiah."

"I understand you feel that way. But why do you have to take Holiday with you?"

"She should know my people," Ahmed said, pouring himself another glass of wino from the white cardboard box sitting on the secondhand Plexiglas coffee table. The surface was cluttered with Solberg family knickknacks, including a picture of Kim, Holly, and her grandparents.

"Why not just set up a dinner at your mother's house?" Kim asked. She paced restlessly around the room, picking at clutter. "What else is going on?"

Ahmed leaned back against the couch cushions and pursed his lips. "I never thought about family stuff until I stumbled into the Temple," he said slowly. "But Holly needs to know she's a Black girl."

"A Black girl?" Kim repeated, lining up playthings against the walls. She used her foot to nudge aside a purple musical alligator whose high tones drove everyone crazy.

"Honey," Ahmed said gently, "you know that when Holiday grows up she will be more than your daughter?"

"She's got years before that happens," Kim retorted. "Holly's a product of both of us, and I spend more time with her than anyone else. Let decide who she is."

"In this country, Black is about not being White. The House will teach her pride and respect for who she is, not hatred for what she isn't," Ahmed said.

Kim looked sideways at Ahmed, her lips pursed. She thought of a glittering Mexican palace and filthy American barrios.

"Okay," she said at last. "Fine. You can take her tomorrow?" She flopped down in her mama's drab olive green side chair.

"You can come?" Ahmed asked, and there was that smile she'd been missing.

"Make it a father–daughter thing," she told him, returning his smile. "There's a sale at The Grove."

"Cool. Maybe after church we can all go to Samantha's On the Pier?"

The couple exchanged tender kisses as they cuddled on the couch, watching America's Got Talent, and finished the wine.

"This race thing is complicated," Kim mused. "Growing up in the Valley, Black people were just chocolate-covered White people. Now I'm in love with a real Black man and we have a lovely daughter. We should've talked about this stuff before we fell in love."

"It all happened so fast. I think we're good."

"We're out of wine," Kimberly said as she stretched out a leg and toed at the wine box.

"You have to trust me, sweetheart." Ahmed kissed the top of her head. "There's another one in the cabinet above the fridge." He stood up, grabbed the dead soldier, and pimp-walked into the kitchen for the reserves.

· · · ·

Sunday morning at Ahmed and Kimberly's apartment was usually good for Sunday newspapers and pajamas all around until well after the noon hour. This day, it was time to dress Holiday in a beautiful dress covered with an assortment of her favorite cartoon characters and style her hair into carrot-colored Afro puffs with bright-orange silk ribbons. Ahmed picked out the blue suit that he sported three days a week to the accounting firm. He added a white shirt from the bargain warehouse and a tie he'd gotten for Christmas from his grandfather. He splashed on a dab of designer cologne out of habit.

The temple was just ten minutes from their home, so the trip was easy for Holiday. Before she could whine, cry, or feel the first pangs of carsickness, they pulled up in the parking lot of the temple. Ahmed left his daughter in her car seat until he unfolded the stroller. When he had the cart ready, Ahmed turned his attention to Holiday, scooped her up, and lowered her down into the stroller. He remembered that there was little room in the temple to store the stroller during service. It occurred to him that most mothers and fathers of young children Holiday's age carried the toddlers in their arms until they reached the pews. Then proud fathers would scoot down the narrow aisles to their seats, holding their children against their chests like hard-won prizes.

Ahmed folded the stroller back into the trunk and carried his daughter into the temple.

Inside the House of Jeremiah, Ahmed greeted several of the men whom he had last seen at the mass wedding. Each one stopped politely and clicked his heels together in a solemn gesture while bowing at the waist and cupping his hands as if in prayer.

"As-salem Alaykum."

"Alaykumu s-Salem."

To show respect, Ahmed put one hand over his heart while he cradled Holiday with his free arm. In a matter of minutes, he had found his brother Franklin and Nana Rey near the front of the church.

As he settled his daughter next to Nana Reynolds, he spoke with his brother as Grandmamma fixated on her red-haired grandbaby.

"Look at this angel...such a cutie," Nana Rey cooed. "Give me some sugar." She wore a grin from ear to ear.

Nana gave Holiday a big wet kiss as Holly gently hugged her grandma's neck and kissed back.

Franklin, wearing a blue bowtie, looked proudly at his niece as he gave his brother a shoulder tap and handshake.

"The minister is glad you're here," Franklin said proudly. "He's going to acknowledge you from the pulpit."

"Really? That's cool."

"Holly's got your uncle Herman's nose," Nana Rey said as she lifted the girl into her lap and adjusted her yellow skirt with images of Patty the Duckling printed all over it. "She's a Reynolds baby. No doubt."

Holly giggled as she was bounced.

The minister delivered the sermon about self-reliance and community empowerment, quoting from the Quran and the Bible. The congregation admired and loved their national spokesperson. He was comfortable in the pulpit and earnest in his interpretation of the Scripture.

"In John 1:12, the Scripture reads, Blessed is the man who remains steadfast under trial, for when he has stood the test he will receive the crown of life, which God has promised to those who love him."

Nana Rey nuzzled the top of Holly's head. Holly squirmed and cuddled back into her.

"This reference on its surface speaks directly to how we can maintain faith in Yahweh while meeting the challenges of living. Yet underneath this direct reference is the trust God has in us. We must appreciate the power that he has bestowed on us and the reliance on each other he commands."

Franklin leaned over just enough to bump Ahmed's shoulder.

"In every one of our personal challenges, there's resounding evidence that Yahweh has put the barrier in front of us. Not only to prove his love and understanding but also to demonstrate our own trust in him. The power of Yahweh is within us. Let the people praise him." The minister raised his hands in benediction. "The power of Yahweh is within."

"The power of Yahweh is within." The chant in the temple was thunderous.

As the congregation returned to their seats, the minister turned to smile at Ahmed and Franklin.

"Meeting the challenges of life with both faith and confidence is what we all should thrive for. Today we have a man whom I found in the streets of South Central who now follows the principles and values of our faith and trusts his own ability. Please say hello to Ahmed Reynolds and his lovely daughter, Holiday, along with his brother, Franklin, and their mother, Nana Rey."

Ahmed stood up with Holly in his arms as the group applauded. His family rose with him. He heard Franklin sniffing back tears as they resumed their seats. The minister concluded the sermon.

"It's up to all of us to show the strength and fortitude that Yahweh instilled in us. Through both the good times and the bad. Underneath them is the glory and trust in God. Show him the praise and glory of our courage, in all circumstances. Let us pray."

After the service, the minister and the Reynolds family walked together toward the parking lot. The minister talked about the birth centers.

"Brother Ahmed, I understand you have a great job and a lovely young lady to come home to, but how would you like to come back to work for The House? I need someone to keep the books and help review the financial operations of the center. Can we count on you?"

Before Ahmed could answer, Nana Rey whispered to Franklin.

"This gal's head is a mess. Her mama needs to learn how to do a Black girl's hair," she said, and she pulled a small brush from her purse.

. . . .

Across the plaza, Jimmy Blair watched from the roof of a warehouse as members of the temple poured out onto the street. He was alone with an M24 sniper rifle on his shoulder and was fully aware that the next ten minutes of his life would change it forever. From behind massive air-conditioning equipment, Jimmy focused his sights on various men and women who stood outside the church.

His instructions were simple; kill a mixed-race child, kill Minister Kublai Khan, leave the manifesto and escape—all in less than sixty seconds. The question Blair had, as he prepared the sniper rifle that would shatter bone and tear through flesh, was how long it would take his targets to wander into the kill zone.

He relaxed when he saw her—a high yellow carrot-top toddler in a yellow skirt, being carried by a dark-skinned man in a blue bowtie, standing next to Kublai Khan. She was the one.

Sixty seconds. He focused on the minister. The group stopped short of the parking lot and lingered in the zone as Blair estimated wind and distance. He briefly regretted that Snap wasn't with him. Everything had been easier with him.

Maybelline, why can't you be true…

Fifty seconds.

BANG.

BANG.

Bowtie collapsed on the sidewalk and Carrot Top fell in a heap like a small bag of potatoes. The first shot blew out the left side of Bowtie's head and exploded the rear of his skull. The second shot ripped into Bowtie's throat, leaving a gaping hole where his larynx once was.

Fifty-five seconds.

A huge Black man in a blue suit shoved the minister underneath a parked SUV and fell on him to shield him from fire.

Forty seconds.

BANG.

A third shot ripped through Carrot Top's skirt and petticoat and embedded itself in the stonewall around the parking lot. As soon as the girl hit the ground, a dark man in a blue suit scooped her up and tucked her under his arm like an oversized football. Running in a crouch, he sprinted to a blue Civic. Blair followed him through the scope as he scrambled into the car and tossed the kid into the back seat.

Thirty seconds.

Blair swiftly reassembled the rifle and put it in its carrying case, pulled the manifesto from his breast jacket pocket, and set it on a box top, anchored by a lump of stone with a black cross chiseled on its surface.

Ten seconds.

Blair walked quickly to his jeep, parked beside a lonely garbage can in the warehouse parking lot. Once inside with the window down, he texted the manifesto web address to a short list of well-known news reporters. Then he threw his burner into the trashcan, rolled up the window, started the engine, and pulled out.

Long before the cops arrived, he was already speeding east on the freeway.

. . . .

Inside the kill zone, Khan's second guard quickly called for an ambulance. Nana Rey sobbed and screamed uncontrollably as she slumped over Franklin's corpse.

"Laud have mercy—my boy!" she cried.

The minister and Nana Rey prayed over Franklin as his blood leaked into the cracks of the sidewalk. A crowd gathered. The ambulance arrived as the minister covered Franklin's disfigured head with his coat. The bloody hole in his right shoulder proved that one stray sniper bullet had actually reached its intended target.

. . . .

When Ahmed reached the parking lot of his apartment complex, he pulled into his stall and with his free hand finally released his daughter from the back seat of the vehicle. Inside the apartment, he immediately took Holiday to the restroom to clean her up and change her dress. Kimberly was out running errands. When she returned, the two were in the living room, where their child slept and Ahmed watched television. From the look of shock on his face, Kim knew something was wrong.

"What happened at church?" she asked.

"I don't want to talk about it right now." He stared blankly at the television screen.

"Really? Where's the dress Holly was wearing this morning?" Kim frowned. "Did she have an accident?"

"No—I just threw it out."

Kim wondered whether Ahmed had noticed that she was watching a Korean soap opera without subtitles. She wouldn't have bet money on it.

"Liar," she said. "What happened?"

Before Ahmed could respond, his cell phone buzzed on the coffee table. He didn't move.

Kimberly picked up the phone and answered it.

"Is Ahmed and Holiday all right?" a man's voice demanded.

"What do you mean?" Kim frowned. "Who is this?"

"This is Marcus. Minister Kublai Khan's assistant...The minister is working with the police about Franklin's murder today. Are they both okay?"

The temperature in the room seemed to drop fifteen degrees.

"I'm sorry," Kim said. "I'll need some details."

The details were short and ugly.

"Are they all right?" Marcus demanded again.

"Yes...both of them," Kimberly said, and hung up.

Then she freaked out.

"There was a shooting at the Temple? Why didn't you just tell me?"

"Franklin's dead and they tried to kill our baby." Tears started to flow down Ahmed's cheeks.

Kimberly knelt in front of him, putting her face between Ahmed's and the screen. "You should have told me," she said, trying to make her anger sound gentle. "They said your mom has been sedated. She's at Drew Medical Center, but they think she's gonna be released tonight. Are you okay?" She cupped one side of Ahmed's face, giving him a point of contact.

Ahmed plunged forward into Kimberly's arms and wept.

"Why were they trying to kill her?" he sobbed. "We've got to get out of here."

"I know," she said calmly, feeling the steel inside her harden. She had only fuzzy memories of an alley in Juarez, but she knew she had been in a place like this before. She knew what needed doing. "We'll find a safe place," she told him. "Together."

After Ahmed fell asleep, Kim turned on the news, switched off the sound, and watched the sun set on the House of Jeremiah Temple in South Los Angeles. The plaza was lousy with cameras and police in every overhead helicopter shot. At the warehouse, the closed-captioning said, the investigative team looked for evidence. Inside the temple, the minister answered questions by the detectives.

The focus quickly turned to the Christian Soldiers.

Before nightfall, news of the manifesto had broken, and Kim watched over her sleeping husband and daughter as a nationwide discussion about race and the safety of the country's mixed-race children began.

38

Marking the Spot

The White man has been both the provider and master of all he surveys. Throughout the history of the world, White men have helped establish great cultures and economies that none before or after them has ever matched.

–Christian Soldiers

Pastor Dalton opened the meeting the first meeting of The Christian Soldiers with a short prayer.

"Father in heaven, forgive us for our many sins and indiscretions. We are your humble servants with a crusade in your name. We will lead the children of Jerusalem back into the holy land as we seek your vengeance against the people of Babylon. Control our hands to strike, our eyes to shoot, and our hearts to share your victory with the world. Amen."

The men sat and looked to Pastor Dalton for further guidance.

"Let's pay tribute to Brother Blair for his deed at the devil's sanctuary. His courage was unquestionable. His discipline was unrelenting. Perhaps he can speak to the failure to strike the mocha child. It was unfortunate, but he claimed one soul in the battle." Dalton locked eyes with his congregants as he stood above a relief map of the central coast of California.

"My scope malfunctioned," Blair said calmly. "I'm responsible for the result. Three shots fired and one in the skull of the nigger carrying the child. The minister and the half-breed child escaped. After leaving the manifesto, I exited the warehouse by the back parking lot and escaped in traffic." He held his arms tightly folded across his chest in shame.

"What can we learn from this?" the pastor asked as the Prather brothers stared at the map, actually seeming interested in learning more about their plans. This was the first time Dalton had laid eyes on them.

"I have recalibrated the scope and acquired six semiautomatic rifles and the same in handguns, with an ample supply of rounds," Blair reported. "We have a secluded shooting range in Montebello to practice for the next assignment."

"Amen, brother," Carl and Mike replied in unison.

"This will be our major victory," Dalton intoned. "Jimmy, please take us through the fundamentals of our plan." He leaned over the map and picked up a red grease pencil to point with.

"Over here," he said, jabbing the tip at a spot on the map "is where we are now, the Cramer Springs Resort. Our transport garage is here. Our ammunitions armory is just down this road."

The Christian Soldiers huddled over the map, their noses brushing the edge of the antique parlor table in the basement meeting room in the shuttered resort. Dalton marked a new spot on the map with a scuff of red lead.

"Brothers, here's our next assignment," he said. "The birthing centers of Kublai Khan."

39

The Reckoning

Look to the ancient nation of Babylon to know that when the races mix, the final effect will be chaos and debauchery. Do rabbits mate with pigs? Do butterflies enjoin themselves with the filthy moth? In biology and science, there is the natural selection of each species that protects the world from chaos and destruction.

–Christian Soldiers

In the six weeks since Franklin's murder, Ahmed spent very little time with his family. It was how he eventually found himself, one bright Saturday morning, walking up to his mother's home in South Central.

Ahmed entered the small house near Normandie and 51st Street. He found his mother sitting at the kitchen table with a glass of grapefruit juice and a fifth of Beefeater's Gin at the ready. She was dressed in her undergarments and a worn housecoat bought at the Swap Meet, and she was already several sheets to the wind.

"Hi, Nana," Ahmed said by way of announcing himself. "How are you doing?"

"Get a glass and have a drink with your mama." She didn't look at him.

"Have you eaten yet?"

"No, baby. Just had some grapefruit juice and my medicine."

"You mean that bottle of gin?" Ahmed suppressed a groan. "How about I make you some grits and eggs? You got any bacon?"

Ahmed opened the refrigerator door. Inside he quickly found the makings of a country breakfast. In little time, he had a black cast-iron skillet on a hot stove, with some thick-cut country bacon cooking and a pot of water boiling for grits.

He got a six-ounce jelly glass from the cupboard and poured himself a short dog, giving consideration for the time of day and the quantities of liquor that Nana had already consumed. He just wanted to get through the meeting without arguing. The taste of gin gave him a dose of courage.

"Nana. I don't see you enough."

"You never come by to see your mama," she replied. "I think you and that White girl of yours are scared to come south of the freeway. Look at you, all dressed in White people's clothes like you forgot what it is to be a Black man from South Central."

"Mama, I didn't come here to argue."

"How come?" she spat. "I know it wasn't to cook me a cheap-ass breakfast from my own refrigerator. Why didn't you bring some of that Jew food? Like those little potato cakes or some bagels with cream cheese and lox? Or are you saving your money to take care of that kike hoe you live with?"

With an effort, Ahmed kept his voice soft and gentle. "Mama, you shouldn't talk like that about Kimberly. It ain't right—"

"Don't burn the bacon," Nana interrupted, pointing to the skillet full of swine.

Ahmed turned his attention to the stove, put on the grits, and turned the bacon over. With his back turned to his mother, he changed the subject.

"So how are Franklin's children doing?"

"They're as good as can be expected. The girls are with their mother and I got the boys here. Your dad is out with them now, so we could have some time together."

"What can I do to help?"

"You can grow a pair of balls," she grumbled, "and leave that girl with her babies and come back to the Temple. It's time you show people what you're made of. With the racist bastards killing people, you need to come back home where you belong."

"And abandon my family? I can't do that."

"Then come back to the Temple," she retorted, "and help the minister protect the birth center from those White devils. The House is putting together a security team now to go protect our babies. You should be a part of the men of the church. Kublai Khan needs you. Boy, he pulled you out of the dirt, and now it's time to pay him back."

"I'll think about it." Ahmed poked at the bacon with a spatula. Not quite done yet.

"You're one sorry-ass player," Nana Rey snarled. "Don't you understand what's happening? It's what White folks call a reckoning. They are trying to wipe us out and you have as much to do with the problem as anyone. Now it's time to be with your people."

"I said I'd think about it," Ahmed repeated.

"Do it, or don't bother to come around here again."

The bacon sizzled its way to completion. Ahmed finished buttering the toast and served Nana Rey. Together they ate in silence. After finishing the dishes, Ahmed headed back across the Santa Monica Freeway.

. . . .

In the days after visiting his mother, Ahmed relaxed back into the routine at the accounting firm and never called the Temple about the job at the birth center. One evening, as he and Kimberly watched the news about the race war, his phone rang. He answered, but said nothing, the product of long experience with heavy breathers and robocalls.

It was neither.

"This time," a strange, deep voice growled, "the next bullet is for your daughter. We know where you live."

The line beeped off. Ahmed lifted his eyes to Kimberly's, and saw they were wide and dark. She'd heard everything.

The news was turned off. The conversation turned to options.

"We could move to Juarez," Ahmed suggested. "We can be there in twelve hours. We'll leave tonight."

Kim frowned. "I don't know. Do you really think the person on the phone would actually hurt us?"

"Absolutely. They've tried to kill our baby before." Ahmed shook his head. "I'm not giving them another shot at it. We've gotta get out of this crazy city."

Kimberly rushed as fast as she could to pack a few bags, resting a hand on her swollen belly whenever she had a moment in case the baby decided to protest the sudden activity. Ahmed peered out of the small living-room window like he would be able to deflect a sniper's bullet with a glance.

They ended up spending the night at Kimberly's mother's place and getting Ahmed a new cell number. After a few days, they returned to their own apartment as their panic passed.

. . . .

In a duplex apartment in lower Beverly Hills, Chris Fitzroy and Adam Porper shared what was left of a bottle of single-malt whiskey with a friend and laughed about the prank they had just played on Ahmed.

"You two are assholes," the friend complained. "Pay me already. I got rehearsal tonight."

. . . .

Ahmed got Kim thinking. She took her phone and went into the bathroom to call her stepbrother.

"I'm glad you can help," she told him. "We want the trouble to stop."

"I'll call a friend of mine at the telephone company," Hermando assured her. "He can check on your papi's number and tell me who made that shitty call. All I need is the date and time." Kim could hear the patter of water behind his voice. He must be sitting near a fountain at the Rodriguez villa in Juarez.

"That's very cool," she told him. "I owe you one."

"No big thing. It's all I can do. Can't have people scaring my little niece."

"You're sweet," Kim said with a relieved sigh. "Thanks, big brother."

"You gonna tell papi about this?"

Kim shook her head even though Hermando couldn't see her. "Ahmed likes to give help, not take it. Not even from family."

"Family's all we've got," the voice on the other end of the line replied.

"Yeah," Kim said softly. "Sometimes, it is."

40

Satay at Chow's

The White Man is the great father of a master race that reigns supreme when the purity of his genes and intellect are kept intact. Today we watch the slow but methodical destruction of his species by those that say that through diversity and inter-breeding the world will be more equal. Throughout history, such rationale has been proven false and is a threat to all that the White Man holds dear.

–Christian Soldiers

Amid the rolling hills in charming single-family ranches lived artists, musicians, and farmers, surrounded by a selection of resort hotels stretching from San Luis Obispo to Pismo Beach. The House of Jeremiah purchased the property, stocked it with medical equipment, and had it registered as a retirement home. The medical facility had a guard gate installed to control the flow of traffic in and out of the birth center. The addition of three dozen disciplined security men from the Los Angeles Temple made the birth centers almost impenetrable.

It was early dawn when Minister Kublai Khan spoke to the assembled team. He told them that his new friends at Homeland Security had tipped him that there was a likely threat against the birth centers from The Church of the Christian Covenant. Audio surveillance had confirmed that Pastor Dalton was meeting with a paramilitary group, plotting against The House of Jeremiah. The minister was confident that his team could rebuff a ragtag group of religious zealots, but not without casualties. This called for an extra shot of confidence.

"Today we are charged to protect our freedom to worship as we see fit. It is our right as citizens of America to protect our property and personages also. Today, we can support our faith by trusting our lord Yahweh to protect us from the evil intentions of a violent few. Each one of you is the keeper of the flame of our faith. Please be strong and exhibit the courage to command our survival and turn back the forces of evil that are lurking in the hills around us."

The soldiers chanted, while brandishing their side arms and automatic rifles in outstretched arms toward the sky.

"The power of Yahweh is within us."

The Minister's chief commanders assembled their troops and headed toward their appointed positions around the perimeter of the birth center. The nurses and doctors of the secluded clinic continued their routines of attending to the infants and mothers on the second floor while monitoring the vital signs of the women still in waiting. On the third floor of the resort, there were five birthing suites where the women and their families awaited the next round of births. The first floor of the facility held the daycare center, along with sleeping quarters and a cafeteria to feed the men, women, and children of the operation.

With his security troops in place, the minister headed to Los Angeles for meetings and the opportunity to see Chaka for lunch. They met at a popular white-tablecloth restaurant in Beverly Hills. It was Mr. Chow's, the most expensive Chinese food in Los Angeles. Chaka was already sitting at their favorite table, munching on an order of chicken satay when he arrived. She was finishing a call when Kublai Khan took a seat next to her. They greeted each other with a kiss.

"How's it going?" she asked.

"Smooth enough. The center is still on the human-trafficking watch list. But they have been good about the Christian Soldiers investigation."

"And your shoulder?"

"Never been better," he said, flexing his arm so that his bicep bulged against the fabric of his tailored sleeve. "What doesn't kill us makes us stronger."

"They tried to murder you," she said, reaching out and touching his hand tenderly.

"But there's been a breakthrough," he answered.

"A breakthrough?"

"You know Pastor Dalton of the Christian Covenant?"

Chaka tilted her head. "He hates Black people."

"He's behind the Christian Soldiers and he's wanted for questioning." Kublai Khan smiled broadly. "They raided his church and he's on the run."

"I heard a childcare center in Lancaster was destroyed last night," she remarked. "Hate is like wildfire. Be careful." She took a delicate sip of her iced tea.

"That's why we must be brave," the minister said as he reached into his inside breast pocket and opened his right hand, palm up, on the table. On his ring finger was a beautiful diamond ring. "Speaking of which."

Chaka stared down at his hand.

"Will you marry me?" Kublai Khan prompted.

Chaka was silent.

"Honey. I said will you marry me?"

"What's got into you?" Chaka said, finally, with a clipped laugh.

"That's not an answer. Or is it?" He closed his hand and slipped the ring into his pocket.

She lifted her eyes to his. "Sweetheart, did you get the help we talked about?"

"I did," Khan said, looking up to catch the eye of the waiter. He wanted something strong.

"What did you do?"

"I've been seeing Reverend Ricky," the minister confessed.

Chaka was aware of the notable life coach but was a non-believer.

"Learn anything?" she asked with a cursory smile.

Khan sighed heavily. "I had a spiritual insight. I wanted to be like my dad, even though I knew how he mistreated my mom. I never knew any different. I looked to him to learn how to treat a woman…even when he was abusive."

"What do you mean?" Chaka's eyes narrowed.

"He hurt my mother. Often beating her in their bedroom."

"How did you discover this?" Chaka asked.

"Reverend Ricky took me on a visualization journey. I saw my childhood. I didn't realize how much I hated my mother for leaving me." He reached out again, took Chaka's hand, and tucked the ring into her palm.

"How do you feel about that?" she asked.

"I had a satori moment. I experienced knowing she was right to leave," Kublai Khan said. "My purpose is clear now. And I want you with me."

Chaka dropped her gaze and studied the exquisite stone for a moment. Then she closed her eyes briefly, shook her head, and pushed the ring back into his unresisting hand.

"What will happen with us?" Chaka asked as she met his gaze again.

"I think I'm a better man," he assured her. "This won't happen to us."

Chaka pursed her lips, clearly unsure. "I don't feel safe with you. Maybe in time I will."

Khan leaned forward, his eyes pleading. "I want a life with you, now more than ever. Do I frighten you?"

Chaka sat back. "Just at the wrong times," she said warily. "You know I will always love you." A tearful smile spread over her face. She discreetly wiped her eyes with the white table napkin.

"I can control this," Khan insisted. "Only with you I feel… whole." He took her right hand with both of his.

"I'm sorry," she told him gently. "But I can't marry you. Your spiritual journey comes first. Then we'll see where things go." She silently signaled to the approaching waiter to hold off.

Minister Kublai Khan sat silent. The tightness in his chest lifted his arms inches off the table and caused his hands to form fists that slowly tapped the tabletop without his volition. His throat clenched and his mouth became parched. His eyes remained open, unblinking. After an eternity, he relaxed his right hand, reached for the water glass, and brought it to his lips, causing the ice cubes to rattle loudly. The water he sipped cleared his throat and brought his vocal chords back to life.

"I don't believe you," he rumbled. "You're *abandoning* me at a time like *this*?" He stared down at the huge ring, and then squeezed her right arm hard, just below the elbow. She winced before pulling it out of his grasp.

Khan looked up in surprise and quipped.

"Too much? Too soon?"

"Give me time to digest it all."

After lunch, Chaka went back to the office to become absorbed in anything but love while Minister Kublai Khan and his security men returned to LAX to fly to Monterey Regional Airport and then return to the birth center by nightfall.

41

Foot on the Gas

We are that invading army and our duty is to kill off this impure seed and create chaos and destruction among this forsaken tribe.

The Christian Soldiers

Today was Family Day for Star. She was looking forward to seeing Aunt Marie Ann and talking to her attorney about her case. Then it would be off to see Grandma and help her tend to her vegetable garden—ending the day with dinner with her parents. But first, there was breakfast for Cleo.

"Today we're bringing you a special report. *The Race Riot Rampage—Madness Grips Los Angeles.* Let's go to Cristal Carmichael in South Central." The morning news anchor was scrubbed, pressed, and coiffed for the occasion. Hoshiko sat in her small Manhattan Beach sublet, drinking green tea and wondering when the traffic reports would come on in spite of the civil unrest. She fed her ruddy Abyssinian her gourmet chicken livers and hearts while Cristal reported.

"Since the Christian Soldiers' attempted assassination of Minister Kublai Khan of the House of Jeremiah and the discovery of the *White Man's Manifesto,* a spree of racist graffiti, assaults, and outbreaks of looting and rioting has led to a dusk-to-dawn curfew and the involvement of the National Guard."

Star rubbed the velvety spot between Cleo's ears as the reporter droned on.

"Mayor Timmons has been criticized for setting a ten-mile perimeter around the heart of the Black community, where most of the destruction has been contained. Some feel the boundary serves to let South Los Angeles burn while the rest of the city goes unscathed," Carmichael said.

Star scoffed under her breath, picked up the remote, and thumbed the TV off. As the picture blinked out, her cell rang.

"I wondered if you were going today," Ty said. "I have something for Marie." "That's not going to happen. You know how she feels," Star advised. She stood up and walked to her kitchen sink to fill Cleo's water bowl.

"I don't know what else to do," Ty whined. "She returns my letters. Tell her—" He sighed. "No, don't."

Star ignored the invitation to drama. "Got to go," she said brusquely. "Remember, I'll pick the girls up, same time at Grandma's. Same as always."

"I know the drill. Thanks for nothing." His voice was sour.

"It's the very least I can do, you piece of shit," Star said, and pressed the red icon on her cell and dropped it into her purse.

· · · ·

When Star was led to the visiting room, she was seated in a booth against the pale-green wall and stared through the cloudy Plexiglas partition at the empty gray steel chair. After a moment, a door opened and Marie Ann walked in and sat down. She was dressed in a bright-orange jumpsuit with her thin black hair braided in corn-rows. She forced a smile when her eyes met her niece's. As one, they both picked up the black phone receivers and spoke into them.

"How are my girls?"

"Did you get the pictures?" Star asked.

"Yeah. I really like the one on their bikes," Marie Ann said, pushing back the long braids that flowed against her drawn face and tired eyes.

"You eating, right?" Star asked.

"Sometimes. How's Grandma?"

"Everyone's good. Ty called. Said he had a gift for you?" Star said.

"Fuck him. Oops—you've already done that."

The women laughed wickedly until a guard gave them a stern look.

"You think we should forgive him?" Marie Ann asked.

"I will if you will."

"I got time." Marie Ann sat back in her chair. "You see-ing anyone?"

"Nobody special. Just kissing a lot of frogs." Star kept one eye on the clock on the wall.

"What's with the mixed-race riot talk?"

"I stay out of LA. My dad says folks have lost their minds," she said, and pushed back in her chair back against the rear wall in a feeble attempt to stretch her legs. The taut telephone cord restrained her movement.

"You're closer to Los Angeles than you think," Marie Ann replied.

"So who did your hair?" Star asked, pushing her feet against the barrier.

"Just a girl on the block. We call her Mick," Marie Ann said. She fingered her braids, row by row.

"That's a strange name," Star remarked, leaning forward on her elbows.

"Think about it," Marie Ann said, and then pushed out her tongue until it touched her chin.

Again the ladies laughed in spite of the guard's stern look.

"You seem to have the right attitude," Star said. "I don't know how do you do it."

"Buddha says focus the mind on the present moment," Marie Ann said. "And let your love flow outward." She beamed.

"I got it." Star cocked an eyebrow. "When did you become Buddhist?"

"I'm not. Jesus said some cool shit too." The woman in the jumpsuit flipped her braids back over her shoulders.

"You seem at peace or something."

"I forgave myself and the madness lifted," she answered.

The blare of a buzzer signaled the end of the visiting session.

"The craziness is out there," Marie Ann warned. "Don't give away your power." She took the receiver off her right ear, signaling her impending compliance to the guard, but left it close enough for her to hear her niece.

"I will," Star promised and then continued, "Do you need anything?"

"More books."

"I know what you like. Drama. Thrillers. Anything else?"

"Just the will that says to them: Hold On."

"Kipling? More poetry. Got it," Star said, stood up, and reached out to spread her hand against the glass. Marie Ann mirrored the gesture, and they touched without touching.

"Love you." Marie Ann said as tears moistened her shallow cheeks.

"Love you more," Star said. She stayed where she was as her aunt hung up, and watched the guard escort the prisoner through the interior door and back to her cell.

• • • •

The ratty-headed Rastafarian wore a green, red, and black knit cap with his dreads piled high inside. He peddled scented oils and incense to the concerned citizens looking for a solution to the presence of federal troops in their community. Jeremy Talbert sat at the back of the stage, watching the brother hawk his wares through the crowd and listening to Reverend Harper as he addressed the rally.

"We will meet with the Mayor and tell him we need protection and not occupation," Harper said while the press corps in the front row snapped away and held their recorders as far as their arms could reach. The concerned women assembled near them nodded their agreement. A rail-thin old gentleman standing in the middle of the crowd stroked his brow with his thumb and index finger and listened in disbelief.

Jeremy studied them all from his seat. He had lost interest in being stood up like an off-white mannequin. No longer was he asked to speak about injustice; all he did was sit next to Harper and bear witness to his ramblings. He said nothing until a reporter from *The Sentinel* ascended to the platform after the speeches were done. She wanted answers.

"What's next for you?" the petite woman asked, holding out a low-end digital recorder.

"Nothing," Jeremy said softly. "Some school and maybe lacrosse."

"But what about the investigation?" the reporter asked.

"None of this will bring Sidney back," Jeremy replied. He glanced over at Harper, waiting for the bigger man to swoop in to take over, but there were half a dozen microphones in front of the reverend's face and there would be no competing with that.

The newswoman seized the initiative.

"Can racism be stopped?" she asked.

Jeremy stood up, not looking at her. "Can you stop the rain?" he replied. Then he stepped off the platform and headed out of the park.

• • • •

Jeremy wandered down Vernon, thinking about Sidney. As he walked, his thoughts became words and escaped his full lips.

"You were one crazy nigger," he murmured. "Always down on yourself. Looking for trouble. I guess you found it." As he crossed Arlington, his phone buzzed. He looked down to see his mother's picture and a text notification.

"*Where are you?*"

He thumbed a response as he hopped up on the curb. "*Just left Rally. Going to Jamie's house.*"

"*When are you coming home?*"

"*Uncle Rod drive me home later.*"

"*Call me when you get there.*"

"*K.*"

He put the phone in his pocket as a black Monte Carlo low rider pulled to the curb and two bangers in hoodies stepped out, moving toward him.

"Get that White boy!" the heavyset one screamed as the two caught Jeremy on the run and tussled him to the curb.

"Hey!" Jeremy struggled against their grip, trying to twist free. "Wait—I'm a brother!"

"Like hell you are! What you doing this side of the freeway?" said the other thug as he kicked Jeremy repeatedly in the stomach. The fat one took to Jeremy's back with his worn-out Timberlands.

"Ohh! Stop! Okay! I'm White and my daddy's a cop," Jeremy pleaded.

The smaller hoodlum picked up a pipe from a mound of trash and swung it at Jeremy's head.

They kept up their assault until Jeremy's blood dripped into the street. Winded from the onslaught, the men jumped into the standing getaway car and peeled out, headed deep into the neighborhood with only the stench of burning rubber left to mark their passing.

Jeremy heaved himself to his feet and staggered off the sidewalk, using the pipe as a crutch. He was trying to rise up to walk when a muscular arm reached out to him.

"Steady, man," said a gentle voice.

Jeremy's eyes were just beginning to open and focus when he saw that the voice belonged to a young Black man in a barber's white smock. The man could have been his brother—green eyes, ivory skin, and brown curly hair to go with his broad nose and full lips.

"What was that about?" the man asked.

"They thought I was White."

"No shit," the man snorted. "They call me JR. I should take you to a clinic."

"No, just my cousin's," Jeremy said as he steadied his arm and pointed east. "He's close."

"Let's get you there. The night brings out a lot worse than those punks."

"Th—thanks, brother," Jeremy mumbled.

"Any time. Brother."

. . . .

Looking through the rearview mirror at the concrete and glass edifice of the jail, Star couldn't help but sense how precious freedom was. She couldn't imagine living contained, retained, and sustained by strangers who had dominion over her every move. A call to Marie's attorney was the least she could do given auntie took the murder rap for her.

"Jerry, she's rotting in there," she said as the wind across her convertible whipped through her raven hair.

"She's serving eight years. And that's a gift," Jerry said from his cluttered office in South Pasadena.

"Now what?"

"A writ of appeal, like I said. And remember what I told you?"

"Time is money. That's cool. I'll get it."

"I'll need it up front. Sorry," Jerry said.

"We're good for it. How much?"

"Let's do two thou. Need it before the clock starts again, little lady," he warned.

Star thought again. She mouthed her aunt's words to herself.

Don't give away your power.

"Jerry," she said. "We're going to go in a different direction. You're fired. Have a nice life." She ended the call with a tap on her earpiece.

Star pressed a button to raise the roof of her convertible as she pulled onto the freeway. The wind noise reduced, she tapped again and then spoke.

"Call Attorney Rowan," she commanded her Bluetooth device as she slipped into the fast lane at eighty miles per hour.

· · · ·

Every BMW loves 91 Octane. Anything less makes them ping like a pinball machine, so Star found the most expensive gas she could find in Gardena. Next stop was Grandma's house. She placed the gasoline muzzle tip gently into the gas spout as if her car really had feelings. In the brisk late-afternoon air, she pressed the assorted buttons and waited for the sweet smell of dead dinosaurs as she wrapped herself in her thin cotton sweater.

Five dollars clicked into eight as the pump turned slowly. Behind her, she heard another car pull up, with the stereo blaring loud-head banging music. She turned toward the newcomers as her pulse quickened and adrenaline flooded her veins.

"Look at that!" A longhaired Asian man with a thick Fu Manchu mustache and a soul patch stuck his head out the window. "A half-breed soul sister. Bet her daddy's a Jagger."

From the passenger seat, a shaven-headed man hooted with delight.

Star pulled her brown sweater tight against her stomach and held one hand inside. Then she took two steps toward the car and stopped.

"Yeah, you right," she said coolly. "And he gave me this piece to deal with assholes like you."

The men froze.

Star turned on her heel and flung herself into the driver's seat of her car before they could take time to think. In two short seconds, she whipped her sportster from zero to sixty, pointed toward Grandma's house. She heard the snarl of their engine fade away as she blasted down the highway again, and she smiled tightly. The punks' hooptie was no match for her beautiful bumwa.

With a grin on her face, Star imagined the boys giving up the chase and the broken hose of the pump pouring gallons of expensive petro onto the gas station's pavement.

· · · ·

The road to Van Nuys was littered with fast-food drive-throughs, but the boys had to have a Pickaninny Burger before going to their late-night booty call. The ebb and flow of traffic in the drive-through moved like a hamster hump in a python.

Fitzroy sputtered and coughed as he paid homage to the pipe of hashish in his hand.

"This is some good shit."

His chest puffed like a blowfish from the contents of the glowing amber bowl, but the hacking continued.

"Have a sip," Porper said as he handed his buddy a pocket-sized bottle of VSOP cognac.

"Thanks, bro," Fitzroy said as he pulled his white Peugeot forward a few feet and stopped before the order speaker, modeled to look like a toothy grinning Negro man in blackface, red and white lips and top hat.

"Welcome to Pickaninny's. How's your mammy? Can I take your order?" said the speaker.

"Two spear-chucker burgers and a couple of coon fries, please," Porper shouted from the shotgun seat into the face of the minstrel.

"Lots of napkins," Fitzroy added. "Love that chili sauce." He pulled forward.

They fed on the best that Pickaninny's had to offer from the parking lot of the near-famous establishment where the shit-kicking grins of jiggaboos illuminated the outdoor countertops.

The White boys got comfortable in their car, listened to the frenzied electronic strains of Muse, and carefully unwrapped their burgers. They methodically rearranged the pickles and lettuce so the sandwiches looked the way they did on television ads. Fitzroy and Porper peeled back the cheese paper carefully. They gorged on the massive double patties and steel-cut French fries as they watched a group of teenage girls prancing about a nearby table.

"Can't beat Valley girls," Porper remarked around a mouthful of beef.

"Too tame. I like West Side ladies," Fitzroy said with a piece of dill pickle stuck between his teeth.

"Too close to the riot shit going down," Porper replied. "Plus the place is flush with Persians. They're rich sand niggers. It's safer in the Valley," he added.

"Word. Just hit it and quit it, I say," Porper said, taking a sip of beer from the tall can in the cup holder.

ZZooft.

ZZooft.

ZZooft.

ZZooft.

Four silenced gunshots shattered the car windows. Red holes appeared in the temple and chest of each man. They slumped in their seats, their meals still warm on their laps as their bodies began to cool.

Two shadowy assassins walked casually out of the twilight, smoking cigarillos with their heads in hoods and their Glocks concealed underneath their baggy black jackets. The younger man spoke.

"Yo tengo hambre," he said, eyeing a red neon sign that shouted Emilio's.

With a nod, Hermando and his security chief pulled off their hoodies and gloves, rolled the guns inside the bundles, and dumped them into a nearby trashcan. They pulled out the tails of their collared shirts, combed their hair, and casually walked inside the tiny pizza joint.

42

A Suite Awaits

The White race must protect itself against the dangers of impurity and moral uncleanliness. This destruction must be a strike upon the heads and bodies of the mongrel races' offspring. These seeds carry the damaged genes and traits of their mothers and fathers. Our duty is to bring about the holy solution our father once prayed.

It took a short text from Kublai Khan for Ahmed to give up on Los Angeles.

"Do you want the job?"

"Yes."

"Can you be here ASAP."

"My wife and child too?"

"Of course. Sunday?"

"Yes. We're on the way. Thx."

"So, what arrangements have been made for us? They know I'm pregnant…what about Holly?" Kimberly asked as she settled her rump more firmly into the hot brown plastic car seat cushion for the five-hour trip.

"We have a suite waiting with all the accommodations," Ahmed said, keeping his eyes on the meanderings of the Grapevine.

"What about medical care?"

"The minister always does things first class. There's even a twenty-four-hour daycare center. It really could be a good place for us while LA cools down."

"So our new baby will be born there?" Kimberly said as she watched housing subdivisions slowly morph into oilrigs and farmlands.

"It could be worse. Think about it. The birth won't cost us a penny as long as I help the minister with his books and records."

"That's something. I hope they show this White girl some love." Kim caressed her huge baby bump.

"Of course they will. You won't be the only White woman there—I would never let anything bad happen to you." Ahmed smiled at her sidelong. "Besides, they're all about mixing it up."

After midnight, the Reynolds's Honda pulled up to the security gate. They were cleared and preceded to the main entrance of the renovated vacation resort. There were sandbag barriers that limited entry to a narrow path in the middle of the entrance arch. Inside, the family was led into the birth center.

The large open lobby was accented by highly polished red terra cotta Spanish mission tile, leading to a front desk attended by medical staff dressed in blue scrubs. Black men in dark suits and bowties patrolled the hallways with small automatic weapons in hand. Doctors and nurses in starched white coats and dresses scurried about, attending to the hundreds of women and babies in beds and operating rooms in the four floors above them. With little fanfare and attention, Ahmed and his family were led to a birthing suite on the second floor.

After dining on beans, rice, and baked halibut, Ahmed met the staff of the clinic while Kimberly received an entry exam and Holiday played in the childcare center. It was in the business center that Ahmed saw Kublai Khan.

"Brother Ahmed, both your ladies are getting pampered now after a long trip," the minister said.

"Is Kimberly all right?" Ahmed asked as he sat next to Khan in a small office space cluttered with stacks of paper files and a late-model desktop computer.

"The doctor says it's any time now. She's resting. He's still anxious to see her medical files," Khan said as he glanced impatiently at his desk phone. Then he shook his head and stood up. "Let's take a walk."

He was out of the door in seconds and heading down the hall. Ahmed hastened to catch up.

The two men briskly walked down the hallway to the stairs and headed to the nursery. They strode down the stark white corridor, glancing in at rooms where new mothers nibbled on hospital-grade dinners. Some cradled their babies and enjoyed the healthy cries and whines coming from the newborns as Khan got to the point.

"The first thing tomorrow, I need you to work with Brother Peterson," Khan said. "I need you to comb all our files for information concerning two women."

"Who are they?" Ahmed asked.

"Not important. Just be meticulous. If you find them, or you find anything out of order, call me immediately." Khan stopped at a plate-glass window, peered in, and admired the infants in the room beyond while the nurses passed slowly and attentively among them. Then he turned to Ahmed, jerked a thumb at the room full of bassinets, and said, "You're going to have as beautiful and healthy a child." He walked away from Ahmed and left him admiring the babies and thinking of his own.

Later, up in the birthing suite, Ahmed sat with Kimberly, Holiday on his knee. They talked about their future together.

"Holly will be a great big sister. I love the way she helps me with housework," Kim said, looking at her daughter lovingly while Holly scurried to get away from her dad and engaged herself in the plastic toys she had mysteriously collected in the short two hours they had been there. Everyone at the center seemed to have a soft spot for small children, and Holly was running out of steam as sleep approached.

"I think it's a boy. That would be so cool. A little me and a little you." Ahmed stared into space, imagining what it would be like with two kids instead of one.

"It won't matter," Kim said firmly. "We'll be great parents."

"I'll have to work on it. Never wanted somebody to call me daddy until I met you," Ahmed said, touching the bed sheet covering her. The fetal monitored beeped assurance that the unnamed arrival was strong and vital.

"I'm going back to school for my degree. I want to be a graphic designer," she said, looking into Ahmed's eyes for approval.

"Whatever. We'll make it work."

"I know. That's why I'm here, silly," She said as the fetal monitor beeped an odd, disturbing tone, and Kimberly convulsed in pain and pulled her legs up into a fetal position.

"Uggh…Ohhh!" Ahmed jabbed the call button. Then ran to the hallway and shouted.

"Help us! She's in pain!"

A nurse ran into the room and began checking Kim's vital signs.

"Where's the pain?" she asked.

"My chest. My head hurts," Kimberly moaned.

The attendant opened her gown and turned to Ahmed. "Take your child to the care center."

Ahmed took the hint and scooped up Holly. He walked with his daughter to the elevator, looking back at Kim as the nurse applied a cold compress and straightened out her legs.

Holly chose that moment to speak her first full sentence.

"What's wrong with Mommy?"

Ahmed gripped her tiny hand ever so tightly and walked into the lift while a doctor and a nurse hustled toward their birthing suite.

43

His Wife...His Child

"The people of Babylon must bear the consequences of their guilt because they rebelled against our God. They must be killed by an invading army, their little ones dashed to death against the ground, their pregnant women ripped open by swords."

–Christian Soldiers

As the Christian Soldiers prepared for battle, Pastor Dalton nodded off on a flea-infested sofa and dreamed in black and white.

His Aryan troglodytes, armed with forged swords and spears, stormed the fortified gates of the majestic castle while giant catapults heaved balls of fire that exploded against the dark granite walls of the edifice. Inside, howling Komodo dragons guarded the charcoal-hued sentries that patrolled along the parapet.

"Onward toward the light!" Lord Dahl commanded his troops as a super-Trog named Blar lead the behemoths into hand-to-hand combat.

"I will rip out your soul and feed it to the dragons!" Blar screamed as he swung his giant sword toward a sentry. Dragon breath burned against his snakelike skin.

The groans and grunts of the Trogs grew stronger as each dragon was slain and the Khan's troops grew thin. The harder the sentries fought, the more evident their loss became until, through the pitch-blackness, Dahl saw a glowing sunset appearing on the dark horizon. From its apex appeared a golden chariot led by two winged horses. Inside, the Khan was at the helm.

Guts and body parts flew as the monstrous Khan guards fought off the inhuman Trogs before they could reach the basilica.

"Forge ahead!" Blar bellowed. "Never stop moving forward!" he screamed as he saw his mighty legions overpowering the inferior forces of the Khan. He too saw a glowing ball of fire on the hill.

"Never stop," pleaded Dahl as he raced ahead to the presence of Khan, who was dressed in an exquisite black kimono, shining against the night sky as smoke and fire burned beyond him, giving the warrior's immaculate white dreadlocks an air of invincibility.

"So, Tucker, we meet on the battlefield," Khan said as he swept his long sword gracefully in an arch and ended up with knees slightly bent, his exquisite sabre held high above his head with both hands.

Dahl circled to his left and held the finest Tarzarian steel sword in the kingdom high in anticipation of a fight to the death. He watched Khan dismount and slowly move toward him, straight as a bee's path.

"Your men are prepared to take the castle but not win the battle," Khan rumbled. "They're just puppets that I command on a long string. Where's your left flank?"

The men suddenly dropped their weapons and fled back across the castle walls.

The mighty Khan's guards, battered and slain by the Trogs, rose again and stood alive and unscathed in the spots where they were killed. The dragons howled again as the remaining Trogs abandoned the battle. Pastor Dahl and his loyal captain Blar were alone, facing the translucent, glowing image of the Khan. Blar was first to reach him.

"Stay back, Pastor. I will slay our enemy," Blar promised as he charged the image of the Khan.

"You need not attack. I will kill you from here," Khan said, and he reached out and captured the virtual image of Blar running toward him in the palm of his hand. Then he closed his fist and Blar vanished. Dahl saw whatever happened…happen.

"I beg you, Master Khan. I want to live," he wept and placed his hands together in a prayerful gesture.

"Silence. Your fate has been decided by the babies you seek," Khan said as faces of the newborn children danced bodiless behind him.

The Pastor saw the bloodless smile of the unmerciful Master as the sword was drawn behind him and he came forward with great speed toward Dahl's head.

Dalton forced his eyes open before contact, and the shouts of Sergeant Blair echoed through his head.

"Pastor. Pastor! The men are ready. We must make our attack before first light!"

. . . .

On a gentle hillside above the birth center, Jimmy Blair was poised to pick off anyone coming through the courtyard, but the House of Jeremiah soldiers were masked by darkness and black fatigues, so Jimmy made a command decision to storm the facility from the rear while the frontal attack took place.

"Load the trucks and ATVs," he ordered. "Our troops in front know what to do." "We're good to go," Dalton assured him over the radio. "The plow will strike the front gate in thirty seconds. Make the rear attack work."

The men in the rear navigated the border wall only to be greeted by snipers in the courtyard. As Christian Soldiers and Khan's men were mortally wounded, a few soldiers entered the rear of the building. They stormed the halls, bearing machetes and automatic weapons, searching for the children.

Blair caught a nurse's aide near the elevator by Blair.

"Tell me where they are. You don't have to die," he said menacingly.

She shook in silence as Blair slit her stomach with his hunting knife from one end to the other. Her blood squirted onto her blue smock, leaving a purple-red path along her belly.

"This didn't have to happen," he said. He let the nurse drop to the floor, clutching her stomach and staring down the hallway in the direction of the nursery. She winced in pain before fading into unconsciousness.

"Dumb bitch," Blair said as he reached for his wireless. "We're on the inside," he announced. "Pastor, what's your location?" He walked down the darkened hallways with three of his men at the ready, searching the unoccupied rooms.

"We've reached the front gate and headed inside. Where's the nursery?"

"It must be in the basement. Meet y'all there," Blair said, wiping the blood and perspiration from his brow with the checked handkerchief he carried in his hip pocket.

Then he paused.

Away down the corridor, he noticed a stairwell heading down. At the top of the stairwell stood six of The House of Jeremiah's finest and Kublai Khan. They hadn't seen him yet.

Blair showed his teeth in a smile.

• • • •

Dalton and the five other soldiers were jammed inside of the snowplow's cab, bullets pinging off the blade in front of them as Carl floored it. When the plow hit the ornamental steel gate, it crumpled like a cheap folding chair before the whole mess slammed into the stone guard gate and the two men inside stopped shooting and raced for cover.

"Yippee-ki-yay! We're in," screamed Carl as he leaned out the driver's side window and took aim with his rifle. Mike yanked his brother back inside the cab.

"Don't kill us, you idiot!" he barked. "Save it for them!"

The slow-moving snow removal vehicle hit the sandbags and the soldiers scurried for cover against the faux brick barrier lining the driveway. The Christian Soldiers scrambled out of the cab, but automatic gunfire snarled out from inside the center and flew over their heads.

"Wait 'em out," the Pastor ordered while keeping his head down.

"Preach, if the boys are inside, we gotta help!" Carl complained.

"Khan has the babies hidden. Blair will find them," Dalton said and ducked farther back behind the plow blade.

Automatic fire rattled the air as the gate guardsmen circled back and caught Dalton and his men in a crossfire. Mike Prather went down with two high-caliber rifle shells and a small-caliber pistol bullet in his back. He stumbled forward and then fell in a heap in front of this brother, who then tried to drag him to cover. New shots rang out. Dalton's semiautomatic rifle sang in virtual unison with handguns carried by Brother Timothy and Carl.

"Brother, don't leave me now," Carl said as Mike's scared eyes faded and he coughed up blood.

"Bet…I'm with you," Mike said, gripping his brother's hand palm-to-palm.

"Hold on," Carl begged, his voice barely above a whimper.

He felt it when Mike died in his brother's grasp.

Carl gently laid Mike's head on the cold morning grass as another salvo ripped the predawn air. The rear guard returned fire and caught Carl in the shoulder and back. The force of the blast spun him around as he tried to dive over the sandbags for cover. The cry Carl made as the AR-15 shell landed in his back sounded more like a plea for help than a warrior's verbal indifference to pain.

"Little brother, you didn't die for nothing! Aggghhh!" Carl screamed as the guards riddled him with automatic fire.

Carl never made it over the pile. His bullet-mangled body landed on a row of sandbags and the security men adjusted fire to greet someone else who felt lucky. But the Christian Soldiers were excellent shots, and more and more guard positions fell silent.

For minutes that seemed forever, the killing field went quiet as smoke and the stench of gunpowder filled the air.

Then:

"Move out!" Dalton shouted as they looked for better cover inside a side door to the center.

The three surviving Soldiers left the corpses of the Prather brothers and followed their preacher into the birth center.

. . . .

"Ms. Solberg had a seizure and can't be moved," said the doctor as the commotion upstairs grew louder.

"The hell she can't!" Ahmed snapped back. "No child of mine is going to be born in a combat zone. My family and I are out of here." He helped Kim put on with her pants as Holly looked on.

In minutes, Ahmed had found a safe exit and was guiding Kimberly toward it with Holiday in his arms. A stray Christian Soldier attacked them, holding his machete high in the air.

"Die, mongrel pup! Die!" the soldier yelled as he lurched toward Holly.

Ahmed dropped his daughter's hand and sprang at the marauder's chest like a Rottweiler after a rabbit. He grabbed the attacker's wrist and tackled him to the floor. Ahmed ripped the machete away from the soldier and pushed the sharpened edge against the man's throat as he held him down.

"My wife…my child. You bastard," he snarled as he slashed the soldier's neck and left him bleeding while his family ran for cover.

Inside the second-floor stairwell, Ahmed could see the rear exit door that led to the parking lot. Two more soldiers stood on the first level, obviously looking for the nursery. The hollow emptiness in his belly and the emotional void in his heart were evidence that there was more murderous work to do.

"Can you hold on a few more minutes?" he asked Kim as he put Holly into her arms. She nodded woozily as she leaned against the door of the second-floor stairway.

"I'll wait. Be careful," she said.

"Be back in a flash," he replied, and headed out to do his job.

· · · ·

Ahmed listened to the Soldiers chatting lazily as he crept up on them.

"I guess there's another stairs down besides this one. Must be over there." A Pall Mall smoker pointed toward the south with his filter less cancer stick.

"This one's secured. Let's get on with it." A man dressed in a new set of discount duck-hunting camo hefted his gun meaningfully.

"Calm down," Pall Mall said, and dropped his cigarette to grind it out with his boot as the stairwell suddenly went pitch-black.

The men stood still, obviously waiting for the emergency lighting to kick in.

It didn't. Ahmed, standing by a light switch above them, had seen to that.

"Shit. I can't see my fucking hand," the smoker said.

"I'm over here, you idiot," Camo replied.

"Damn. Let's go up and see if they got lights," Pall Mall suggested.

The sound of Ahmed's machete was more whoosh than thump, leaving blood, sinew, and loose flesh on the stairs. Soon the sounds of two feet and the moaning of the dead were the only sounds left in the dark.

As the Reynolds-Solberg family left the building, Ahmed led them to the car. Kim and Holiday crouched low until the car reached a service road out of the complex and turned onto a dirt road, heading toward the highway.

"Can you make it, baby?" Ahmed asked, keeping his eyes on the road.

"Where are we going?" Kim mumbled back.

"Hold on. I got an idea." He punched the gas, sending the car surging forward into the predawn gloom. Behind him was only the absence of light.

"Stay on the floor. Until I think we're safe," he said.

• • • •

"Protect the nursery with your life," Kublai Khan said, positioning his men two by two along the dark corridor and inside the delivery rooms and the adjoining nursery.

Minister Khan steadied his P229 handgun and shot the first soldier he saw, a lanky man with sandy-brown hair, bloodshot eyes, and an M-24 at the ready. Khan caught a quick glimpse of the name stenciled above the breast pocket of the man's fatigues: BLAIR.

Shot in the shoulder, Blair stumbled at the top of the stairs as his men raced down them to greet the first wave of Kahn's men.

"Meet them in the middle," Khan commanded.

The men attacked while Khan fired upon the man at the top. The Minister stood in the doorway to the nursery while babies cried for attention behind him. One attacker fought with a guard, who hacked off the soldier's hand with a machete another Christian Solider had dropped in battle. The man on the middle stairway tier leaped over the rail and landed on Khan.

"You ape!" he shouted. He rode Khan's back and struggled to get his large blade around the minister's neck.

Khan pulled the soldier's left arm forward and, using his own body for leverage, hurled the soldier over his shoulder onto the floor. Before striking the man with a fatal elbow to the neck, the minister looked into the soldier's eyes and saw the fear and anger that would kill him if given a chance. The Christian Soldier seized on the minister's pause and wiggled free from his grip. Back on his feet, he grinned in relief and grabbed his sidearm. He stood above the minister with his gun cocked at the ready.

"Come with me. The Pastor wants you," the soldier said and waved his pistol in a direction away from the nursery door.

Kublai Khan had no choice. He surrendered.

"Through that door, back up the stairs," the soldier commanded.

At the first-floor landing, the soldier said, "You call yourself a man of God?"

"That I am. You call yourself a Christian?" Kublai Khan replied.

"I am. Sanctified," the man said with a touch of regret in his voice.

"And yet you plan to kill babies in his name?"

"Yet *you* try to betray God's rule?" the man retorted.

"Is that what your preacher tells you about me?"

"You believe in Christ?" the soldier asked as they reached the ground floor and he looked around, probably seeking a secure path to the front lines.

They started slowly down a dark, poorly lit hallway.

"I have my faith," Khan said. "Even as I walk this path with you."

"But do you believe?"

"Yes. I do. Do you?" Khan asked.

"I said I was saved."

"Then why did you call me an ape?"

"You didn't like my battle cry? Could have called you a nigga?"

"Thanks for the concession," Khan said. "Son, what's your name?"

"They call me Nate. But I like Nathaniel."

"Do you read the Bible, Nathaniel?"

"Not really."

"There's a Nathaniel in it."

"So?"

"Read his story sometime. I want you to see me as just a man."

"And if I do?" Nate said in disbelief.

"Then something good could come of this madness," Khan said as they reached the main building.

Pah…ting. Pah…ting.

Nate stumbled as he was hit, leaving Khan an opening to kick him in the groin before knee-dropping him and stomping him in the throat. Nate squirmed and gasped under Khan's boot as a guard ran up.

"Minister, you all right? We have to get back to the nursery." The guard pointed back to the babies. Khan paused and looked down at his injured foe, who was busily stewing in his own blood.

"Yahweh is in you," he said, pushed Nate against the wall, and ran back to fight.

．．．．

The sounds of Soyun's groans rang out from the birthing suite.

Her baby began to push through as the attentive doctor looked on and his nurse waited for orders.

A whiskey laced blues song bellowed from a radio, drowning out the battle outside.

You gonna trust me

Or your lying eyes?

No matter what you think you saw

I know that I wasn't there

Not my skin or my nappy hair

You gonna trust me

Or your lying eyes?

What you think you saw

It's just a filthy pack of lies.

"*Ohhhhh* my God!" Soyun yelled, drowning out the commotion just outside the delivery room while still leaving the background guitar strokes vibrant and luminating.

The anguish on the Korean woman's face turned into a smile the instant she saw her healthy brown baby. The nurse cleared the newborn's airways and wrapped the baby girl hurriedly in a light blanket before placing it in a bassinet near Soyun's right side. The baby cooed with surprising good nature, considering the pop of gunfire and the yells emanating from beyond the door.

"She's beautiful," the Chinese nurse said.

"Can I hold her?" asked Soyun.

The nurse reached down carefully to transfer the child.

The double door sprang open and a sandy-haired soldier burst through the door with a machete held high. He brought the blade down in a sweeping arc above Soyun as she reached to embrace her newborn. The nurse screamed and twisted her body into the path of the machete while the doctor stabbed the intruder in the neck with a surgical scalpel.

Then something popped, and the sandy-haired man collapsed, a look of shock permanently etched into his face.

· · · ·

Kublai Khan's pulse raced as his heart quickened and he took aim at Blair from below the stairwell and shot him in the back of his head. Blair fell and his machete clanged against the floor and slid under the hospital bed.

Another shot rang out, killing another Christian Soldier at the door. As Khan raced into the delivery room, past his man, a booming amplified voice rang out throughout the birth center.

"FBI. Put down your weapons."

· · · ·

The agents stormed the room and the center. The siege was over. FN SCAR assault rifles were trained on the remaining Christian

Soldiers, including Pastor Dalton. Kublai Khan spoke to Agent Miller on the front lawn while the staff attended to the wounded.

"Thanks. I knew you were tracking Dalton, but…" Kublai Khan paused to put his hand on the chest of a passing victim on a gurney, one of his men who had survived the attack.

"Just doing my job," Miller said, standing on the grass in his new-smelling riot gear as Dalton and the remains of his soldiers were being put into a transport in handcuffs and ankle bracelets.

"Can I say something to the Pastor?" Khan asked.

"Go for it," Miller urged as he signaled to the officers to stop.

The minister looked at the defeated pastor and looked into his soul before speaking.

"I will pray for you," Kublai Khan said.

The guards waited for a response.

"Save it for someone who gives a damn," Dalton snarled as the guards led him to the transport.

Khan and Miller watched as the four remaining Christian Soldiers were loaded up and driven away through the small crowd of neighbors that stood around the gate, gawking at the spectacular commotion. Nate limped toward another transport as Khan approached him.

"You're a good man on the wrong path," the minister said.

Nate seemed to ignore him, concentrating on walking. He stumbled on the sloped lawn and Khan grabbed his arm to steady him. Nathaniel nodded approvingly.

"Thanks, pastor…I mean, Minister."

"You're welcome, Nate." Khan nodded gravely at him as he was struck by an idea. "I'll send you a Bible when you get where you're going. You read that story now, hear?"

Nate blinked at him in surprise nodded, and allowed himself to be guided into the van without another word.

Agent Miller turned to rejoin his agents and said to the minister, "You're good to go."

"I'm sure your upcoming inspection will find things in order," Khan said.

"Won't be one. They found those girls—or their bodies anyway—in Seoul," Miller said from over his shoulder as he reached his black SUV. "Somebody's gonna have questions for Reverend Hung, but it won't be me."

44

A Safe Space

Ahmed knew that he had to get somewhere. The contractions were coming closer together, and there wasn't a hospital in sight. He made it to the highway and headed north. He remembered talking with Susan Morgan at the ad agency about her folks in Coalinga and what it was like growing up there, so he called her from the car.

"We can be there in forty-five minutes," he explained. "She's sleeping quietly right now, so I think we have the time, if we're lucky. Got our daughter Holly with us. She's twenty months." His voice wavered from the stress of fighting desperadoes just to get on a dark, lonely road. He could hear the uneven breathing of both Holly and Kimberly. Their tone and cadence was different, yet somehow also the same, like two singers in harmony.

"They'll get you taken care of," Susan assured him.

"Send me the address, and I'll look it up and make sure we get there. Let them know she needs a doctor since she had a mild stroke or something," he said.

"Will do. My ma Val and my poppa Jerry will be waiting, and if Dr. Whitlow is in town, I'm sure he will come and help out."

Ahmed said goodbye, and he tried to stay calm and focused.

"We'll be there soon," he said into the darkness to Kim. "Just breathe and relax. Stay awake." He carefully kept his distance from a pair of speeding tanker trucks that rattled the Civic with the wind of their passing.

"Okay, baby. Just get us there," Kim said.

"You breathe, and I will sing to you. What song would you like to hear?" Ahmed said clearing his throat.

"Can't think right now. Anything," she said.

They both were silent for a moment until Kimberly chose.

"How about some Stevie Wonder?"

Ahmed tried to remember a Stevie Wonder song but couldn't at first. Then his heart felt a perfect choice. He gathered himself to sing.

"You are the sunshine in my life...that's why I'll always stay in town.... You are the Snapple of my eye, forever you'll sway in my heart."

"That was lovely," Kim said.

Holly woke up giggling. "Daddy's trying to sing," she informed her mother.

Ahmed hoped for better reviews before he went for the second verse.

"AAAHH—!"

Kim went into a convulsion and Ahmed took the next exit.

• • • •

Ahmed stopped on the front yard of a small wood-frame house with a large, weathered barn in back. As he brought the car to a stop, a petite woman with short silver-gray hair ran to the car. Behind her was a man in his late seventies, running not far behind.

Val shouted instructions. Behind Jerry was an elderly man with a stethoscope around his neck.

"Turn the car off and help your wife!" Dr. Whitlow shouted. "Jerry will help you carry her in. Val will get your daughter. There's no time to spare. Are the contractions more than five minutes apart?"

"Yes!" Ahmed cut the engine and scrambled out, already hurrying for the door. "They seem to be about twenty minutes apart. During the last one, I think she had a seizure," he added as Jerry and Dr. Whitlow opened the rear door and carefully got Kim to her feet.

"Let's get her to the guest bedroom. Jerry, you got her?" Whitlow asked as he pressed fingers to Kim's wrist and glanced at his watch to take her pulse.

"We got her, Doc." Jerry steadied her as they slowly walked toward the open-air porch and the open front door. "Ambulance is on the way, but it'll be a while."

. . . .

Inside the bedroom, Kimberly barely noticed the embroidered ivory, rose, and aster handmade bedspread with matching down-stuffed pillows. Over the spread was a translucent blue shower curtain. The room was neatly arranged with high-school pictures and cheerleading trophies, presumably belonging to the towering redheaded girl in the pictures. Near the bed was a card table full of medical supplies. Kimberly's eyes focused on a prom photo of the red-haired girl and a handsome White boy in a frame on the nightstand while the doctor checked her heart. She tried to find the face of her boyfriend in the room.